A TREASONOUS PATH

Tom Walsingham Mysteries
Book Two

C. P. Giuliani

Also in the Tom Walsingham Series

The Road to Murder

Death In Rheims

A TREASONOUS PATH

Published by Sapere Books.

24 Trafalgar Road, Ilkley, LS29 8HH,
United Kingdom

saperebooks.com

ISBN: 978-1-80055-713-0

To my mother, who never fails in her support and encouragement — and shows book covers to her friends in lieu of grandchildren's pictures.

ACKNOWLEDGEMENTS

Being asked — rather out of the blue — for the best way of stabbing someone through the back so they won't be able to cry out … well, I suppose it may make for a slightly alarming experience. Therefore, I'm grateful to Massimiliano Monari — not only for showing me how to plausibly choreograph a gruesome murder, but also for not calling the police.

Other than that, the usual suspects: my mother, Milla the Idea-Bouncer, everyone at Sapere Books, and the staff at the Biblioteca Baratta always deserve my thanks.

Also, thank you Massimo Marcomini, and everybody at the Teatro di Palazzo d'Arco, for cheering me along, and bearing all the patience it has taken.

PROLOGUE

18th of June 1583, Salisbury Court, London

The man woke to pain and blackness, not knowing where he was.

The close air, the smell of anchovies, the burning in his belly…

With a moan, he turned on his side, curled himself around his stomach — and wished he hadn't. He took a gulp of air, and with it the smell…

Oh Saint Fiacre!

Mouth filling, he leant over the pallet's edge to retch. Nothing but spit and bile — and not his pallet…

A cot — yes, the scullion's cot in the back kitchen. He'd routed away the boy, hadn't he — too tight in the chest, too weak to climb all the way to the garret. And now look at him.

It was a great effort to push himself on his back, wheezing and rasping, each breath harder than the last, his legs heavy as logs, and his hands…

He shouldn't have eaten the Scot's sweetmeats.

He shouldn't have drunk the dregs of the wine.

He shouldn't have… Oh Saint Fiacre give succour — the candied rhubarb! The filthy taste. His mouth still burnt with it. His tongue. His teeth.

He couldn't breathe.

If only he could sit up…

If only he…

When his mouth filled again, he tried to turn — and couldn't. He spat in the pillow, wheezing and gasping.

Help!

But no sound came from his mouth.

Help!

Belly aflame, mouth agape, he lay flailing his heavy hands.

Help, all the saints! Did no one hear?

And the last thing in his mind was the sturgeon from the market — still alive, flopping weaker and weaker, bulge-eyed on the stone slab in the scullery…

CHAPTER 1

20th of June 1583

Thomas Walsingham shook the letter to dislodge yet another fly, and carefully swallowed the curse. His father's cousin, Sir Francis Walsingham, Secretary of State to Her Highness the Queen of England, wasn't known for his tolerance towards swearing. Or, for that matter, towards displays of impatience great and small — not even swatting at a fly. Much less when he himself sat waiting at his writing table.

That it was stifling hot in the little dark-panelled study, that not even the slightest breeze entered, though the window's iron casement was thrown open, that the flies did in abundance — none of this seemed to disturb Mr. Secretary in the least. He just sat in the high-backed chair, eyes fixed on Tom, and waited.

Tom gave a last, narrow-eyed frown at the letter's signature — a false name, since no "Henry Fagot" resided with the French Ambassador, Monsieur de Castelnau at Salisbury Court. But then, the whole matter was a rigmarole: a mysterious informant writing his letters in bad French, and hiding them in an Italian fencing-master's hat. Almost too fanciful to be true — and yet...

This was the third time, since returning from France late in May, that Tom had been summoned to the wood-panelled study, and set to read this fellow Fagot's papers, and then made to unpick their meaning under his great cousin's Sphinx-like scrutiny.

"So, Thomas?"

Tom took a good deep breath and straightened away from the windowsill. "So the French Ambassador's servants are smuggling in Catholic books, but that is more an embarrassment than anything else," he said — slow and considering. "Either this Henry Fagot is not very good at telling what is important, or he has a grudge against the Ambassador's butler and cook."

Sir Francis gave the tiniest nod. "Both things, quite possibly."

"Then there is 'Foulair'… who is William Fowler, the 'very traitorous Scot' — and this comes from the Ambassador's secretary. Another grudge, perhaps? I wonder if Fagot, whoever he is, knows that Fowler is your own man, Sir? Whether he does or not, a strange warning."

"Indeed," murmured Sir Francis. "But I'll say that Fowler's reports have grown somewhat thin these past weeks. He writes of trifles, complains that he is of no account to Monsieur de Castelnau. I wonder if he still is my own man at all."

So perhaps Fagot and his secretary friend were right? And yet… "And yet, if he had turned coats, he wouldn't complain," Tom pointed out. "He would never say he is of little account. On the contrary, he would do his best to seem useful."

"So he would — for all that he never showed much efficacy. What else?"

"According to Fagot, the Spanish Ambassador is visiting often with Monsieur de Castelnau. I'm sure the Señor Mendoza would very much like to see the Duke of Anjou married to an Infanta."

François of Anjou, brother and heir to the King of France, who was sometimes engaged to Queen Elizabeth and sometimes not, much to the disapproving frustration of Sir Francis.

"Yes, yes — this will need watching. We do not want a tighter bond between Spain and France — now less than ever. Still, whatever Mendoza whispers, 'tis hardly likely to be more than that yet: whisperings. And so tell me, Thomas: what would you say is most relevant among Fagot's tidbits?"

"I would say two things." Tom dropped the letter on top of its stacked fellows on the sill, and stood a little straighter — his sweat-drenched shirt coming briefly unstuck from his back under the doublet. "Lord Howard and Francis Throckmorton are doing the work of the Queen of Scots, *in primis* — and are doing it under the French Ambassador's roof."

"Yes — that is most alarming." There were two quills on the table, and a small penknife. Sir Francis carefully adjusted them in a tight row before he looked up again. "You know this Francis Throckmorton from Paris?"

"Both him and his brother."

"Would you call them friends?"

"Hardly," Tom said. "In Paris, we used to fence in the same hall. Throckmorton is a Catholic, no doubt — and does nothing to disguise it — but I wouldn't have thought him a traitor."

Sir Francis shook his head with a little sigh. "His side of the family has always leant towards Rome. At another time, I would call what Fagot says a youthful vagary — but now…" There was more adjusting of pens and knife — a thing of painstaking precision. In another man it would have looked like fiddling. "There have been letters from Scotland. 'Tis much doubtful that the Earl of Gowrie will keep the King under his influence for long."

All the air drained from Tom's lungs, from the whole room. Gowrie, who had all but kidnapped young King James, and kept Scotland, if not quiet, at least more amicable to Protestant England than to Catholic France…

"But if the Earl falls —"

"*When*, Thomas — not if. When Gowrie falls, there is no telling what the King will do, and much less the Queen his mother, with her party. You see why we *must* know what Howard and Throckmorton do at Salisbury Court."

And see Tom did. Gowrie and his friends had no love for the Papist Queen of Scots, and were well content to have her imprisoned in England, but once this changed, Mary Stewart's partisans would rally. And what France would choose to do then…

"But you said that two things struck you in the letter. On Howard and Throckmorton, I agree. What is your *in secundis*?"

Sir Francis's words startled Tom out of his black forebodings, and he floundered for a moment. "Oh. Yes. Yes, *in secundis*, there's the matter of the secretary."

"Yes, the secretary. That would be…" Sir Francis ran a fingertip down a sheet of tightly written notes. "Claude de Courcelles. He spent a few years in Scotland before he was sent here, and now he's ready to sell his master's secrets — or so Fagot would have us believe."

"It struck me as astounding before; now I find it a boon. Supposing it all can be credited…"

"Indeed." Sir Francis nodded, more to himself than to Tom, and in the brief silence, the creak and clatter of a wheelbarrow made itself heard from the small garden, along with a man's soft humming. "For the crux of the matter remains this: can we trust this Fagot — or Fagot?" It was pronounced in the English way first, then French-wise.

Trusting a fellow who disguised himself under a false name, and who had written unasked to inform about the French Ambassador and the whole household…

Tom shook his head and stepped away from the window, and from the sunlight pouring in slantwise. For days Fagot's riddle had been buzzing inside his head like the most persistent of flies. "I wish I could fathom it better," he said. "It baffled me from the beginning that Fagot would offer intelligence without the certainty of reward, without even a sure way to be acknowledged — and that he would do it in this manner. This Italian, this fencing master who found the letters — can *he* be trusted?"

Sir Francis Walsingham was not prone to shrugging, but there was a suspicion of it in the tilt of his head, the raised eyebrows, as though his patience was running thin on this whole affair. "I will not claim that I trust Rocco Bonetti very far," he said. "But if he were playing tricks — either of his own counsel or someone else's — I trust him to weave a better tale than finding the letters hidden in his hat."

"Or someone would weave it for him." Tom sighed. "This Fagot seems fond enough of secrecy and riddles. But now … trying to buy the Ambassador's own secretary is a horse of another colour. It's exposing himself to discovery. Why would he take such a risk? And why is he writing in French when he doesn't have enough of the tongue? He could never imagine he'd pass himself off as a Frenchman, surely? Unless…" And then something shifted in Tom's head, like a piece falling into place.

"Unless?"

There was a gleam in the dark grey eyes observing him over the steepled hands, and Tom fell silent and cleared his voice. Now let his new notion not be utterly foolish. "Unless, in truth, he is a Frenchman who is trying to pass himself off as one who is *not* a Frenchman."

"Yes. A good thought," Sir Francis said, and Tom's shoulders unknotted a little.

"And who do you think, then, this devious Frenchman to be?"

Question after question, posed like riddles, surely, because it was not to be thought that Sir Francis wanted a lowly courier to shed light on such matters. But riddles were a game Tom liked.

"The secretary, Courcelles himself, perhaps," he mused. "As seasoning for counterfeit intelligence on behalf of the French Ambassador? They must know that we'll wonder who Fagot truly is, though. After all, how many live in Salisbury Court who are not French? Who are not French *and* would know such things —?" Oh Lord, look at him: such blathering keenness! And pacing to and fro, even. "Your pardon, Sir — I…"

"Not at all, Thomas, not at all. Asking questions is never an idle exercise." There was something in Sir Francis's voice that could have almost been a smile. "Do sit down, though, before you give yourself a calenture."

And this was the second hint of praise today. There was a chair before the empty hearth, and Tom sat in it, feeling a little pleased with himself. He was under no illusion that these conversations were anything but a test — and yet, that they were, and hadn't stopped, and comprised secret news from Scotland — all of this seemed good for his prospects. And perhaps — *perhaps* he wasn't doing too badly.

He had another question — but would it sound like fishing for more praise, if he asked it now? He hesitated for a heartbeat, listening to the bees buzzing in Lady Ursula's roses outside. "But there is still Fowler…" he ventured.

"Fowler? What of him?"

"If Monsieur l'Ambassadeur doesn't trust Fowler anymore, Sir, why would he warn you against him —?"

A sudden burst of voices rose outside, and Tom stopped short. Men's voices raised in argument, loud enough to be heard even through the thick door to the gallery and the staircase.

"Would you see what's the disruption, Thomas?" Sir Francis asked, more curious than angry.

Tom went to the door and opened it, not surprised to find Davies, Sir Francis's huge Welsh guard, standing squarely at the top of the stairs, big enough to block the view, but not the high-pitched voice clamouring for Mr. Secretary.

"What is it, Davies?"

The Welshman barely turned and made no sound, moving half a step aside, to let Tom see.

And a sight it was. Down a few steps, on the landing, three men were tangling. Two were servants of Sir Francis — wiry, fierce Wat Williams and squat Nick Skeres. Between, and half beneath, them was a thin young man in black, collar askew and eyes wild — the one with the reedy voice.

"Yer Honour, hear me!" he howled, squirming madly in the two men's hold. "Yer Honour, I beseech —" He yelped when Williams cuffed him on the head.

"Hold your noise, Fowler!" the man ordered — and was obeyed, although Skeres's stranglehold might also have had to do with the sudden compliance.

Fowler! Speak of the devil — but this panting, scrawny, bulge-eyed creature with the womanish voice — was this really Henry Fagot's traitorous Scot?

"Bring in Mr. Fowler, Davies."

They all started, for all that Sir Francis had not raised his voice in the least. He stood on the study's threshold, dark and straight against the sunlight inside.

"You also, Thomas. And Wat."

Tom found himself enormously pleased to be included in whatever was to happen. Wat Williams, instead, looked dour. Not that Williams was ever the most friendly of men — but right now he had the air of one who would do murder without a second thought.

They all trooped in after Sir Francis. There was one truly uncomfortable chair in the room. Davies moved it before the table, and dropped Fowler in it. The Scotsman, who looked to be Tom's age or little more, sagged in the seat, gasping and blinking like a scared frog, with Tom and Williams on either side of him — Williams glaring and tensed, as though about to cuff the man again.

He didn't even wait for Davies to go before exploding, "I cannot begin to guess, Master. I taught him better than to come barging in here..."

Fowler flinched, and Sir Francis raised an eyebrow. "I've no doubt that you did, Wat. But perhaps Mr. Fowler will want to explain himself?"

There were several gasps, and much dry swallowing, until Tom had an itch to cuff the fellow himself.

"Yer Honour!" Fowler squawked in the end, and then cleared his throat. When he resumed, his voice was still whitish, very Scottish in colour, but firm enough to understand. "Yer Honour, they tried to murder me!"

CHAPTER 2

Fowler had earned everyone's attention — and it struck Tom that there were men working in the garden who didn't need to hear the Scot's wailings. When he moved to pull the casement shut, Fowler flinched again, and Williams uncrossed and recrossed his arms.

Any impatience of his own, Sir Francis hid. "I'm glad to see that they failed," was all he said. "May I ask who *they* are?"

"But they didnae!" Fowler leaned forward, clutching at the tapestry on the table. "Fail, I mean. They didnae fail at all."

There was a snort from Williams, and a small frown from Sir Francis, and Tom couldn't help himself. "You look hale enough for one murdered," he murmured.

Williams snorted again, very softly.

Fowler turned on Tom with unexpected ferocity. "'Tis not me that they murdered! They tried, and failed, and killed another!" He went back to Sir Francis, all fierceness gone, and moaned: "Yer Honour, the French Ambassador's butler is deid!"

They were all rather speechless, Sir Francis, Williams, and Tom — and Fowler kept looking from one to the other, head swivelling on his thin neck. Why, the fellow was named beyond perfection: most fowl-like in his round-eyed expectancy.

Tom bit down an unseemly urge to laugh, and grasped for something — something in Fowler's extraordinary utterance. "The butler," he said under his breath. "Monsieur de Castelnau's butler." One of the men who, according to Fagot, were smuggling Popish books into London. He leant against the table, to look Fowler in the eye. "You say that someone murdered the butler at Salisbury Court?"

The Scot blinked. "Aweel, no…" He took a breath, as though to say more, and then settled for a firmer, "No."

"But you said…" Tom stopped, and sought Sir Francis's eye, and a nod of permission to press the matter — and, as he did, Williams beat him to it.

He caught Fowler by the shoulder, less than gently. "You said they did in the butler instead of you."

"Aye — but not the butler." Fowler squirmed free of Williams's grasp. "'Twas the butler's man."

This time Tom didn't wait. "And someone murdered him?"

"Aweel … he's deid." Fowler looked away with a one-shouldered shrug, like one who was beginning to doubt he'd made a marvel of himself.

"How dead?"

The answer, when it came, was whisper-soft. "Deid in his bed, this past night…"

Williams exclaimed in disgust, and pushed past Tom to grab Fowler again. "You come here, where you should not!" A shake. "You raise such a din they heard you down in Surrey!" A shake. "You push yourself onto Mr. Secretary — and all because a foreign servant *died in his bed*?"

Fowler shrank, but held enough of his ground to squeak in one great rush: "Aye, in his bed — but after he ate the sweetmeats I didnae touch, and aye, he was just a servant — but I, I'm Mr. Secretary's intelligencer, so who is it ye reckon that they'd poison?"

Williams clicked his tongue in disgust and stalked away — and Tom wondered what he knew of Fagot's latest letter, for this small, nervous creature seemed hardly up to intelligencing, and yet…

Sir Francis must be thinking much the same. "I would not entirely dismiss Mr. Fowler's concerns, Wat," he said. "He did make enemies at Salisbury Court."

With a small shrug, Williams stood back, like a soldier stepping into rank, unconvinced but obedient.

As for Fowler, let his eyes bulge any more, and he'd be picking them up from amidst the rushes. He reddened with the suddenness of a lantern lit. "So I did!" he bristled. "Douglas, most of all, and others, like that Italian Giordano Bruno..."

"Oh yes, this Bruno is at Salisbury Court, is he?" A new frown appeared on Sir Francis's brow, for this particular Italian had come to London with a name for uncommendable religion and closeness to the French King. "And he is your enemy, too?"

"Not *my* enemy as such." And here was a different Fowler — a little less the blabbering fool or, at least, one who could consider things. "But he doesnae like that I was of the Kirk of Scotland. He says 'tis ignorance that makes a rift between Protestants and Catholics, and that the Kirk is more ignorant than most, and —"

Sir Francis was quick to stem the flood. "Yes, yes — we are aware of Giordano Bruno's ways, but this may concern someone else. Have you met, at Salisbury Court, a man by the name of Henry Fagot?"

At Fowler's frown and shake of the head, Sir Francis nodded to Tom. "If you please, then, Thomas?"

Now let all his study of those letters serve him well! Tom crossed his arms, drew straight, and gave a concise telling of the mysterious Henry Fagot with his questionable French, and his unsolicited intelligence — though not in any detail, except for what concerned Fowler himself and the dead man. "So you are very traitorous," he concluded. "*Fort traistre*, in the words of

Castelnau's secretary. Also, it seems that the butler traffics Popish books, so perhaps his man did too."

He watched Fowler closely while he talked. He watched him turn flabbergasted, then indignant, then blank, then rueful, then aggrieved, and then bury his head in his hands.

"I dinnae ken," the man moaned. "I've never… Why would Monsieur de Courcelles call me traitorous? As for knowing all the ministers in Scotland, this fellow mistakes me for Mr. Douglas. Aye, so he does. 'Tis Douglas's counsel the Ambassador seeks, not mine. I … he … I…" He looked down and murmured, "His Excellency doesnae trust me the way he did…"

"Still, Douglas was not there in April — when this Fagot first wrote about you."

Fowler looked up and gaped at Tom, as though he had spoken Greek. "But then, why…?"

And this was as far as Wat Williams's patience went. "Because, Lord knows how, you fooled them all, and the secretary thinks that you take Scottish coin, or maybe French — that's why, you lackwit!"

Fowler's voice climbed to shrillness. "And for this, they'd murder me?"

"This we do not know," Tom hastened to say, before Williams exploded in earnest. "You said the dead man ate sweetmeats that were set for you. You dined at Salisbury Court, I take it?"

"Aye!" Fowler lit up, all nodding eagerness, and made as if to clutch Tom's sleeve. "Aye — that I did. And Barbier — that's what he's called. Was called. Clement Barbier always liked to come upstairs as the servants cleared the table. To see they don't dawdle, he said — but what he saw to was snatching broken meats, and draining the wine left in the cups. Aye, well. The other night I left my tart — and Barbier took it."

"Are you sure? You saw him do it?"

More earnest nodding. "I'd dropped my kerchief, so I went back for it — and saw Barbier slap a servant lad who tried to take my tart."

"And then this Barbier died. Do you know how?"

Again the Scot shook his head, and said, "In his bed."

Small wonder it was that Williams barked: "Ay, so you've said — but how?"

When that earned nothing but more shaking of the yellow head, Tom cut straight across Williams's grumble. "They must have called an apothecary. Do you know what he said?"

There had been a toy duck, when Tom was a child, a thing of painted wood, handed down from Edmund and Guildford, with a round nodding head, painted a bright yellow, and even rounder eyes. Gawain, they'd called it — or at least Tom had, his sisters settling for Duckling instead. Well, Duckling had nodded its stick-like neck just the same way as Fowler did — which was most distracting.

"Aye, that they did," Fowler said. "A French fellow, the Ambassador's own physician — who called it asthma. Barbier being fat and wheezing, the sort who'd stop breathing and die in their sleep. But surely ye must see, ye must…"

And it must have struck him as he said it, just how feeble it all was, for he let it trail.

For a dozen heartbeats there was silence in the small, stifling room, but for the faint rasp of a rake in the gravel outside, and Williams taking a long breath and letting it out through his nose.

Sir Francis had let Tom and Williams manage things between them until this. Now he leant forward. "Do you have any reason, Fowler — any reason besides the tart and your own fears, to see foul play in this man Barbier's death?"

Fowler looked down at his twisting hands, and then up again. "I would say no, Yer Honour," he said, "but that there *is* the tart, *and* now this Fagot's slanderous words — and I dinna ken how the twa of them make a reason…" and he fell quiet, the picture of desolation.

Sir Francis gave him the slow nod that Fowler likely did not know for deep consideration. "You don't know, and neither do I. And because I don't know…" He looked at Tom over Fowler's head. "Because of that, my kinsman will visit Salisbury Court, and see whether he can find out."

Tom worked hard at keeping his jolt to himself. "Yes, Sir," he said, as impassive as he knew how.

And why this should afford such glowing relief to Fowler, Tom didn't know — not until the Duckling sat up straighter and launched into another stream of babbling. "Aye, Yer Honour — then I can withdraw, seeing that I'm under suspicion there — and I may go one last time, and introduce him to Monsieur l'Ambassadeur, as … not as my own kinsman, no, for there's naething of the Scot to him — but as a friend from Paris, belike, a fellow student. Were ye ever in Paris, Mr…?"

"Walsingham," Tom stepped in the fool's first pause. "And yes, I was in Paris a long time, and met countless men there who could turn up at the Embassy any day."

And so crestfallen did Fowler look, that Tom wondered at the man's choice of occupation.

"No," Sir Francis said. "When Thomas goes to Salisbury Court, it will be under his own name. Monsieur l'Ambassadeur is an old friend, after all. It will not be unseemly that I send to him my cousin back from Paris. But you will be of assistance to him in other ways, Fowler, I have no doubt — for as long as this takes."

And there was no mistaking the firmness of the order, nor the quality of dismissal that coloured the words.

Fowler rose uncertainly, looking from Tom to Williams to Sir Francis again. "But Yer Honour," he tried, "if I am thought a traitor at the Embassy, if the Ambassador doesnae trust me, I cannae well continue my attendance…"

"Oh, if Courcelles thinks you a traitor he should warn us against, he is unlikely to tell anyone else, is he? And if the Ambassador has doubts about you, it would seem most suspicious if you were to disappear now — all the more if there is something in it about that servant's death."

Braver men had quailed before that one raised eyebrow. Fowler lowered his head, and murmured, "Aye, Yer Honour."

"And, Fowler…"

Up shot the yellow head again. "Aye, Yer Honour?"

"Remember: you never met any kinsman of mine."

Fowler gave Tom a good look — as one making certain of another's semblance and committing it to memory — and then, with another "Aye, Yer Honour," he let himself be herded out by Williams.

Williams was back in a trice, half scowling and half sheepish. "I cannot think what ails him, Master," he half growled. "He never was too sharp-witted, but…"

"Fear, Wat. Fear is what ails him — the worst of maladies. Next to a lack of wits."

Only those who knew him well would have known the irritation in Sir Francis's voice, in the slightest clipping of the words.

Tom did — and so did Williams, who raked a hand through his short-cropped hair and blew out his cheeks. "I cannot think… Coming here like this!"

"And never getting a whiff of Fagot," said Tom. "Or the smuggling … or old Mendoza's visits, it would seem."

Williams glowered, and would have bitten back, but that Sir Francis spoke.

"Indeed. And this, also, you will observe at Salisbury Court, Thomas. See whether you can find out who signs himself Henry Fagot, and judge for yourself the matter of this man Barbier — but also observe in what standing are held both Fowler and Archibald Douglas. One claims to have the Ambassador's ear, the other to have lost it. Monsieur de Castelnau has always seemed to me inordinately trusting — but it's hard not to wonder."

In truth, Tom also rather wondered how he would accomplish this Herculean list of tasks during one visit. Still, this was his own to wonder — and he bristled at the doubtful look of Williams — and bristled even more when Wat's words echoed his own thoughts: "A good many things to observe, Master…?"

For one so new at this sort of game, hung unsaid. And how did one answer to that, how did one answer *before Sir Francis*, without sounding arrogant or petty?

"Thomas is not wholly untried in the art of observing. Nor in that of sifting through the flexures and joints of murder." Sir Francis raised a hand to stop Williams when he took breath to speak. "We don't know that there was murder done — but nor do we know there wasn't."

Williams held his ground. "Even if they do know Fowler for your man, Master — they'd never poison him, would they?

Use him, that I'd understand. Show him what they want us to know..."

"Indeed, Wat. And this is why, if anyone in Salisbury Court is resorting to poison instead, we want to know the reason. Whether it is to silence a Queen's man, a spy of Mary Stuart's, or a smuggler of Catholic tracts. Oh — and while we are at it, there is the Italian Bruno. A nuisance of a man, I'll say. A bare week lecturing in Oxford, and he made plenty of enemies calling him a madman."

"He had a name for spirit and sagacity, in Paris," Tom added.

Sir Francis's frown darkened. "Deservedly, no doubt, since a good many pay heed to him who should not — beginning with the King of France! His Majesty is said to like the fellow's talk of conciliation between Protestants and Catholics. And this is why, Thomas, you will observe in what regard Bruno is held at Salisbury Court."

And here was another item for Tom's Labours — but Sir Francis's good words were enough to make one take on the full dozen. *Thomas is not wholly untried in the art* — and, being not wholly untried, he ventured another point.

"About this, Sir. If there was poison used, and if the butler's man was the one meant to die, we might keep an eye on the inn in Southwark that Fagot mentions?"

"Oh yes — the place where they keep the smuggled books. What does Fagot call it?"

"*Le Croissant.*"

"The Crescent." Sir Francis raised one questioning brow at Williams. "Wat?"

Williams frowned in thought. "There is an inn called the Half Moon, in Bankside. Right across the River from Salisbury Court. A tad brazen — or else very foolish."

"I don't imagine that Monsieur l'Ambassadeur is party to the venture." Sir Francis readjusted the papers on his table into a neat stack, a usual sign of dismissal. "Place a man of yours there, Wat. See whether anyone from the Embassy goes there — or the one who sells the books… Herson, was it? As for you, Thomas, Monsieur de Castelnau, if I recall, celebrates his birthday in July. Choose a gift for him, will you? A book of Latin poetry, I would say — something you can discuss pleasantly enough to earn an invitation for dinner."

CHAPTER 3

They descended the stairs in unfriendly silence, Tom and Williams, side by side but for Williams's longer legs. To keep quiet and avoid poking at wasps' nests would have been the wise course — but Tom didn't feel overly wise right then. Blame it on the heat, on his cousin's words, on the task before him — and most of all on the stinging thought that Williams was right in his doubting. After all, Tom's acquaintance with murder and those who did it boiled down to one harrowing journey to Paris and back, two years gone.

"Speak your mind, Williams," he ground out, as soon as they were out of earshot from the study.

He could have bitten his tongue when Williams only threw a glance over his shoulder and asked, "What about?"

"You don't think I'll do any good by going to Salisbury Court."

There was a shrug of the broad shoulders this time. "Master says you will."

So he does, was what a level-headed man would have said. "But you don't."

Three steps down ahead, Williams stopped and turned to look up at Tom, his craggy face schooled to blankness. "I don't question Mr. Secretary's orders," he said.

Tom, who had just lately wondered to himself why Sir Francis had chosen Fowler to be sent to the Embassy, opened his mouth and closed it again — hoping that he was flushed enough from the heat to conceal the blush creeping its way up from his neck.

Wat Williams snorted a little, before changing the subject. "I think I'll send Skeres to the Half Moon. He's just the sort to blend in well across the river, and knows what French sounds like, if nothing else. 'Tis your notion, Mr. Thomas, so go find him, and tell him what to do. And when you're done, send him to me," he called over his shoulder, and off he went, with that slouching, loose-boned gait he had.

Tom watched him go, calling himself names under his breath. They'd known each other for years, Wat Williams and he — or known of each other, neither taking much heed. Unlike many others in the Service, Williams didn't seem to resent Tom's kinship with Sir Francis, not enough to be wary of him. It had suited Tom well enough, while they crossed ways on the couriering routes or in the corridors of Seething Lane once in a long while. But it was an irritation now that Williams was installed as a man of all business, and Tom was…

And Tom was what? What was he doing in London, truly? Nigh on four weeks — he hadn't spent this long in England in years, and then there were these lessons, testing, tutoring with Mr. Secretary himself — and now this Gordian knot to unravel at the French Ambassador's house.

He loosened his collar, and squinted up the staircase, up at the summer light that slanted through the oriel overhead. He ought to be happier, cheerful about his prospects. Wasn't the task a clear sign of his great cousin's trust?

All things of great promise — if only he could charm his way into more than one dinner at Castelnau's table, enough of them in fact to find his bearings there … and, come to think of it, what would he wear to all those dinners, with most of his fine clothes, his Court things, still in Paris, and no money to have new ones made…? Not that he'd have the time — which was just as well, seeing that he was already in debt to two fine London tailors…

A very foolish quandary, and one that Sir Francis's wife would know how to solve — but Lady Ursula was away, at Barn Elms for the summer with little Frances, and there was nothing for it.

More than a few days of this, and he'd look like another Fowler — a beggarly wormer of secrets.

It was with the sigh of a less than cheerful heart that Tom resumed his descent and went in search of Nick Skeres.

Nicholas Skeres, who at twenty looked even more like a Minotaur than he had at eighteen, was very glad to be whisked away from the sweaty chore of beating carpets. When he heard of his new task at the Half Moon, however, he was less so.

"And what do I do there?" he asked, flushed crimson from his hard work, and fanning himself with a sodden kerchief.

"Nothing much. You say you are to meet your master there. You pretend to wait, and keep your ears well open for anyone speaking French, for any talk of a dead Frenchman, of Papistry, or books. You see whether an Englishman called Herson is around. You play the lackwit, nose about… Lord, Skeres — but you stink! Go wash, will you?"

The lad grumbled that Tom would smell like no rose himself, after a day of beating poxy carpets — but obeyed. Things had not changed much since the journey to France: Nicholas Skeres grumbled, and then did as he was told.

Tom followed him to the scullery yard, and stood well away while Skeres went about his ablutions, snorting and spraying, and sluicing pailfuls of well water over his head. There came giggling from the scullery door, and Skeres tossed his rag of a kerchief that way, sending two girls running, swallow-shrill.

He bellowed after one of them: "Saw you, Maggot, I did! And I'll see more of you, come night!"

Tom rolled his eyes. "And, I was going to say, you gossip with the inn girls… Don't!" He stepped away, but not fast enough, as Skeres shook himself like a wet hound, spraying water across half the narrow, cobbled yard. "A cursed barbarian, that's what you are!" Tom shook his dampened cuffs. "Did two years in a proper house teach you nothing?"

The lad grunted as he dragged his dirty shirt back over his head. "And do I get to drink while I'm there? A right strange servant I'll look, if I don't 'ave meself a cup now and then."

"You could always be a Puritan."

This earned a fat, ringing laugh. "Bless you, Master — a Puritan! And 'ave you ever seen a soul gossip up to a Puritan — even another one of them?"

And what could one do, but laugh back? "And that's a fact. You'll have a little money — but not to drink it away yourself. You'll have others drinking — and talking."

"All friendly-like, eh?" Skeres tapped his nose knowingly. "'Tis to do with that Scot as came 'ere?"

Ah, now — wouldn't they all like to know just that! "Not that you know," Tom said, sombre again.

"In the Bedlam, that's where I'd lock 'im."

"No, you would not — for you never set eyes on him. Mark well: you never heard of him — or Mr. Secretary, or me."

A wise humming. "Or of dead Frenchmen, or Popish books — you worry none, Master." A tapping of the head. "I 'ave it 'ere."

And he looked so wise, so pleased with his own cunning, as to give a man misgivings. "See that you do — and keep it there. Now off with you to supper, and be ready to go in the morning."

Throwing his rag over his shoulder, Skeres made for the scullery door — and stopped, turning to frown at Tom. "But if there's a dead Frenchman, why don't you go yourself? You speak French like an 'eathen, and you're good with dead folks — and the French are still folks."

"Good of you, Faithful Dolius — but I'll be elsewhere."

"And if I find out what you want? 'Ow do I tell you?"

"You tell Williams. Go find him, by the way. He knows where the Half Moon is."

"I know by meself."

"And he'll give you the money."

It was no great wonder when this last won the lad's grumbling acquiescence. "Not that I like 'im, mind you — money or no. The way 'e orders everyone around, you'd think 'e was your uncle 'imself."

"Cousin." There were times Tom wondered why he bothered to make the point — with Skeres most of all.

"Bragging and bragging and bragging that 'e was with Mr. Sec'tary in France back in the day … as if you must trust a man because 'e went to France! You go to France all the time."

Tom swallowed a laugh. "Yes, well — you've been there yourself, and look at you! Still, whatever else he is, Sir Francis trusts Wat Williams — so there is the smallest chance that you're mistaken, Skeres. Now go find him."

And, with a pitying shake of the head, and an even more pitying "Ay, Master," off went Nick Skeres.

Tom looked up at the square of hazy sky over the courtyard, smelling the summer air, thick with rotting things, and smoke, and the river, and turned Skeres's question over in his mind: what did the goings-on at the Half Moon have to do with Fowler, indeed?

CHAPTER 4

What did the bookselling at the Half Moon have to do with Fowler, and with the death of the butler's man? With this question and a few others jangling in his mind like many-coloured pieces in a bag, the next day at mid-morning Tom stood under the sun before the French Ambassador's door in Salisbury Court.

He stood there in his blue doublet and his best high-crowned hat, and fumed, and glared at the porter. The porter stood by the door, feet planted wide and arms crossed, and glared right back.

Fagot's Jehan Folk or Foxe, quite possibly, the trafficker of Popish books. *The worst of the lot*, the mysterious spy called him… Even without ever seeing the others, it wasn't hard to credit the description.

"I can only suppose that you have not caught the name, fellow," Tom said in French, striving to keep his voice level. "I am sent by His Excellency, Mr. Secretary Walsingham." He repeated the name, as slow and clear as he could. "Sir Francis Walsingham, secretary to Her Highness the Queen, and a friend to your master."

The Frenchman jutted out his bearded chin. "Monsieur said so two times already. And Monsieur can go on saying it till he's hoarse. I'll let Monsieur in when I am ordered to."

He was a short, wiry fellow in the blue and yellow of the house of Castelnau. He wore the livery coat open in the summer heat, and held his too-wide shoulders to a truculent tilt, enough to make a lamb bristle.

Tom was no lamb, and besides, the day was stifling, the sky turned into a lid of blinding haze. "I very much doubt your orders are to leave your master's visitors out here," he snapped — and evenness be damned.

The porter scowled harder. "I'll let Monsieur in when I'm ordered to," he repeated, squaring himself on his feet in a manner that, together with the dark flush and the squinting eyes…

"Are you in your cups, fellow?"

Behind Tom, the servant lad shifted with a crunch of gravel under his shoes. Adjusting a tighter grasp on the boxwood case, quite likely — the young fool. Did he think they'd fight their way inside —?

"Foulques!"

The voice made them all jolt. The porter, Tom noted in passing satisfaction, jolted the hardest. A French voice, soft but forceful. A woman's voice.

And sure enough, from the gloom inside a woman emerged, and stopped just behind the threshold.

"What is this, Foulques?"

The porter shrank before the woman — and well he might. There was something to her tall, straight carriage, to the small frown creasing the white forehead, to the stillness of the hands joined at her waist — something that Tom was much tempted to call queenly.

"It's nothing, Madame." Foulques was struggling with the buttons, tugging his coat in some semblance of order. "This gentleman would see Monsieur."

"And you leave him out here?" A slight deepening of the frown, a slight rising of the last word — nothing else.

It was enough to send Foulques into a squirming sullenness. "I sent the boy with the letter to Monsieur Claude," he said, before he inched closer to the lady for what he must have thought was a whisper, tilting his head twice Tom-wards, very much like a bird. “He is an Englishman.”

“A rare sight indeed, in London,” said the lady — an eyebrow raising in graceful irony — and only then she looked from the porter to the visitor.

She had the largest, darkest eyes, so deep, so unsmilingly serene…

Tom doffed his hat and bowed low. “My name is Thomas Walsingham, Madame,” he said in his best Court French. “As I was trying to explain to your man, here, my kinsman, Mr. Secretary Walsingham sends me to pay his compliments to Monsieur l’Ambassadeur.”

A hint of a curtsey and a twinkling of keys revealed a chatelaine at the lady’s waist. “Monsieur Walsingham,” she said, slowly, as though trying out the name — and, for a wonder, pronouncing it well. “Monsieur l’Ambassadeur will be most glad of your visit.”

She stepped back from the threshold, without a word or a look for Foulques. None was needed. The porter retreated with an ungracious bow that did nothing to conceal a very black scowl, and Tom was admitted into a gloomy, panelled passage, and from there to a hall. He blinked, half blinded after the milky brightness outside. He made out tapestries hanging above the wainscot, a staircase that led to a gallery on one side, and a row of painted screens on the other. There were two diamond-paned windows facing towards the court, and more light came from above the gallery. The air was heavy, thick with the river’s dankness and the green scent of crushed rushes.

"I hope you will forgive such a discourteous reception, Monsieur," Tom's rescuer said. "I know that Monsieur de Castelnau will be most distressed to hear of it."

Tom assured her that he would not have the Ambassador bothered with such a trifling matter. He assured her in more flowery words than he strictly needed, and all the while studied the woman with the chatelaine. Austere black attire, and plainly bound auburn hair under a black widow's coif. A housekeeper of sorts — and yet, by her manner, not quite a servant. And these large eyes, so dark they showed no difference between pupil and iris, pools of obsidian serenity…

Oh Lord! Had he been staring? "I bring…" He'd never lost the servant lad, had he? But no — a glance over his shoulder revealed the liveried boy, who hastened forward with the finely carved case. "I bring Mr. Secretary's greetings, and a small token of his friendship, Madame…" He lifted the last syllable — not quite a question, should she choose not to answer. But she did.

"I am Madame de Bochetel," she said. "And I'm afraid that Monsieur l'Ambassadeur is busy at the moment. Shall you partake of a little refreshment with Monsieur de Courcelles while you wait?"

Which was, considering, not much of an answer — nor, likely, was it meant to be. Tom knew enough, though, to recognise the name as the same as that of the Ambassador's wife. Madame de Castelnau had been born Marie de Bochetel, a stricter Catholic than her husband, by all accounts — and a devoted friend to that rabid champion of Catholicism in France, the Duke of Guise. She was known to still linger in Paris. Had she sent ahead a widowed kinswoman to keep house in her absence? A poor relation, perhaps, now leading the way up the staircase of polished oak — tall, and straight, and distantly courteous, her steps near soundless on the wooden stairs.

A learned man, Sir Francis had called Monsieur de Castelnau — so that the abundance of books in the small green parlour was no surprise.

Also, though not always, a peculiarly trusting one, for one in his position, had come after that — and, as he considered the man's secretary reclining across the fireplace, Tom had to wonder.

There was no other word for the languid pose of Claude de Courcelles, half stretched in the lion-footed chair, *fanning* himself, like some Roman emperor of old.

"It is this abominable, abominable dampness," he kept saying, and each time he sipped more wine. The refreshment promised by Madame de Bochetel had come in the form of fine claret wine in even finer Venetian cups of green and gold glass, and for a small while now Tom and the Frenchman had been sitting together, and partaking of it, and studying each other.

For there was no doubting that, for all his languid ways, Courcelles was observing the visitor just as closely as the visitor was studying him. He had long lashes, and long, limp, much-beringed hands, and a discontented pout, and wore bronze-coloured silk pinked at the sleeves to show the most startling green, and a pearl earring, and enough perfume to drown a cat, and his huge ruffle was starched yellow, and his hair curled and oiled, and, having known him for less than half an hour, Tom disliked the man from the bottom of his heart.

"Abominable — would you not say? One hopes all London summers are not —" a flopping of the hand that held the fan — "like this."

It would have been easy to dismiss the man, but this was Castelnau's secretary, willing to betray his King for English money — or so Fagot said…

"I've grown more accustomed to French summers myself, these past years," Tom offered — the scantest morsel of either bait or reassurance. "But London seldom tastes this sort of heat — and never for long."

And there it was, the gleam of alertness in the hooded eyes. It was a quick thing, carefully masked behind the lowered lashes. "*Vraiment?*" The long fingers played with the fan's mother-of-pearl handle. "But yes — you speak too fine a French — Monsieur Wal-sing-ham."

The slow emphasis on the name, another of those searching glances, and then more playing with the fan, the rings… Not that Tom had expected the man to state their mutual interest with open cheer — but what was the use of playing things this close? Surely he must see what use Fagot would make of his willingness? Well then, if it was more prodding that he needed…

"Thank you, Monsieur." Tom smiled. "One learns good French, living in Paris. I'll wager you and I have mutual acquaintances there. Also here, perhaps…"

Had he not been watching, Tom might have missed the change, the minute stiffening of the fingers, and the sudden, blank glance. He was rather proud, if truth be told, of how seamlessly he let his smile widen. "…for I keep running into people from my Paris days, you wouldn't know how many."

An ability to seem harmless, Thomas, will always stand an intelligencer in good stead, said Sir Francis's voice in Tom's head, echoed by the laughter of Watson, the Paris friend, also a Service man, who had used less charitable words.

So Tom played harmless, and chattered of his Paris days — *tickle-headed, Tityrus, not witless* — and behind that screen wondered. Were they being watched? Was Courcelles afraid? Was he playing some hidden game? Was he even the right man? Had Fagot lied…?

The scrape of Courcelles's chair startled Tom out of his chattering and his thoughts. He rose himself as a door opened, and a tall man walked in, a hand extended in greeting, and the warmest smile on his lined, dark-complexioned face.

"Monsieur Thomas Walsingham, is it? Well met, Monsieur!" The laughing eyes went to the cups and the pitcher on the small inlaid table. "We have made young Monsieur Walsingham welcome, have we, Claude? His uncle is a very good friend of France and of myself."

Cousin. Tom swallowed the correction, and bowed, and smiled at Michel de Castelnau, sieur de la Mauvissière, who could call Sir Francis Walsingham a good friend of France with such unmingled warmth.

The Ambassador was full of apologies for the long wait, and it was a while before Tom could assure him that it hadn't been long at all, and that Monsieur de Courcelles and he had filled it with the most pleasant conversation. Out of the corner of his eye, he saw the secretary sketch the smallest bow — although it could have been a nod made larger by that cartwheel of a yellow ruffle, and he imagined more of that shuttered keenness in the long-lashed eyes.

But there went Castelnau again, amiable and genial. "Sir Francis commends you as a student of the Latin poets, Mr. Walsingham — and for this reason you were chosen for his errand."

Latin poets, yes. There would be time later to reason through Claude de Courcelles's baffling conversation. Now to earn a

French dinner. Hercules, his Second Labour — not that the first had been accomplished by half.

"I am the bearer of Sir Francis's good wishes on Your Excellency's birth-tide, and a small token of his friendship…"

On a sideboard, as fiercely lion-footed as the chairs, lay the case. A fine thing, it was, inlaid with a pattern of trees and birds. With the smile of a child given sweetmeats, Castelnau lifted the hinged lid, and exclaimed in pleasure at the sight of the book.

And well he might. Tom had spent a good part of the previous night poring over the exquisite manuscript of Horace's Odes — a small treasure from Sir Francis's long-ago Italian travels … and this morning he had shared with his great cousin a small sigh to see it go.

For the cause of the Queen and England, Thomas.

Castelnau lifted the book from its nest of green velvet, and carefully opened it. "*Mais c'est merveilleux!*" he murmured, and a marvel it was. Roughly the size of an octavo, illuminated lightly, in colours so vivid they glowed, still imbued, one would say, with long-gone Italian sunlight. Even Courcelles crowded at his master's shoulder to look.

"A most generous gift!" Castelnau's eyes sparkled, and he shifted to English. "If you are a poet, Monsieur Walsingham, you must find yourself the words to express my thanks to Sir Francis — for my tongue fails me." He spoke it well, if heavily coloured with the French accent — and with a kind of elegant stiffness. The English of books and Court speeches, learnt in almost a decade of being in London and never of London.

Tom bowed a little. "No poet at all, Monsieur l'Ambassadeur. Only a lover of poetry…"

"Ah, yes — so your illustrious kinsman says, a lover and a keen student, are you not? Sir Francis speaks well of your taste and knowledge."

He would have written it at any rate, Tom admonished himself — and yet could not help the wave of warmth that always came with every hint of praise from Sir Francis… "Mr. Secretary is too good," he murmured.

Castelnau chuckled, and patted Tom's arm — by which he knew he must have blushed.

"We all know, do we not? That Sir Francis Walsingham is most rigorous in doling out praise. But I intend to probe your taste and knowledge myself, Monsieur — for you must stay and join us for dinner."

Hercules, his Second Labour — how he won himself a seat at the French Ambassador's table.

There was still the affair of demurring, of not wanting to impose on the hospitality of Monsieur l'Ambassadeur…

But, as was to be expected, Castelnau would hear none of it. "It will not be a very bright affair, you understand," he said, reverting to French. "Not much to entice a young man like yourself, fresh from Paris. But…" Laying the book back in its case, he took Tom's elbow and steered him towards the door and out to the gallery. "We shall discuss Horace to our hearts' content."

Courcelles followed, looking a good deal less amiable.

And discuss Horace they did, all through a meal of *troute royale*, asparagus in a buttered sauce, *carpe à la Florentine*, melon and figs, and more wine in Venice cups. Years in Paris had given Tom a good head for wine — but Castelnau's Rhenish was quite strong on a head that had to covertly observe, and think, and discourse on poetry — and do it in two languages, neither its own.

Tom sat on the Ambassador's right — in honour of Sir Francis, no doubt — and on his other side was the small Italian, with bright eyes and a bright voice, Giordano Bruno. This fellow who misliked poor Fowler, and mocked English ignorance, was equally as erudite as their host, if less keen on Horace.

"*Sol Oceano subest*," he quoted, eyes burning, "*ad ortus solis ab Hesperio cubili*, but only *dum rediens fugat astra Phoebus*... Horace's sun sinks under the Ocean in the Hesperian West, then takes a turn, then rises again..."

Tom's Italian was better these days. Watson had seen to that — and a certain Florentine girl in Paris — but discussing the skies still took a good deal of consideration.

"And would you seek natural philosophy in a poet whose rising Phoebus chases the stars from the sky?" he asked, slow and careful.

Bruno waved the objection away. "No, no, I would not — but if I do, what do I find? And mind — some Pythagorean magi had seen the truth long before Horace's time. And yet, what does the poet give us, eh? What but the commonest man's Ptolemy?"

Castelnau chuckled, a fond uncle watching clever nephews at play. "Do not hope to sway our Doctor Bruno from his stars and his sun, Monsieur Walsingham — unless you have an argument to oppose?"

"Only that..." Tom started in Italian, and then turned to French — oh Lord, and what should he know of stars turning around the Earth or otherwise? "Only that perhaps, when it came to the skies, Horace *was* a common man..."

"*E bravo, Signor Walsn'am!*" Giordano Bruno had the merriest laugh, although, whether it was for Tom's rejoinder or for the plate of almond tarts a servant placed before them, was hard to tell. The Italian heaped tarts on his plate with a child's glee, and, as the Muses and Fates would have it, Castelnau turned to answer his left-hand neighbour.

A pause, at last. Tom drew a breath, and sipped his wine, and sat back a little, like one who was enjoying a fine dinner and finer conversation, and was not taking his first chance to observe his table companions. It was, indeed, a small gathering — though an interesting one. Bruno himself, to begin with — with his notions of magic and religious conciliation… Across the table, in conversation with the Ambassador, sat the Scot Archibald Douglas. Tom remembered him at Seething Lane, more than half a prisoner, less than half a guest of Sir Francis until recently… Courcelles came next, Distemper in bright silks, picking at his tart, nodding now and then to the Englishman on his left — a youngish, apple-faced fellow, with a domed forehead and a scraggly yellow beard…

"You have met the Signor Scory?"

Tom turned to find Bruno twisting his mouth, eyes fixed on the Englishman, as though the name tasted sour.

"A Bishop's son — he never tires of saying so. One'd think that Bishops are Kings on your chessboards. Are they?"

"It depends on the Bishop, I suppose," Tom said, earning another of those glittering laughs.

"As everywhere, as everywhere. But this one, he didn't raise his son too well. The Signor Scory said to me just yesterday that the moment his father dies, he will take his money and run to France — and he can hardly wait. Unchristian and unfilial both, no?"

"Nowhere is it written that Bishops must make the best fathers…"

Bruno threw another unfriendly glance towards Scory, who was busy eating fruit and still bending Courcelles's ear. "Where

I come from, most would tell you that somewhere it is written that Bishops should make no sort of fathers at all…" A narrow-shouldered shrug. "Pay no mind to me, Mr. Walsn'am. Mr. Douglas says I like to hear the sound of my voice. He may well be right, Mr. Douglas." He tilted his head towards the Scot, still deep in conference with the Ambassador. They looked much like a scene in a play, Castelnau beaming with that benevolent warmth of his, and Douglas, in black from head to toe, sitting sideways, his red head tilted, smiling skew-whiff in his beard like Devil listening to Man.

"A most sharp-witted man."

"Is he?" Tom inquired — in that way of idle conversation that seeks no answer, for there was no telling who at Salisbury Court knew of Douglas's recent sojourn under the roof of Tom's own cousin…

If Bruno did, he kept it to himself, and gave another shrug. "The Signor de Castelnau values his words very much, for one thing. But do have a tart before I devour them all. I am a glutton for them."

Tom accepted the pastry — the Cook here might be a smuggler, but made the finest almond cream — and, as he ate, he studied the Italian: the small frame, the vivid face, clean-shaven but for a narrow moustache, the quick smile, the eyes that changed from guileless to the most burning intenseness between one heartbeat and the next, the bright, sing-song voice, the gossiping manner…

"Do you have no French at all, Doctor? It must be lonely in a French household in the midst of an English city…"

Bruno smiled, a nodding, knowing smile that creased his cheeks and hooded his eyes. "Ah, but I do. I do have French, and I do feel the loneliness all the same. There are those who understand Italian here, speak it, even — His Excellency being one — but French is expected, and…" A small sigh. "Your company today has given a very great pleasure to a homesick man."

And, Tom noticed, he did not shift to French. As though what French he had were so foreign, so distinctive, so similar to that of Henry Fagot…

"*Votre pardon, Monsieur…*"

A servant leant over Tom's shoulder to fill his cup, frowning in concentration as he poured, like one not well used to the task. New at it, perhaps, just stepped into the dead man's shoes? Would Clement Barbier be pouring wine, had he not died the other night?

Now that was going to be an awkward subject to broach. No amount of Horace would bring up the death of a servant… Tom blamed it on the French wine when he caught himself sifting his memory for a suitable line, something that might steer the gossipy Bruno in the right direction… The wine, most definitely — and a good thing that the Italian was distracted by his right-hand neighbour, a quiet fellow in the soberest black broadcloth.

The Ambassador inquired after Sir Francis's health, and then about Tom's own French travels, and the conversation dwindled after a while, like that of men looking to go after their own business, until Castelnau rose, to take leave of his dinner guests. He had a smile and a pleasant word for each, until he seemed to notice a gap in the company. "What has become of Monsieur Fowler, I wonder?" he asked as they left the dining chamber in a loose knot. "Have you heard from him, Monsieur Scory?"

Tom had been rather wondering the same — another question he could not ask. Interesting, though, that the Ambassador should ask this Scory in particular…

That gentleman just shook his head, however, and hoped that His Excellency would forgive his ignorance of Fowler's whereabouts. "I cannot say that I am much acquainted with him in truth. Mr. Douglas would know more, I think?"

Even more interesting was the malicious flash Archibald Douglas didn't bother to hide. "Because Scot should befriend Scot, Mr. Scory?" He had a beautiful voice, this Douglas, mellow and honeyed, for all its Scottish tinge. A liar's voice, Tom's mother would have called it. An intriguer's, most certainly. "Ye must know little of my country, if ye believe it."

Castelnau laughed heartily at this, exclaiming that all Europe knew the Scots for a most contentious people... It seemed plain courtesy to laugh — although the whole company must have known that Douglas had been party to the murder of Mary Stuart's English husband, Lord Darnley, and not just that... Courcelles wasn't laughing, nor was the quiet man in black, Bruno's other table neighbour — who, when he felt Tom's eyes on him, shook his head.

"The man knows no shame, does he?" he murmured in French — and was the first to excuse himself from the company.

It was a while before Tom could do the same, armed with Castelnau's profuse thanks that he should convey to Mr. Secretary, and, most importantly, with an invitation to come again and partake of dinner on Sunday.

"We have not yet finished with Horace, my good Bruno, you, and I," was the Ambassador's salutation, and then Tom was entrusted to the butler Girault's care.

This exalted personage saw Tom not to the main gate he had entered in the morning, but through a different door, into a narrow, beautifully kept garden that sloped away from the house and down halfway to the river. It was walled on three sides, and on one corner there was a wicket gate. "To Water Lane, Monsieur, and thence to the water stairs…" After this, Girault squared his shoulders, like one preparing himself for an unpleasant task.

"I am told that Monsieur met with an unfortunate accident on his arrival," he announced. He was a big, jowly fellow, with an ample girth and a manner of sombre importance — a veritable Minos among butlers.

Under this austere scrutiny, Tom had the most unreasonable notion that he himself was somehow to blame — as though he were going to let a French smuggler cow him!

"Your porter, yes. A rather unpleasant fellow — but I am sure it won't happen again."

The beginning of a scowl was quickly rearranged back into solemnity. "No, it will not. Monsieur is most generous. The man Foulques has not been himself, lately, but he will be rebuked…"

And then there were steps running down the gravelled path from the house, and the scowl was suddenly back, like a mastiff turned loose, directed at someone beyond Tom's back.

"Where were you, Rowley?" the butler barked in much accented English. "Monsieur wants a barque."

Rowley proved to be a sturdy lad of twenty or so, who, cap in hand, skidded to a brief halt, only to hasten to unbolt the gate.

Tom followed him into the narrow, sloping lane, flanked with garden walls on one side, and the passage-riddled boundary of the old White Friars on the other — the boy grumbling all the time under his breath. Once he threw a glance over his shoulder, and, turning back, pulled a face. It took no turning to picture the butler, watching from the little gate, a statue of disapproval.

They emerged onto the stairs, where young Rowley's boat — a small, one-man sculler — waited, moored to a pole. Tom paid his half-groat to the Water Gate, and off they went, the lad rowing with a will.

In the hazy light of midafternoon, the Thames gave a blinding glare, dotted with crafts large and small. Across lay Bankside, a row of houses huddling right by the water — among them the Half Moon Inn, where Skeres was, one could hope, keeping his eyes and ears well open. The wherryman would know which of the mud-coloured houses was the inn… A good look at the lad, though, at the brow knotted beyond the effort of rowing, steered Tom on a different course. Because perhaps, if this particular boat served the Embassy, then…

"A little brisk, is Monsieur Girault…"

Young Rowley let out a snort that Nick Skeres might envy. "A bully, Master, that's what he is. A bullfrog, and one who mislikes the English — but then, I say, why didn't he stay in France? A nasty piece of work, that one. A pity that they didn't put *him* out of the way!"

So there — almost too easy. Now just let the lad have a loose tongue…

"Out of the way?"

"Why, Master, they made away with a fellow at the Court, didn't you know? Old Girault's man. Now, Barbier was a greedy braggart with a roving eye — but still, 'tis a pity they didn't aim a tad higher, I say." And young Rowley grunted as he leant his whole weight on his oars, with the air of one who had said his piece.

Now, there are two ways to keep a man talking, Thomas: to believe him, or to disbelieve him. And this boy bubbled with it all, like badly bottled ale, ready to bite at the smallest bait…

"Come, now! You never mean they did murder?"

"Didn't they!" The bait taken. "They are all French in there, Master — French and papist! They'd think nothing of poisoning even one of their own." Rowley paused in his rowing, to lean over his crossed oars in earnest confidence. "I've a sister as works there. Wed to one of them, fool girl, and she knew him. The dead man. Knew him myself, come to that: a big ruddy fellow, well fed…" Rowley mimed a paunch. "They don't just up and die, that sort. Stopped breathing — ha! Stopped breathing my foot!"

Stopped breathing… Tom pointed out that the oars would not row themselves, and sat back to consider while the chastised lad resumed his efforts. Stopped breathing…

"Well, men do stop breathing, you know," he said after a while.

Rowley made to cross his oars again, but thought better of it. "Ay, that's what they said, for Barbier was a fat fellow, wheezing when he climbed the stairs… But I say, he climbed no stairs sleeping, did he? You don't get blue in the face by sleeping."

Tom pulled a disbelieving face. "You never saw him, did you?"

It was diverting to watch Rowley chew on the temptation to lie. At length he had to admit that no, he had not seen the dead Barbier — but his sister's gossiper, the kitchen maid, had been the one to find him, in the cot in the kitchen parlour. "Just like a haddock, Master: all cold and stiff, with goggling eyes and mouth agape — and all blue. Near gave the girl a calenture, it did…"

And at that point the sculler rocked, caught in the faster current that rushed towards the bridge and its great, looming arches. The boatman cursed cheerfully, steering his small boat in the foaming turbulence, away from the waterwheels, as he made ready to shoot the arches.

As they passed one of the huge stone starlings, and the roar of the river grew deafening between the pillars, Tom gripped his bench a little tighter. The rush of childish glee that flickered in his stomach with the speed and din, he quenched, and made himself ponder instead blue-faced servants, cots in the back kitchen, and tales passing from mouth to mouth — and also the wind-changing nature of secretaries. Much like the river, though, his thoughts kept running, and eddying back on themselves, to that blue, gaping mouth... His bag of many-coloured pieces was as loose as when he'd entered Salisbury Court, and now a good deal fuller — but he knew where to seek one answer at least.

CHAPTER 5

All the way to Scadbury, Tom debated with himself. It was well over two hours' ride, what with the hot summer day, and not wanting to overtire the horse — and, if one was entirely honest, a certain sluggishness in the going. Because certainly he didn't need to go all the way to Chislehurst for this — but then, who was there to ask of poisons, someone knowing, someone who would not think ill?

He frowned at the cherry-pickers in the orchards, and at the hawthorn hedges bright with ruby-red haws, and considered the wisdom of befriending some apothecary or physician, if this sort of task was what Sir Francis had in mind for him… And thoughts of Sir Francis, and what he might have in mind, led to thinking of Tom's father, and of that note asking why Tom had been in London since May, and never seen it fit to pay his respects to his parents…

And so it was that, well before midmorning, Tom was crossing the small bridge over the moat at Scadbury, under the gatehouse and into the dear old paved courtyard where his sister Mary's peacocks cawed and fluttered. He dismounted, swatting his hat at the beautiful, stupidly fierce birds, and there he stood, weighing in his mind his assigned quandary, and with the notion that having a word with old Cicely was a good enough reason to ride home, until the side door opened, and an elderly couple hurried out to meet him.

There was much smiling and fussing from Turley and his wife, who dragged Master Tom to the cool stone-flagged kitchen, and fed him new bread and cheese, and currants from the orchard, and Mrs Turley's home-brewed ale — no matter how he said he'd broken his fast in Seething Lane.

"They starve you there," Mrs Turley clucked, squeezing his shoulder to make sure under jerkin and shirt — and then Tom's sister Mary came rushing in with a basket of cherries, all laughter and teasing, and for a while it was like coming home.

For a little while — only until Mary, sitting across the kitchen table, and plucking cherries from the basket, said how Father would not like it that Tom had come when he was from home.

"He's not much pleased with you," she informed him, stopping to dispose of a cherry stone. Once, Mary would have just spit the thing in her palm. Now she daintily covered her mouth...

Tom reached to tweak a dark curl at her temple. "So Mother has been making a lady of you, I see," he teased, more to divert the conversation than anything else — and he half repented it when his sister's eyes darkened. Was Father not much pleased with her, either — still unmarried at eighteen?

And no matter how slight or unmeant Tom's hit had been, Mary was quick to strike back. "Up to your ears in debt, Ned says," she sneered, and grabbed a handful of cherries.

Tom watched Mrs Turley protest that there would be none left for making jam. Mary shrugged — so much for being made a lady — and in his heart Tom cursed his brother Edmund most unchristianly. Not that he could deny the debts, and Fates send that they only knew of the ones in London — but still...

"Ay, well, he can say that to my face, if he's at home," he said, and pushed himself to his feet.

Mary shrugged again, and said that Ned was out riding but would be back for supper, and then went back to her cherries with a vindictive sullenness to make milk sour.

And so, having found out from the head-shaking Mrs Turley the whereabouts of his mother, Tom went in search of her — his homecoming well and truly finished.

It must have been out of laziness that they still called it the old pantry — for it had been decades since Tom's grandmother had taken it over for her stillroom. But there was nothing lazy about it — a small, whitewashed room, with busy workbenches, and jars, and pestles, and drying herbs, hanging in bunches from the beams of the low ceiling, and mounds of freshly harvested lavender everywhere. The air had a scent that was green, and heady, and sweet…

As children, Tom and his brothers had been banned from the old pantry — and, as a result, had crept there as often as they could.

Dorothie, Lady Walsingham, who was never to be found idle, was also rarely to be found well content, so it was no great wonder when she turned from her lavender, and the old servant, and the child, and exclaimed in displeasure at the sight of her youngest son.

"Oh, Thomas!" was her salutation. "What will your father say?"

Nothing good, that was for certain — but then, so he would have if he'd been home, and Tom was about to say so, but bit it back. Instead, he watched as his mother dusted her hands on the apron she wore over a dark everyday kirtle, tilting her head — struck perhaps with a thought to offer a warmer welcome to the son she had not seen in months. And as she rose to do so, bracing herself on the long working bench, Tom was struck by a thought of his own: his mother was old. Not as old as Cicely, who hovered back, a smile on her wizened apple face — and yet somehow older, as though, of a sudden, the bearing of fourteen children and the losing of eight were weighing her down, twisting her into a brittle thing…

He picked his way to her, among piles of baskets and benches heaped with drying herbs… Before he could say a word, the little maid — his brother Guildford's one child — rushed to clutch at her grandmother's skirt, watching the newcomer with round, half-frightened eyes.

Lady Walsingham clucked at her. "Tush, sweetheart, 'tis just your Uncle Tom." And then to him, smiling only half in jest: "There. A stranger to your own niece, that's what you have become." And then to Cicely: "Take her away, Cicely…"

And Tom could have held his breath, couldn't he, and waited, and let the nurse go, and sought her out later… But no, he had to go and call to her. "No, wait, Cicely — I need a word with you. I've come for —" and he stopped.

"With me, Master Tom?" Cicely laughed her old, hearty laugh. "Bless you, whatever for?" And then she waddled to gather the child. "Now, you come with me, Dot, and leave Master Tom with his Mam, eh? Off we go to feed the peacocks…"

All cheerful bustle, she was — not that it served to smooth Lady Walsingham's frown.

She waited until nurse and girl were gone, before turning back to her son. "You've come for a word with Cicely," she repeated, with a perfect evenness Sir Francis would have liked. "Have we been harbouring another one of Mr. Secretary's spies in our herb garden?"

One of… Tom gaped. What did his mother know? How did she…? And to speak so openly…?

She laughed, at last — that quiet, half-weary laugh and shake of the head Tom had known all his life as an infrequent thing. "Never look so startled, Tom dear." She reached to pat his cheek. "Didn't Sir Francis teach you better? Or do you think your mother is a dolt, blind and deaf?"

Hadn't Sir Francis taught him better, indeed? Mr. Secretary's trusted man — and here he was, blurting out things, and gaping like a gudgeon before his own mother…

"'Tis being at home." He returned the smile — if a bit ruefully. "It makes me a boy again."

And if he'd hoped this would please his mother, he found himself mistaken again.

"Home!" She threw up a hand, and turned back to her harvest, briskly fussing with the stems. "Home, you call it, the place where you come as a thief, to have a word with a servant? And you'll rush away as soon as you're done, will you not? Back to France again, before your father can set his eyes on you?"

Not squirming was a feat. Tom picked a dark red petal from the nearest bowl of drying roses. What relief he'd felt at his father's absence had already died the death of foolish thoughts. "I didn't know Father would be away — and not to France, but yes… I'm for London in the morning, on Mr. Secretary's business."

With a great sigh, Lady Walsingham turned around, a bunch of lavender in her hands, and gave her son a long, hard look. "I hope, Thomas, I truly hope that Mr. Secretary's business will keep you well and long, for your father is not growing younger, and Edmund…" *And Edmund has little patience for his brothers.* "As long as he stays unmarried, Guildford will be his heir — but…" *But what of you?*

Tom crumpled the petal between his fingers. It gave a sweet smell of summer afternoons. What of him, indeed? What of third sons, all over the realm? But then… "What should I do, then, Mother? Smooth up Father into bequeathing me a substance? Do away with my brothers and leave myself the heir?"

Lady Walsingham huffed. "Don't be cockapert, boy. And don't be foolish." She waved a hand at him, much in the way of one surrendering. "Go find your Cicely, if that's what you've come for. And what your cousin wants of her, I cannot think — nor want to know."

In her own little cottage behind the house, Cicely sat Tom by the cold fireplace with a bit of dinner — pickled herrings, a well-buttered manchet, and ale to go with it — much as she'd done when the child Master Tom had been in disgrace.

She had sat by him then, hands on her ample stomach, pursing her lips at his childish woes. To look at her, it made no great difference that he was now a grown man, seeking her knowledge of herbs.

She frowned deeper and deeper, though, as she listened to what little Tom knew of the dead Barbier.

"And was he old?" she asked when he was finished.

Tom hadn't thought to ask. "He was the butler's man — so he won't have been too green a lad…" Although, how many underlings did Girault have? "He wheezed climbing the stairs, they say…"

Cicely laughed, and slapped her well-padded side. "If wheezing up the stairs killed folks, I'd be long dead and buried, child!" And then she sobered. "But then, there was one of my cousins as died of it — rest her soul. Not of the wheezing alone, mind. She'd cough, and spit sometimes — and had more trouble of it at night — and then one morning we found her cold in the bed. And she only a little maid of nine or ten. I mind me, Her Ladyship's doctor — your Grandmam, that was — called it a thing as happens."

At Tom's hum of sympathy, the nurse just shrugged. "'Twas long ago. You know as that he coughed and spat, your Frenchman?"

Another thing to find out… *And, pray, your dead servant: he used to cough and spit, perchance?* But more and more it looked as though the murder of Clement Barbier was all in Fowler's megrims. Still… "Was she… Your little cousin, was she blue about the mouth when you found her?"

Cicely's brow creased. "A bit, about the lips."

"But inside the mouth? The tongue? And was she bulge-eyed?"

The faded eyes grew sharp. "Master Tom, it does my heart good to see you at home, mind — but … you never rode all the way from London so as you'd ask old Cicely of a dead foreigner and a dead child."

There! A Service man these past four years, Sir Francis's own pupil — and here he was, read like a hornbook not only by his mother, but his old nurse as well…

With a rueful sigh, Tom sat back in his chair. Had the ceiling always been this dark and low? "Ah, but I did, Cicely. I did — for I'm not sure about this man's death, and things may be so that I can't go and ask an apothecary in London…"

"Ay," Cicely nodded, her wise, wobbly-chinned nod. "For you can't know who was the one as sold it."

Tom sat up straighter. "The one who sold what, Cicely? What herb is there, that could kill a man like that?"

It was disconcerting that, instead of answering, the nurse pushed back her stool, and stood, and began to fuss with the empty trencher, the cup, the knife. She picked up the jug, found it still full, and put it down, and all the time she never looked Tom in the eyes. He waited while she turned the cup in her hand, over and over.

At length she looked up. "'Tis nothing as an honest man would sell. Or buy."

"A poison, then?"

"A herb. The sheep sometimes will eat it in a meadow, and turn up dead, blue in the mouth, the tongue. And bulge-eyed, and I reckon as it'd kill Christian folk the same — but…" Cicely was back at her fiddling.

And what troubled her was not hard to guess. "But this herb, would there be any reason to have it about the house?"

She shook her head. "It has nothing good about it, hemlock."

Hemlock. Tom had no Greek, but there were books in Sir Francis's library, of Greek Plato's works turned into Latin, where one could read of fellows put to the death for corrupting the young. Put to the death by drinking cicuta — and that was hemlock. A witch-like thing, too, wasn't it? A thing of half-remembered tales told on dark evenings, of warnings that all country children heard, either in manor house or cottage. And a thing to distemper old nurses and wise women alike, to judge by the way Cicely scowled, and twisted her apron's hem.

Tom rose and leant close to kiss her on the cheek. "Don't fret now, Cicely — don't fret. No one will put hemlock in my wine. I'm only to unpick the reason why that fellow was killed — if he was."

"Ay? And if he was, there is the man as killed him. How will he like to have his reasons unpicked, that one?"

There was, indeed, that. "But then, the butler's man could have died like your cousin, couldn't he?"

Cicely clicked her tongue, and it was clear as day that she cared very little how Barbier had died. She grabbed his hand, and held it tight between her own, old and worn. "Now, mark you, Master Tom: hemlock has a foul stench, like cat's piss. No matter as how you dry it, boil it, steep it — it will always keep it. 'Tis sharp and strong. So always mind you what you drink and eat. Like cat's piss."

And this, too, was worth a question or two at Salisbury Court — for perhaps no one remembered Barbier complaining of foul-tasting tarts, or perhaps someone might…

"Like cat's piss," he repeated, and offered grave thanks, and a graver promise to look after himself. And then, trying not to wonder why his old nurse would know of boiling and steeping deadly poisons, he went off to himself, to cogitate what he had just learnt.

They supped in the tall, cool cavern of the great hall, where no number of candles ever dispelled the gloom, and no amount of company or noise ever filled the space under the truss-beams.

The six of them sat at the table under the musicians' gallery and, no doubt, to anyone watching them from across the hall, they must have looked and sounded like Virgil's Aeneas and his wandering companions: supping on the shores of the Harpies' island — and lost.

Six of them in all — Tom and his two brothers, Lady Walsingham, Mary, and Guildford's bashful wife, big with a second child. Of the two brothers, Edmund, the oldest, was more like Tom in appearance, fair-headed and blue-eyed, while Guildford favoured their stockier, darker father. Guildford had welcomed Tom warmly; Edmund had not.

Mary must have tattled of Tom's challenge in the morning — Mary always sided with Ned — and now there Edmund sat, with no qualms about discussing his youngest brother's debts at supper. Discussing them in great detail.

It would have been worse, had Father been at home, would it not? It must be so. It may be so but, by the time the carps on sops and the goose were served, Tom was very much doubting anything could be much worse than Edmund's gloating censure.

"…One'd think you dine at the French King's table, the gold you squander!"

A man of reason, Thomas, does not squabble. Men of reason count in Latin until they can govern their temper — or at least their manner… "Not very often, and not at the King's own table — but I do dine at Court, now and then, and at the Ambassador's house a good deal more —"

Edmund's snort cut him off. "The exalted company my brother keeps — and he only a courier!"

And devil take reason! "Ay — Mr. Secretary's own trusted courier, and his kinsman, and…" And his solver of deadly riddles — but that one Tom had the sense to bite off.

"And does Mr. Secretary know his trusted kinsman is a gamester?" Edmund sneered around a mouthful of sopped bread. "For it cannot be all clothes, can it?"

A shot in the dark, this one — and easy to answer. "Cards are forbidden in France — except at Court, and there they stake whole fortunes on a game. No sport for third sons, be sure of that." That the lesson had been learnt at one lesser table of la prime — to a very high cost, they need not know, need they?

Only, Edmund was no fool. "You are not in France now, it seems to me…" He held up a hand when Tom would have protested. "Cards are not forbidden in England, and one who plays the gentleman at the primero table —"

"I tell you I don't —"

"Enough!" Lady Walsingham snapped, glowering in displeasure at both quarrelsome sons. "Let us just hope that Thomas knows to deserve Mr. Secretary's trust better than that — and be finished with this." And, in the same manner of queenly displeasure, she turned to the gawping serving lad, and bid him bring the lampreys.

For a short while there was only the clink of knives and the clatter of plates, and the creaking of the truss-beams above, and the screech of Mary's peacocks from the garden.

"Let those cackling pests run wild much longer, Mary," Edmund growled, "and I'll wring their necks myself, to the last!"

It was an old argument between brother and sister, and one that made Tom trade glances with Guildford, and a huff of laughter — but tonight there was venom in Edmund's words, put there by Mother's rebuke, and Mary… Never be it said that Mary Walsingham was one to give ground: Mary struck back.

"Ay, for Tom's wedding banquet," she sneered. "If he deserves well enough, then Mr. Secretary will trust him to marry Cousin Frances — and then, Ned, you'll have to pick thanks with him!"

And at that there was uproar — as much of it as six persons can make, one of them as good as speechless.

Edmund laughed loud and unpleasant, and Guildford exclaimed, "Why, Tomkin!", and his wife looked up and about like a startled pheasant, and Tom's mother said, "Tush, Mary!" but her eyes narrowed at Tom.

And Tom stared back in horror at them all. If this should find its way to Sir Francis's ear… "Baggage, Mary! Baggage, all of it! There will be no thank-picking, and Frances is meant for better than my penniless self, and I'm no currier of favour, and —"

"*And* you are blushing."

A plague, a curse, and a penance — that's what little sisters were! And to make matters worse, blushing he was… Blushing that Mr. Secretary might think him a self-serving angler, that his own family should…

Edmund laughed again, that jangling laugh of his. "Pride is no sport for third sons, boy. I'd curry all the favour I can, in your place. Father may have a weakness when it comes to you, but it doesn't mean that others will."

And he sat back, crossing his arms like Scipio at Zama — a victor at the end — and there went Tom's allowance, such as it was, the day Father…

Tom threw his napkin — all reason fled. "Well then, I'd better earn my keep at Seething Lane, had I not?" He rose, and bowed stiffly to his mother. "I'm for London at cockcrow. Madam…" And then he just couldn't help himself: "The French Ambassador awaits me for dinner."

And off he stalked — the more fool he.

It was Guildford who found Tom outside, pacing in the tall grass by the moat, and throwing pebbles in the turbid water.

"Is that true, Tomkin?" he asked from the bridge, laughing voice carrying over the moat. "The French Ambassador?"

The last handful of pebbles plopped in the water. "Not that I'd stay even if it weren't. I've had enough of Scadbury to last me for a while. And you —" Tom pointed at his brother — sulking like a scolded child, good Lord save him! But then… "Not even you sided with me!"

Even in the golden twilight, Guildford's grimace scored lines on his brow. "You're for London at cockcrow. I'm not." He held up a bundled napkin. "Mistress Turley sends gifts. Come and eat."

Fine displays of temper fill no stomach — but, in truth, it was something in Guildford's voice that drew Tom out of his sulks. Something defeated.

Mrs Turley's gift was one of pears, four of them, rusty to eye and touch, and the brothers sat side by side by the moat, sharing the fruit between them. Tom wished of a sudden they'd done this as boys. Guildford was five years his senior, always kind to his little brother, but not keen on keeping company with a child. And then there had been Cambridge, briefly, and a few years of his own with Sir Francis…

"So, how are things in Seething Lane?" Guildford asked after a while.

Why, very good. The Queen's own work. A privilege. One could not ask for better… But here, here was the one man who would understand, who would know in a way not even Watson could. To no one else in this world could Tom spill it all. So he did, between bites of pear — he told his brother of Paris, and the routes, and London, and the Embassy, and the other Service men.

"…And they will all be thinking what a fortunate fellow I am — Mr. Secretary's kinsman, it must be easy, must it not? And it's a curse, in truth — and never because of Sir Francis, why, I'd go through fire to prove myself to him — but the others! Oh Lord, the others! You have to prove to them all, too, and prove yourself again, and again, and when you do, they'll just shrug it away, for *what could be expected of him*? And if you fail…"

Tom thrust the pear's core into the moat, the plop loud in the evening silence.

"You mind that big carp used to come up and eat what we threw?" Guildford's eyes never left the wider and wider rings in the water. "My Dottie found it floating belly up, last week, poor old fellow." He sighed, shook his head. "Who would *the others* be, these days?"

Tom gave names... Some his brother knew, some he didn't. "And then there's Walter Williams, devil pinch him! The worst of them all. You know him?" There was a knowing huff from Guildford. "No matter what I do, no matter how well, he'll always look as though I'm nothing but a cross — a very lesser one."

"He thinks you are like me." This said so softly, Tom was only half sure he'd heard it. The sun was sinking low, making the water gleam the hue of copper, but there was light enough to see the shrug, the bent head, the hand crumpling a tuft of summer grass...

"I didn't do too well with Mr. Secretary, you see. Oh, nothing to wreck the destinies of the realm — but..." Another shrug. "Sir Francis never thought to school me in matters of the State. And surely he never dreamt of sending me to uncover foreign murderers. Still, good old Wat will be thinking, here comes another of them — save and deliver!"

It was not easy to share the laugh. And never wondering, all these years, what had sent his brother home...

And whatever showed on Tom's face, Guildford misread, for he sighed, and reached to pat his brother's shoulder.

"But you are not like me, Tomkin. Williams will have to see it, one of these days. Now come." He climbed to his feet, slow and awkward, wincing like one in pain. "It grows damp — and you're off early in the morning."

Did Guildford wish he could be off too? Off to London, to Seething Lane again, to dine with ambassadors and Scottish intriguers, and...

A sudden whim came to Tom. "Did you ever meet a fellow called Scory, Guil? Sylvanus Scory."

"Scory, now..." Guildford hummed in thought. "There was a fellow of this name — a soldier with Leicester, at some time — or so he used to brag... He never takes Sir Francis's money now, does he?"

Tom shook his head. "He dines at Salisbury Court ... on Leicester's say-so, you think?"

"Ah, that's for you to find out tomorrow. And I am thinking: are you attired for the part? We can't have you disgracing the name, can we? Come see what you can borrow of mine." He put an arm around Tom's shoulder, and steered them both towards the bridge. "I'd give you money, but I'm not all that well-heeled myself. Father is going tight-fisted in his old age. He is unwell, and leans on Ned more and more — and Ned... Ah well, you heard him."

They crossed the bridge and the archway, full of shadows so deep that the courtyard seemed light when they emerged. The house glowed in the last dregs of daylight — the ruddy brick, the honey-coloured daub, and the leaded glass of the windows... It had seemed so huge and tall, to a child's eyes...

"I'd better mind what he said at supper, had I not?"

Guildford's arm grew heavier on Tom's shoulder, and there was a sigh. "And all the help I have for you, boy, is a pair of sleeves or two."

CHAPTER 6

Not even the time to enter the courtyard in Seething Lane, and Tobias Chandler, the scrivener, was at Tom's stirrup, saying that Master Williams wanted him. "Straight away, if it please you."

Tom dismounted. In spite of leaving Scadbury at dawn, it had been a stifling hot ride, under the grey sky — and one of less than pleasant thoughts. "And can't I have a pot of ale, first?" he asked, irritably.

Poor Toby's eyes went round — he wasn't thriving under Williams's rule of the house, and yet had not the heart to insist to Mr. Secretary's own kinsman… The sagging of the narrow shoulders, when Tom took pity on him, was a sight to see, and all the way through passages and hall the lad pattered at Tom's elbow like a lapdog, murmuring that Mr. Secretary was away, and —

"And here comes Mr. Thomas!"

Tom looked up to see Wat Williams descending the stairs at a loose-boned half trot.

He thinks you are like me… poor Guildford had said — and Tom drew straighter, pleased when his clipped "What is it, Williams?" earned no other comment than a raised eyebrow.

They were soon ensconced in the cramped downstairs office, the one that smelt of bitter ink and paper dust, next to the room where the cypherers toiled. Williams looked grim.

"Skeres sent word from the Half Moon," he said. "Sir Francis left for Court yesterday, and left instruction that, if anything came, you should be told — but you weren't here. I was about to go to Southwark myself." He ran his hand through his hair, and gave a resentful glare.

About to go himself, was he? "Then I'm just in time to spare you the trouble." Tom held out his hand. "Let me see the note."

"A note!" Williams snorted. "I'd like to have a note. The fool sent an urchin to say a man was done in at the inn."

Oh Lord — an urchin. Didn't Skeres know his letters? Tom had never thought to make sure, to arrange for a messenger in case… Williams, most surely, would have thought of it. "Murdered at the inn. Do we know who it was? If it's anyone from Salisbury Court…"

A shrug. "The brat only said they fished him out of the river. And ay — men fall in there all the time of their own doing, I said so — but…" Another shrug, and an amused gleam in the dark eyes. "*Mr. Skeres* was most particular that murder it is."

Mr. Skeres, indeed! But Mr. Skeres had been there when a man had been fished out of the harbour in Calais, two years ago, and found to have been murdered… And if Barbier had truly died of the hemlock, and not of his own disorders, it would be a very great chance, wouldn't it, to have two murders in three days, one at the Court, one at the inn?

Ah well. "Nothing for it but to go and see myself, is there?"

And Williams could do nothing but agree.

The Half Moon Inn in Southwark perhaps was one of those bustling places at its best — but Tom doubted it. The whole row of dun-daubed houses sagged in the mud, towards the water, as though drooping in the heat. Dampness mottled the walls, and the roofs had a look of shoulders raised against a sneeze — or a blow.

The wherryman knew the right stairs, and also of what he called the ado at the Moon, for news travelled fast on the river — and soon Tom was at the inn's water door. He hesitated on the steps, in something of a quandary. Not a new one: at Salisbury Court he was in the same necessity of asking questions without giving himself away as Mr. Secretary's man…

It had been easier, in France.

As he pondered this, he caught sight of an aproned woman inside, and beckoned to her, asking whether they had one Nicholas Skeres at the inn…

The woman sniffed, and squinted at Tom, pale eyes narrowed against the glare of the day outside.

"Ay!" she said at length, and one would think, by her manner, that there was little joy in having Skeres. "Over at the Falcon, he'll be. With the constable. There was mischief done."

She came to the doorstep, hugging the doorjamb to point to a bigger house, farther in the row towards the Paris Garden stairs, and then scurried back into the inn.

The constable, of course. So the local law was already at work, and they had moved the body…

Before following the woman's directions, Tom had a look about. It hadn't shown when looking from the river, but the stretch of ground between the inn and the water was larger at one end, and fenced like a courtyard, and tapered to a muddy slope upriver-way, where the Half Moon's tottering water stairs lay. Likely the river swallowed part of this unfenced portion in its higher days — but summer left it dry now, the water lapping at its end, fringed with sodden dirt. It was encumbered in part by a heap of kitchen waste, alive with fat green flies, its rotting stench thick in the air. Between the heap and the stairs, the mud was well trampled, and stained a dark red in places, where more flies buzzed, and the Thames made lazy wavelets, like a dog licking the ground behind a butchery… On the other side sat a low building, with a battered gate, and no windows, and the look of a storeroom of sorts.

It looked, on the whole, very much like a place where a man could have been killed — and a shame that they'd moved the body away…

Ah well.

Tom found the Falcon Inn — a larger place, with a gabled roof and a well-kept courtyard. On asking, he was directed to a storeroom across the yard that contained three men. Two were arguing heatedly. The third lay dead, stretched on a bench.

The moment he caught sight of Tom, Skeres lit up in relief. "Oy, Master!" he cried, and then turned, most minotaurishly, on his foe of the moment. "There, see, you dunce! What did I tell you? Mr. Tom Walsingham 'imself. Now ask 'im!"

And so much for discreet dealings…

"Quiet, Skeres!" Not that this obtained more than the usual shrug. The constable's eyes — if this was indeed the constable — had gone round.

"Walsingham?" he inquired, head tilted in careful disbelief. "And this man is your servant?"

"Walsingham, yes. But I'd rather keep that quiet, for the moment." Tom had become better at this commanding evenness, good enough that it had its effect, if not on Skeres, then on the other man, who nodded eagerly, and gave his own name as Constable Pitt, of the Liberty of Paris Manor.

He was a sturdy fellow, a little older than Tom, with big bones and earnest, round eyes in a freckled face. Also, he was either in awe of the gentleman with the illustrious name, or much relieved to have someone else take things off his hands.

How his betters would like his eager showing of the dead body to Mr. Secretary's man, Tom decided, was Pitt's own business.

"Three wounds." The fellow pointed at the forearm, the chest… "And there's another in the back. And if those didn't kill him, then the river did."

"I saw the blood out behind the Half Moon."

The constable looked grim. "And after stabbing him … either they threw him in the water, or he fell in himself. Your man, here, found him snagged under the Moon's fence, right at the end." And there was suspicion in the scowl sent Skeres's way. "Said that he must have been killed there."

Skeres, of course, surged in red-faced protest. "Ay — so would you, if you'd bothered to look, instead of blaming folks!"

"Well, you didn't run to fetch us, did you? And you knew to look for him —"

"That I didn't! Went out for a piss, I did, and saw all the blood by the water… Show me the Christian soul as would not go looking —"

"Peace — both of you!" Tom stepped between. "There's blood enough back at the Half Moon to make clear what happened there — and surely, Constable, you understand why my man was not keen to make his presence known."

One could have laughed at the way Skeres's smirk withered under Tom's sideways glare. One could have laughed — but for the poor corpse on the bench.

Tom bent to watch more closely. The man wore no dagger. A sheath hung empty from the girdle … which meant little enough. The dagger itself could have slid out in the river, or the murderer could have thrown it there after the fight… The clothes — a dark-coloured jerkin over a good shirt and slops, and one remaining boot — were heavy with water and mud. But not… "Did you wipe his face?"

Pitt nodded. "Nobody could know him for sure, he was that muddied."

"Now you know, then?"

"Ay, that's … that was Master Hurston. Barnaby Hurston, as lives near The Beargarden."

"Barnaby Hurston…" Tom studied the corpse. In his late twenties, dark of hair and complexion, prosperously dressed, if not finely — and drowned in the filthy Bankside mud. Or perhaps not drowned — no way to know whether there had been froth at the nose and mouth — but it mattered little. Drowned or not, three stab wounds meant that Skeres was right: murder it was — or at the very least a deadly fight…

Tom took one wrist, turning the hand palm-up towards the light, to find the fingertips discoloured and wrinkled.

"He must have been in the water a while," he said — neither a question nor a statement, the way Sir Francis did. And sure enough…

"'Twas hard to see him from the river, and from land, unless one was looking…" Pitt said.

And across him, Skeres: "There was no blood yesterday after supper. After that…" A shrug.

Tom nodded. "So he was stabbed either in the night, or this morning." Which sounded like a wise conclusion, but was not much help. "Very early this morning, I think, or someone from the inn would have heard the commotion, surely?" He made to lay Hurston's hand across the breast — when he observed the ring on the middle finger. He rubbed the drying mud from it, to uncover silver and a murky dark red stone. Not what one'd call a kingly jewel, but still… Tom felt for a purse, and found one inside the jerkin. A reasonably full one. "Well, that was no robbery, for sure. What was Hurston's trade?"

"A carrier — but, Your Honour..."

Tom looked up from the coins in his palm to see Pitt shifting his weight, face twisted in a grimace.

"Constable Samford, he's gone to fetch the coroner — and when he comes..."

"Of course." Tom slid the coins back into the purse, and put it where he'd found it. "I never touched this poor soul, Constable. I know nothing of him. As for Nick Skeres, here, he's just a servant, waiting to meet his master at the Half Moon. He just stumbled into the place where the murder was done —"

"If it truly was murder..."

Skeres had kept commendably quiet for once and for a wonder — but the constable's doubting words were fire to his short matchlock. "And what's that now, you dunce!" he bellowed. "You've heard Mr. Thomas —"

"Quiet, Skeres!" And the day would come, Tom didn't doubt, when he would say these same two words in his sleep. "It could be self-defence, for all we know — but if it was, why throw Hurston in the river and run?"

After some sucking of teeth, the constable nodded unhappily. "And you're sure 'twas done at the Moon? Right sure?"

"Why, have you reason to think it was done elsewhere?"

Pitt rubbed his nose, and blew out his cheeks, and looked over his shoulder for good measure. "No — or maybe ... 'tis the other way around," he said. "That is ... Constable Samford will wish it had been elsewhere." He shook his head, and seemed to come to a decision. "We was sent to search the place, you see. The Moon, I mean. Only..."

"Only you didn't go?"

Pitt's eyes went wide. "Bless Your Honour, no! Go we did, and found naught, and Constable Samford said the Moon's as respectable a place as you can find…"

And here a snort from Skeres.

Pitt squirmed. "Ay, well — Master Kellett, him as runs the Moon, he's friends with Samford, and…"

"And so the search was less thorough than it should have been." Although, in truth, it may well have been. *The chests with the books are not yet at the Half Moon*, Fagot had written. Not there at the time of the searching — but most likely brought there since. Yes, whether the dead man had been one of Girault's shop-fellows or not, the constable would be less than glad. All the more if his friendship with the innkeeper was of the same nature as that of the innkeeper with Girault. *They have given a great deal of money to the landlord to keep quiet…*

"Reckon we'll be sent to search again?" Pitt asked. "For the books, I mean, you know —"

"I know." Which Tom did, after all, and if the constable assumed that Mr. Secretary had been behind the searching, let him.

He must have, for he nodded solemnly, and, when Tom bent over the corpse again to lift the jerkin and shirt, he made no move to stop him.

The wound in the right forearm was deep, jagged, and gaping wide, the flesh looking more torn than cut. But for the mud in it, surely the bone would show. It was easy to imagine the poor fellow — Hurston, was it? — raising his arm against the assault. Tom straightened to mime the gesture, and bumped into Skeres, who had been peering over his shoulder.

"For all the good it did 'im," the lad muttered, more sombre than usual.

"Or instead he was stabbed in the back first, and turned, and tried to shield himself, and then…"

Then there was the stab in the chest, a good inch in width. Neater than the other, and washed pale by the water, it still looked ugly and deep. Whether it was a killing stab, though… "What of the one in the back?"

"Much like this one." Pitt twisted around to show a point in the right of his own back, neither too high nor too low. "Hereabouts —" he said, and then stopped and blanched as voices were heard from the courtyard.

Tom barely had time to drop the jerkin and shirt, and step back from the corpse before the door slammed open, and a large man barged in.

There was no doubting — by poor Pitt's unease, if nothing else — that this was Chief Constable Samford, a big fellow with a ruddy, jowly face, and a grubby sash of office tied across a barrel chest.

"What is this, Pitt?" he roared. "What are these ones doing in here?"

Tom rounded on him in a show of the haughtiest displeasure. "At long last, then! You'll be the constable? Then you can answer questions. Your man here would not, nor let me go near the body."

It was enough to give Samford pause, the truculence fading as he took in the gentlemanly clothes and bearing.

"He has his orders, Pitt has," he said when he was done with his scrutiny. "And come to that, Master, so have I. Why would you see the body?"

And the tone was respectful enough, if wary — and small blame to the man. Was there any point in concealing Mr. Secretary's name by now? Pitt was sure to tell as soon as Tom's back was turned, if he waited that long… Still, here was the man who had not quite searched for the books… Perhaps it was worth some angling?

"Because of the Half Moon Inn, mostly," Tom said, as inscrutable as he knew.

If Samford didn't quite take the bait, he nosed it gingerly. "We don't know that he was killed there…" he tried, with an effort at a searching gaze.

And Skeres had to take breath to speak, of course, and Tom elbowed him under colour of a shrug.

"Did I say that he was?"

Samford's gaze wavered. No constable of the Liberty of Paris Manor could think to play these games with a pupil of Sir Francis Walsingham's, could he?

He could play other things, though — such as the tortoise, retreating blank-eyed into its shell.

"Ay well, Master — I'll say again: I have my orders…"

The eternal cuirass of underlings. *Safe by Nature's gift* — though the man would do well to ponder the fate of Phaedrus's poor reptile…

"So you do — not that you always mind them through and through when it comes to the Half Moon, do you?"

He tried, poor fellow. He did try to keep tortoise-eyed. He tried hard — and failed. The guilty thought of the landlord's bribe was written large in his demeanour. His luck was just that Tom had no interest in playing the eagle to him — for now.

"No matter, Constable. I shall know what I want to know — without you and your men."

And off he stalked, with Skeres right behind him, leaving Samford agape and Pitt no less so.

It should likely be counted as progress that Nick Skeres managed to simmer all through the Falcon's yard, and out on to the street before he boiled up.

"You let 'im get away with it? Why didn't you tell 'im of Mr. Sec'tary? And of all that blood back at the inn?"

"But will you be quiet!" Tom grabbed him by the arm, and considered where they could go to discuss the matter, other than the public street.

On the one side, the Bankside continued along the lush, rich gardens of Paris Manor, towards the marshy curve of Lambeth, dotted with grazing cows and bushes in all their summer glory; on the other, houses were ranged well away from the river, with their kitchen gardens behind them, up to the bear-baiting where Hurston had lived, and to the huddling houses of Southwark, up to the spire of St. Mary Overie. Right in front of the Falcon, the street angled away, south-bound, coasting the manor's other side and then through more marshy grounds, where London petered away. In all these directions, and from them, people went about their business, on foot, on horseback, either to Church, or seeking Sunday entertainment. A beggar approached them, the side of his face puckered by a hideous scar, wailing of battle in Flanders, and of the thrice-cursed Spaniard throwing boiling oil… Tom sent him on his way with a ha'penny, much to Skeres's disgust.

"There, a-wasting money on a clapper-dudgeon! Don't you know they use pig's blood and who knows what to make those scars? If 'e's a soldier, then I'm the King of Spain —"

"Ay, well — some are easier to put to silence than others. Let's find a tavern, Dolius, so we can speak."

Skeres went from scowling in the way he had when trying to figure out mockery, to a disbelieving look, and turned to where the Falcon and the Half Moon were…

"Not there, you dolt!" Tom snapped, and started Southwark-way at as smart a jog as the Sunday crowd allowed, until he found a door sporting a drooping branch.

Drinking in a tavern of a Sunday, instead of going to church…! It had been a long time since Tom had truly worried about such things — but perhaps because of his visit at Scadbury, his mother's disapproving glower was in his mind as he crossed the threshold…

The place was only half full, and gloomy, and less than clean — the sawdust on the floor having seen from there more days than was seemly. Besides, the bull-baiting was near enough to taint the air with the baying and stenches from the kennels. It would do well, just busy enough, and noisy enough, that they would not be particularly noticed nor overheard.

An unperturbed Skeres took one end of an empty table; Tom called for two pots of ale, and pitched his voice low — but not too much.

Few things are more harmful to the keeping of secrets, Thomas, than an appearance of carrying them.

Skeres, of course, had not had the benefit of such instruction, so he scowled this way and that over each hunched shoulder…

"Now, don't you look so thievish, will you," Tom said.

And look how the lad sat square on his stool, and straightened, and composed his mien to what he must have believed a harmless look. Oh, Jupiter above — and they had sent this one to covertly watch a band of conspirators!

"I didn't tell Constable Samford of the blood at the Half Moon because he knows already — and I want him guessing at what *I* know. As for whose man I am, he won't be left guessing for long, since you told his underling."

Not looking abashed in the least, Skeres sucked his teeth. "Don't know that 'e'll tell, though, that Pitt. Saved 'is hide, didn't you? I'll wager 'e's keen to do you a favour."

Which was possible, but... "But hardly the favour of lying to his chief. We'll do better to assume the local law now knows Mr. Secretary has an interest in the matter. And that he thinks it tied to the Half Moon, since I took such pains to bring it in..." Which, in truth, was beginning to seem less wise than it had in the moment.

Pausing in his effort to shake the last dregs of ale from his pot, Skeres sniffed. "Didn't need you nor Mr. Sec'tary for that, did they? Seeing where the murther was done..."

Or didn't they? "I don't know. We have reason to tie the Half Moon to Salisbury Court — reasons the constables know nothing about — unless Kellett was very forthcoming with Samford..."

"Still," the lad leant across the table to whisper, "still, this one *is* murther, eh?"

Pleased as a fishwife with a fine sturgeon to sell!

"Try to enjoy yourself a little less, will you?" Tom scolded. "That poor fellow is dead — and yes, murdered at the inn — or dead trying to do murder..." And at a strange time, to be at an inn near his house. "He was never staying there, was he?"

Skeres's face scrunched in thought. "Not as that 'e bedded there, I don't think. But 'e was there yesterday. And the day before..."

Was he now? "Are you sure it was the same man, Dolius? Did you see him that well?"

This earned a look of chin-jutting offense. "Didn't I! You fish a man out of the river, Master — and then you tell me 'ow well you see 'im! I've done this before, you know, while you went a-riding 'ither and thither!"

Swallowing the flippancy of whether *this* was fishing dead men from the river, Tom offered grave apologies, and when they were accepted with a grunt, he prodded for more about the dead man.

"The other day, 'e was there about midmorning. Stayed for a while, then went away. By the street door, he went — not river-side."

"And did he talk to anyone?"

There was some humming and sucking of teeth about this. "Can't say that 'e did, no. Unless you mean the landlord, but there isn't a soul 'e doesn't talk to, that one. Was at the tap 'imself, and all who drank 'ad a word or three with their ale."

"And yesterday he was there again?"

"Ay, but for dinner. All cheerful-like, 'e was. All smiles — with these big white teeth, see."

"Did he share dinner with someone, in such good cheer?"

"Ay — and no. There were others at the table, and folks all around. You know 'ow it is, a laugh with one, a word with another — especially the girl."

"What girl?"

"*The girl!*" And one would think, by the lad's manner, that there was but one girl in all London… And so it may well be in his reckoning, for the moment being. Nick Skeres as an amorous swain — and he at the Half Moon not two full days!

"The girl of the inn, I take it?"

"Ay." A pout. "And all a-titter, she was. Some girls are fools like that, they fall for a mouth of white teeth, and Master 'Ur'son this, and Master 'Ur'son that…"

Tom sat up straighter. "What did you say?" he asked, sharp enough to draw Skeres out of his jealous sulk.

"What did I say?"

"Something that the girl said."

"Oh, ay — Master 'Ur'son this…"

The one who sells the books… Master Herson…

"Master Herson!" There was the well-loved sense of pieces falling into place. Not many of them, yet — but still. "That's who he was, your fellow of the white teeth, Dolius! Have you ever seen a Frenchman spell an English name right? If Fowler is Foulair to Fagot — then Herson may well be Hurston! A carrier by trade, did Pitt say? Who better, then, to sell the books out of London? And they weren't at the inn yet the other day, when the landlord only had a few words for Hurston. But yesterday things must have changed… It seems they brought in a few chests right under your nose, Nick Skeres!"

"Not if they had the Angels' help, they didn't!" the lad sputtered, neck tiding crimson, with such indignation that Tom had to shush him. Skeres dropped to a furious whisper. "If you said a purse, now — that I couldn't tell, could I? — but a chest! Cuds-me, 'alf a dozen of them! What do you take me for?"

"Well, you must have slept at night."

"Ay, by a window as looks on the river! And a cart on the street, at night, I'd 'ear!"

"You didn't hear the fight, did you?"

A hit! The Minotaur took breath to speak, and swallowed it, waxing redder and redder…

"No, you did not — and that means one of two things." Tom held up two fingers in turn. "Either you slept harder than you think, or it was truly a murder, rather than a fight."

"I sleep with one eye, always 'ave…" the lad muttered.

And, thinking of one night, at a roadside inn, when Skeres had roused in time to stop the flight of one they thought a murderer, Tom held up a pacifying hand.

"So the chests were here — kept hidden for some reason — until yesterday. Hurston came back at night, either alone or with someone…"

"And they made lard of 'im." Skeres sat back, and crossed his arms in a manner of great satisfaction.

"Either the man came with him, or made an ambush. Now, a brawl would be noisy — but… A stab in the back. Then Hurston turns. The arm. And then the chest…" And indeed, this was what it looked like, *prima facie* — and still… "Still, who did it, Nick Skeres? And why?"

"'E fell foul of 'is cock-mates, and…" The lad dragged a thumb across his throat, clicking his tongue in that way one did to mean "killing".

Killing Hurston, it would seem, and Clement Barbier. For, surely, it would be too much of a chance that two of Girault's men would die in three days — one murdered, and one of a malady? It must be the hemlock, then … and Fowler was both right and wrong: murder, certainly, but never meant for him. But, again… Tom sipped at the unsavoury, lukewarm ale, and pondered. This riverside stabbing and a witching poison… They didn't sit well with each other, did they? Even supposing there was more than one hand behind it all, why kill Hurston in a manner that was plain as a pikestaff, after counterfeiting a natural death for Barbier? Supposing it hadn't been natural, after all — and that particular knot would be difficult to unravel, without a way to question the servants at…

Oh!

Oh, what a plaguey idiot!

Tom jumped to his feet. "Come away, Dolius!"

A startled Nick Skeres followed Tom out of the tavern, calling, "Oy, Master!" and wanting to know whether he'd gone all the way to Midsummer, loud enough that they'd hear him from the Tower.

"I'm to dine at Salisbury Court!" Tom gave a despairing look at the other bank across the trafficked Thames. "To think 'tis just over there!"

"Well then, cross from 'ere and 'ave your dinner."

"Dressed like this!"

Skeres was unmoved, shrugging at Tom's riding boots and third-best jerkin, still dusty from the Kent road. His preoccupation, as he trotted along, was another. "And I go back 'ome, don't I?"

"What?" Tom stopped short. "Not on your soul! You stay at the Half Moon, and keep watch."

"What for? They know I'm with you now. And they've murthered their bookseller. You think they'll be back in an 'aste?"

"They might, at that. Hurston is dead, but we don't know what's become of the books. For all we know, they're still at the inn."

"But what's the good, now all London knows that I'm the man of Mr. Sec'tary's man?"

Did they now? "Pitt knows — and perhaps you're right, perhaps he won't tell Samford. Either way…" It wasn't so much a new thought dawning, as an old one taking on a new colour. "Either way, imagine Girault and his friends grease your palm so you turn a blind eye to their ill doings: would you be all that eager to tell them you may have brought very powerful eyes to look on them?"

And, bless the lad, he stood there in the middle of the road, brow knotted and finger to chin, in consideration so deep, that two over-painted women had to circumnavigate him, laughing at him for a natural and a churl, and he just waved them away without a word.

The Minotaur philosophising.

"'Tis back at the inn for you, Dolius. Keep your eyes wide open, your mouth well shut — and keep measure with the ale."

Skeres gave a mournful snort. "You worry none about that, Master. 'Tis ditch water they sell!"

Which, considering how he had just quaffed the nasty brew at the tavern… "Good!" Tom laughed. "And try not to get yourself murdered, will you? Most of all, drink nothing that stinks of cat's piss." And, after giving the perplexed lad a push westward, off he was like a hare — off to the Paris Stairs, to hail a boat, and shoot the bridge, and pray he wasn't unforgivably late for Salisbury Court.

By what miracle he didn't know, but Tom managed to find himself picking his hasty way up the slope of Water Lane in time for dinner. He was most careful not to soil Guildford's pinked shoes, that matched so nicely the ox-blood sleeves — for, if this kept up much longer, he'd need every stitch of finery he owned and borrowed…

So taken was he with his thoughts that a sudden clatter startled him into a halt. A dozen yards ahead, a door in the right-hand wall opened — one he recognised: the wicket gate to the garden of Salisbury Court. Girault stepped on the threshold and, at the sight of Tom, checked himself.

For a heartbeat, the butler hesitated, eyes sliding sideways to whoever was beside him in the garden…

"Monsieur Walsn'am," he said in his thick, flat voice. A greeting and, no doubt, also a warning to the unseen visitor.

There was a soft word or two from inside, soft but commanding enough that the butler stepped into the lane, making way for a man, and then a second. Master and man, no doubt — the first a crane-like, pock-marked individual, whose dark brown silks had a sober cut and a costly sheen. Behind him strode a lean fellow, fox-faced for all that he kept his head down.

There was a polite exchange of "Monsieur", "Monsieur", and the two men were gone, their backs disappearing down the lane toward the river.

Girault cleared his throat. "Monsieur Walsn'am," he repeated — this time with the slightest colour of reproach. "If Monsieur will be so kind to enter this way…"

He followed Tom into the garden, and shuttered the small gate.

The bolts slid home with a well-greased ease that put one in mind of Francis Throckmorton and Lord Howard. *They never come except at night…*

"This way, Monsieur." Girault herded Tom along the gravelled path. But for a few plum trees and the honeysuckles trained against the walls, it was a rose garden fashioned as a simple knot — the sort one imagined as a lady's refuge. Did Madame Bochetel tend to the pretty bushes that nodded under an abundance of pink and crimson blossoms? The warm air held some sweetness from the flowers, woven with the damp odour from the river. Surely Madame would walk here at a softer hour, early in the morning, steps noiseless, the hem of her dark skirts brushing dew drops from the small box hedges…

"A pretty place, this. Very well kept," Tom said — and wasn't he six kinds of dolt! Fishing for … he didn't quite know what, instead of bending his mind to what piece of his riddles he would pick at over dinner!

All the way through the garden and into the house, and along the dark passage, Girault fretted… Fretting over the late guest, perhaps … or over the late guest crossing paths with the two departing men? Sure as he was he'd never met either of them, Tom had the impression he had not been meant to see them at all…

Ah well — this would have to wait.

Monsieur de Castelnau met them at the great chamber's door, with Courcelles at his heels, and all the appearance of great pleasure at seeing his young friend again.

Tom made his bow. "I beg Your Excellency's pardon — for I fear that I come very late…"

But this the Ambassador waved away. "We enjoy a delayed dinner, today — and not of your doing. We stand on less ceremony of fixed hours. You must remember from Paris how His Majesty the King will take his dinner at ten, at eleven — whenever his engagements will dictate…"

And yes, Castelnau must have been in conference with the man in brown, the nameless fellow who had not stayed for dinner…

With more good-natured reassurances, the Ambassador led the way to the dining table, and indeed the company, more numerous this time — even without Fowler and the noble-faced fellow — and comprised of a few ladies, had all the air of having just assembled there, some still washing their hands in the silver basin. The ladies, three in number, including Madame de Bochetel, were being handed to their chairs, and the servants busied themselves still at the side tables.

It was a much aggrieved Girault that took his place there, carving fowl, and directing his underlings in wrathful whispers.

Tom didn't sit at the Ambassador's side this time — that place being taken by a well fed, youthful individual — a little

Vicomte, it soon transpired, travelling for his instruction in the company of a harried-looking tutor. Of both instruction and tutor the youth seemed in great need, judging by his shallow conversation — of nothing but the merits of French and English women, these latter much wanting — and Tom soon lost all interest in him. Whether anyone in the little dolt's entourage merited more attention, he tried to gather from Claude de Courcelles, sitting right across the table in a splendour of green-blue silk — or he would have tried, had the man been more forthcoming, and had Scory not been at the secretary's side. It would not do to engage Courcelles too much right under the nose of Lord Leicester's man — devil seize him! — and Courcelles… Well, if he had been so loath to converse with Tom in the privacy of the green parlour, why should he be more willing at the table?

Fates send that Fagot drop the play of secrecy — and meanwhile, Tom decided, his best chance was still his right-hand tablemate, the sharp-witted Italian, Bruno.

He found him watching the two ladies at the table — the wife and pretty daughter of the Vicomte's London host. The girl was deep in lively conversation with Scory, while the mother, sitting between Castelnau and Douglas, was as vivacious as her matronliness allowed.

Bruno shook his head a little. "I never cease to marvel at the freedom of your English women," he chuckled. "Your ladies, especially. Those who are of good birth but not very exalted. Look, by way of contrast, at our French Diane: the very figure of quiet composure."

And indeed, Madame de Bochetel sat as though her black garb and her alabaster calmness removed her from the table's general cheer.

"Diana of the moon, you surely mean. Never Diana the Huntress," Tom ventured — for no other reason than that, it stood to reason, learning about the household would help his indagations.

Bruno hummed, throwing his head back a little to squint at the lady. "Do you know, Signor Walsingham, that I am not sure of that? She is hard to read, la Signora Diana. A little of the housekeeper, a little of the poor relation — a cousin by marriage of Madame de Castelnau, you see — a little imperious, a little the humble widowed cousin… The servants do not love her, and our most generous host, you will notice, calls her *Madame ma cousine…*"

Nothing very strange about this last — but oh, the relish this Italian seemed to find in observing his fellow creatures. And in sharing his finds. There had been no more letters after Tom's appearance at Salisbury Court: was this because Fagot had now the opportunity to converse with Sir Francis's man in person?

"You are prodigiously well informed, Doctor, about the household in its entirety."

This earned another chuckle. "Oh, I observe. Doesn't it seem to you that each household is a small cosmos, with its sun and its stars, its planets, its revolving turns and orbits and —"

And whatever else the Italian had meant to say, he was interrupted by a servant boy carrying dishes of golden pastries stuffed with foie gras. The lad leant low to deposit his burden and hastily squirmed away, bumping the Italian's shoulder as he did.

Bruno clicked his tongue. "The way they have all been fumbling these past days, you would think that poor Barbier was a pearl among butlers!"

And remember, Thomas, that an appearance of eagerness is most prejudicial to the gathering of intelligence.

Shoulders loose, eye on the pastries — but for a glance and the slightest frown — and the slightest inflection of question... "I thought that Girault...?"

Bruno nodded. "Yes — yes," he muttered around a mouthful. "Our Girault is the butler proper. But there was this man of his ... and I am sure Girault believes he owns and commands us all — but Barbier was his underling, and ... and let me say no more of him, because he has been dead this past week or so, poor fellow."

"Was he very old?"

"But not at all!" The Italian waved his knife in fervid denial. "Five and thirty, or a little younger — although it is hard to tell sometimes, with such fat people. He just ... he must have taken ill, because one night he took the scullion's cot, and never awoke again. He just stopped breathing, the physician said."

"Rest his soul," Tom said — earning himself only a small, solemn nod. "Do these things come as a sudden seizure?"

Bruno chewed thoughtfully — the academic side of the matter taking hold. "Ah that, now. People choke, I suppose. Or else they have a connatural disposition, an affection..." He stopped, seeing Tom struggle with the Italian words. "A ... a... How shall I say? It is inbred in them more than in others."

Tom nodded slowly, and appropriated Cicely's tale. "I see. A cousin of mine died young in this manner — but all her life she had suffered from coughing fits, and wheezing, and spitting — I beg your pardon. A most unseemly table talk."

Not that Bruno seemed perturbed in the least. "Ah, you think of the asthma! Perhaps, perhaps. I have not been here long myself, but I believe this poor Barbier was much given to wheezing. And now, of course, because of the way he was found — a most unpleasant sight, I will admit — there is great talk among the servants of his staring, blue-faced, blue-tongued ghost wheezing in the halls at night…"

There was a dove-throated laugh across the table, the girl's reaction to some remark of Scory's — and Tom looked up to find Courcelles's eyes on him. A moment, and then the hooded glare shifted sideways, but not quickly enough to hide the unfriendly scrutiny. Had the secrétaire been listening in on Tom and Bruno's conversation?

The Italian had noticed too. He nudged Tom's elbow, and leant in to whisper laughingly: "There is no use, Signor Tommaso. You will never make that one your friend. His own connatural disposition is a most distrustful one."

Make Courcelles his friend! *I have made the Ambassador's secrétaire so much my friend…* Was this Fagot worried that someone might try to get to Courcelles behind his back?

Under cover of an answering chuckle, Tom turned to study the Italian — the knowing eyes, the gleam of mischief in the smile… *Was* this Henry Fagot?

From under his lashes, Courcelles was watching them both again — and, more surprisingly, from her place at the table's end, so was Diane de Bochetel.

Unlike Courcelles of the shifting eyes, Madame did not look away upon finding herself caught. She just tilted her head a little, with a grace that looked at odds with the unwavering black eyes. Tom nodded back — the slightest suggestion of a bow, a hint of a smile — and went back to his foie gras in a manner that, he hoped, did not look pointed.

The pastries were delicious, the crust golden and crisp, the filling delicately spiced… There was no other word for it: it tasted like Paris. Before long, an eating neighbour — as opposed to a conversing one — caught the little Vicomte's interest.

"And is it not a pleasure to eat properly again, Monsieur?" he asked, smacking his greasy lips. "Let me say this, Monsieur: you English do not hold a candle when it comes to fine food. I have eaten barbarously — barbarously! — ever since I set foot on this island. Even in the greatest houses! And I am told you have French cooks — but have them savage good food in your English way... I should not speak to you like this, I think — but Monsieur de Castelnau says that you lived in Paris, so you will understand."

The little prattling want-wit! "I've lived there long enough, Monsieur, to miss good plain English fare at times."

The Vicomte took this as the greatest joke, and laughed heartily. "But surely, Monsieur," he insisted, "you must miss Paris?"

"Surely," was the diplomatic answer — but the fact was that even half-witted stripling noblemen could give a man pause. Did he miss Paris, in truth? He did miss the Thomases, for sure, and the long-leashed half-freedom of a courier's life... Suddenly, the cramped rooms in Paris felt like a distant home. A home he was bound to leave behind for good, sooner rather than later, to be stuck in an England where Scadbury was Edmund's home, and Seething Lane...

Oh Lord, what a fool! If he hadn't been at the French Ambassador's dinner table, Tom would have shaken his head, even laughed at himself. What a fool. And Sir Francis trusting him to uncover secrets...

He nodded at the Vicomte, something like a gracious acknowledgment of a hit, and took another bite of the excellent pastry.

The little dolt laughed again, delighted, and raised his fine glass cup, greasy at the rim. "Here's to Monsieur l'Ambassadeur's most excellent French cook, eh?" he toasted, to far more applause than the sentiment deserved.

And that was when it occurred to Tom that the most excellent cook was, according to Fagot, one of the smugglers. Leduc — or some such name… Was he then also the murderer of Hurston? And, before that, of Barbier? Was a cook in a better position than most to procure strange herbs? Perhaps not — but to slip them in someone's dinner or drink…? Suddenly, the pâté seemed to have all manner of strange flavours…

"Don't you shudder, Signor Walsn'am, to think of our young table fellow as a minister, someday, or a royal favourite?"

Oh Lord! Had Bruno no sense of seemliness? What if the little Vicomte understood Italian? What if anyone heard…? A quick glance revealed the youth obliviously gorging himself on pastries — in a manner so vapid and so witless as to lend weight to Bruno's question.

"Oh, come! He's not *that* well-born, is he?" Tom asked, pointedly lowering his voice.

Eyes crinkling at the corners, the Italian laughed. "I hope not, *signor mio*!" And only then did he bring himself to whisper. "I truly hope not, because intolerance and extremes are not always the breed of stupidity — but…" A tilt of the chin towards the Vicomte. "Stupidity, I fear, knows to breed little else." He shook his head, with a sad smile. "His Excellency would frown to hear me now…"

And whether the frown would be for the lack of charity toward the guest, or the notion in general, Tom was left to piece together for himself — because Bruno went back to his pastries, with his head lowered and a more melancholy manner than he'd yet shown.

Was this one of the Italian's uncommendable opinions, then?

That Castelnau misliked to have such opinions spoken at his table (Hercules, his Lesser Labour accomplished), and that, were it not a matter of religion, Sir Francis might share them, Tom was left no time to consider — as right then the plates were cleared, and a small triumph was brought to the table. The marchpane ship sailing on a sea of coloured jellies caused much praise and exclamation, and by the time this was done, Bruno was firmly entrenched in conversation with the Vicomte's tutor on his other side.

As they rose from the table, Castelnau sought Tom.

"Monsieur Walsingham," he beamed, a hand on Tom's shoulder. "I have neglected you, today… No Horace, no poetry at all — unless that was what you discussed with my Bruno? Ah, but we will make up for it, I promise."

Tom bowed, and smiled away the very idea of having been neglected, and was vague about his conversation with the Italian — Courcelles's cat-like attention coming back to mind.

Whatever the secrétaire had eavesdropped, the Ambassador could not yet be privy to it, could he? Still, when he asked for a few minutes of private speech with his good friend's nephew — or cousin, was it? — Tom could not but wonder…

Once in the hall, Castelnau separated them from the company, and, his hand now on Tom's elbow, led the way up the small flight of stairs, to the green parlour, and, past that, into what must have been the study proper.

It was a larger place — although Salisbury Court boasted no very large rooms — with a fine moulded ceiling, and good light from two glazed windows. The walls were lined with dark, thickly carved cupboards, though, that ate space and drank light, and closed in around two writing tables. The wider one, carpeted with a fine Eastern tapestry, had a high-backed chair, and a very elegant clock, and an inkwell of gilt-bronze in the shape of a prancing horse. At the smaller table, among neat piles of papers, sat a man, busy sanding a freshly written paper. He rose to his feet as the Ambassador entered, bracing himself on the table, and bowing with back-aching stiffness.

"I hope I did not keep you too long from your supper, Laurent?" asked Castelnau, all charm and good cheer.

The man Laurent bowed again, a little less painfully, and said that, if it pleased Monsieur, he had just finished the fair copy.

He looked to be well into his forties, with a powerful build and a scribe's stooping stance under fustian clothes. He had a mane of fair hair just touched with grey at the temples, and a full, equally fair beard that swallowed most of his expression. That he was smiling at the Ambassador, one guessed by the crinkles around the grey eyes. That it wasn't an especially cheerful smile, was just the haziest impression.

"Ah, perfect!" Castelnau said, with an air of great satisfaction. "Seal it then, if you please, Laurent, and then you can go. Meanwhile my young friend will take a seat, won't he?"

He motioned Tom to one of the chairs that fronted the large table, and took the other for himself, instead of sitting in the high-backed chair.

There was a short silence, enough to hear, behind Tom's back, the small sounds of letter-sealing. The folding of the paper, the sizzling of the wax put to the flame…

Then the clerk Laurent came to hand the letter to his master, the seal still soft and glistening, and was dismissed.

"And send our friend to me as you go, will you?" was Castelnau's last instruction, before he turned to Tom and handed him the letter. It was addressed, in a careful hand, to the Right Honourable Sir Francis Walsingham.

"I would have sent a man to deliver it, but then it besought me: who better to be entrusted with such a letter than my young friend, Sir Francis's own kinsman? Oh, not that it contains any great secret — you must be used to carrying far more important papers, eh?"

And this was the Ambassador showing he knew Tom for more than just a Latin-spouting irrelevance. Well, his couriering work had never been a secret — and anyone was welcome to guess at the degree of particularity involved. "A courier carries correspondence of all sorts," he said, and this was accepted with a genial smile.

"*Et bien*, then you will not be offended to carry this one." Castelnau tapped a forefinger on the missive. "It is about a kindness Mr. Secretary did to a protégé of mine — an Italian. I would be grateful to you for conveying the warmth of friendship that accompanies my thanks. The written word does not always carry the fullness of our meaning, does it? Especially across the different tongues, perhaps?"

Across the different tongues…

A knock at the door came right on the tail of that last question. A most welcome interruption.

So! Was this the true aim of this little charade of the letter? Did the Ambassador know of Fagot, then, and of his intelligences in bad French? But if so, why reveal his knowledge to Sir Francis, of all men…?

There was barely a moment for these questions to form in Tom's mind, as the Ambassador called, "*Entrez!*" and a man obeyed the summons — a dark-complexioned fellow of five-and-thirty or so, who bowed low to Castelnau with a brisk gracefulness.

"This, Monsieur Walsingham, is Monsieur Rocco Bonetti — once of Venice, and now a subject of your Queen's Majesty. Young as you are, you must have heard about Monsieur Rocco's fencing school."

"A college, Excellency. Not a mere, paltry school — a college," the Venetian corrected, with the air of one who did so often. He had an accent a little like Bruno's, but a good deal softer — and indeed Tom remembered … oh, did he not! And not just tales of the costliest fencing hall in London — but the man himself, though he'd never met him. Rocco Bonetti, the fellow who'd been finding Fagot's letters in his hat — or so he claimed! What the devil was this, then? Tom schooled his face to the very blankest pleasantness, thankful, for the moment, that the Italian carried on without so much as pausing for breath.

"A college of the noble art of defence, yes — but it is all gone now. All gone. Yet…" Another bow, with much bouncing of dark curls, to the Ambassador, and a long, searching glance at Tom. "Did Your Excellency say Walsingham? I know the name very well. I am much indebted to a gentleman who bears it."

"Monsieur Rocco has been most unfortunate in these last few years, Monsieur Walsingham," the Ambassador explained. "Most unfortunate indeed. He encountered opposition from your fellow countrymen, the disfavour of a great nobleman of your Court, exile, loss, piracy, and sickness. But…" A forefinger shot up, like that of a schoolmaster calling for attention. "Sir Francis's generosity has done much to restore Monsieur Rocco's faith in mankind — and England in particular."

The Italian bowed low, but with the greatest dignity. "Indeed, and all through the good offices of His Excellency. As I said, I am much indebted — and always will be."

And so ambiguous it was to whom the fellow felt indebted, so very much like a play it all seemed, that no recourse remained, beyond taking shelter in the safety of inane good manners. They passed a sugary while, the three of them, assuring each other of the most exquisite gratefulness and friendship — Monsieur l'Ambassadeur beaming with earnest benevolence.

Then Tom was dismissed with his letter and his new doubts — and, if there were any truth to that figure of speech that calls certain thoughts weighty, the wherry he took to carry him eastward would surely have floundered under the burden of them.

CHAPTER 7

It was a very long, very sleepless night that Tom spent in his garret, tossing about in the heat, and turning in his mind the new surfeit of pieces that refused to fit with each other, and trying to turn a deaf ear to the snores of his roommate, young Chandler — which never before had irritated him in such manner.

At some very late point he dozed off, though, until the hooves of horses in the courtyard startled him awake — well past first light.

"Mr. Secretary's back soon," Toby Chandler announced through a yawn.

Tom jolted up. "And when the devil were you going to wake me?" he growled.

Chandler, thoroughly dressed already, shrugged and scurried away.

Tom's mother would have taken ill to hear him curse as he dressed in burning haste, and clattered downstairs still wrangling with his collar — because it was in the evil and perverse nature of linens that his collar would choose this one of all mornings to tangle —

"Oh, there you are, Thomas."

And Tom came to a less than graceful stop, because of course, *of course* Sir Francis stood in the hall to see him late in starting the day — and, to crown the disaster, he was not alone. Of all the days on this earth, Sir Philip Sidney had chosen this very morning to accompany Sir Francis to London.

Sidney, who was an accomplished poet, and a dashing soldier, and a courtier, and a diplomat, and a scholar of renown at eight-and-twenty, and rich to boot, and a knight, and a man Sir Francis treated as a friend and an equal in spite of his much younger age. Sidney, who looked up the stairs like one trying to figure out a strange specimen, began by raising an arched eyebrow, followed by a corner of his mouth, and at last greeted: "Walsingham."

The only saving grace — and a pitifully small one at that — was that Tom didn't stutter when he replied, and even managed to stop himself from excusing his conspicuous lateness.

Even the fact that Sir Francis did not look put out at all only offered the flimsiest relief, and only for the shortest while — only until Tom was told to join his cousin and Sidney for breakfast.

"I am sure you have much to tell of what happened in these past days…"

Oh, didn't he! And now he would have to tell it — the whole morass of conjecture, suspicion, unlikely fact, and questions — in front of Sidney, who was not only all that he was, but also nephew to Lord Leicester, who happened to have a man of his own haunting the Embassy!

And because there was no earthly way to warn Sir Francis of this, Tom was left to follow his betters back upstairs and sit down with them to bread, butter, and herrings — all the time trying to sort through the unjointed pieces in his head, groping for a way to tell his tale and not tell it — and, in fact, wondering what he could safely tell.

A good deal of this anxious cogitation he could have spared himself.

"Sir Philip knows of Fagot's letters, of course," said Sir Francis, when he had taken his seat, dismissed the servant, and started to sparingly butter his manchet.

Of course, and any man with a grain of wit in his head would have known that, otherwise, they would not be having this conversation at all…

So Tom nodded his most soldierly nod, took a good breath, and began his account. He told of the murder at the Half Moon first.

"And there is little doubt that this Hurston is one and the same as Fagot's Master Herson, the seller of books. Being a carrier, he was excellently placed to carry the books out of London to sell. He must have rowed himself to the inn for that purpose. There was no boat when I arrived there, but the murderer may well have cut it loose or taken it away. And then … a falling out with one of his cronies — though what about, and what became of the books later, I do not know yet. But if Hurston was to have taken them, then perhaps the books are still at the inn, while the butler finds another seller. I have left a man at the Half Moon to observe — and to seek the books if he can."

Sidney, who had been listening and eating with an equally keen appetite, gestured with his knife, waving it in the general direction of the river. "The place has been searched already, though, you say? By Paris Manor men?"

So he hadn't listened all that closely, had he? "When the books weren't there yet," Tom said, with some satisfaction. "And even had they been, the constable knew to be less than thorough."

"So you said — but then…" Sidney sat back and mused. "Could the carrier have betrayed his fellows to the law? That would be a killing matter."

Tartarus seize Sidney — this was a new thought. Why had it never occurred to Tom…? "Well, he could…" he began to concede — and then arguments to the contrary began to range themselves in his mind, like good Myrmidons jumping to the fray. "He could indeed — but wouldn't he wait for the books to be there to find? He'd know about that if anyone did — and more than that: he'd also know Constable Samford is in Girault's pay, wouldn't he? And besides…" Not a very neat battle rank, it had to be said — more like carps swimming up as they pleased. Still… "If he'd betrayed them, why would his consorters wait days and days to take revenge?"

"What if they didn't know who their Judas was at first?" Sidney leant forward, breakfast forgotten, a gleam in his eyes.

And if they didn't know… "Then they suspected the underbutler first, and…"

"The fellow at Salisbury Court?" Sidney sat back, stretching his mouth in a doubtful frown. No — worse than doubtful: dismissive. "But that one died a natural death, didn't he?"

And Sidney was Leicester's nephew — and, for all Tom knew, his man, and there was no telling what he knew from Sylvanus Scory, and what reasons he had to dismiss Barbier's death… So he bit back his tentative knowledge of hemlock.

"He might — or he might not," he said instead, dismissive in turn. And that the murder of Hurston itself now argued against a fit of the asthma, he swallowed as well, much as it went against the grain to do so. As dismissals went, he had to be content with a very minor one. "And still, none of this explains why Hurston would betray the presence of the books when the books were not there — and to the Paris Manor men."

Sidney just shrugged. "Perhaps he was not as clever as he thought. People die of that particular ailment. Or else they die of the asthma, and then servants prattle."

"Servants and foreign scholars, then!" Tom snapped — like the churl he was, letting himself be stung into unwary words…

"Foreign scholars…?" Sidney's frown cleared into a boyish smile. "Oh, you mean Doctor Bruno! Staying with Castelnau, is he? You never say my good Giordano talks of murder?"

Unwary words — and inexact, for the Italian had never even hinted at it, only described the dead man in detail that suited well Tom's own suspicions, the same suspicions that he would not voice…

It was a good thing — if not a flattering one — that Sidney never waited for an answer, turning instead to Sir Francis. "Oh, he may have, at that. Giordano Bruno loves a good tale, and has some peculiar notions — but if I've learnt anything this past fortnight in Oxford…"

Sir Francis had thus far sat quietly and listened, half Cato in his praetorian seat, half like one watching tennis-play. Now he held up a finger to interrupt Sidney. "Yes — this Bruno was with you and the Polish Palatine in Oxford, was he not? How long did you say you were there, Philip?"

"I said a fortnight, but in truth … we left London on the sixth, and arrived back at Court … when was that? On the fifteenth."

"Even so." Sir Francis turned to Tom. "He would have been back to Salisbury Court by the sixteenth or so. Do you think, Thomas…"

And here was another thought there had been no time to discuss… "That he could be Fagot? I've been wondering —"

And there went Sidney, laughing out loud. "Why, Bruno, a spy? And one peddling his wares in such a hugger-mugger manner? You have the wrong man there, Sir Francis. Giordano… I will not deny that he may be a little fond of his own voice, a little tactless when it comes to other men's ideas, but he's a fine thinker, all consumed with the fire of philosophy — both natural and moral."

As though philosophers were above such middling matters as the gathering of intelligence — or, for that matter, the need for money!

"That's as may be, but still French is not his birth-tongue, and he is very careful of not using it — at least not with me. And he knows much of what happens under the Ambassador's roof, and of how Courcelles thinks, and…" Tom turned to Sidney. "And you know him best, Sir Philip — but he didn't strike me as one who feels great loyalty to the Catholic cause?"

Had this been a play, Sidney would have considered and in the end conceded the point — but there was no consideration at all, just an amused huff.

"Didn't he! He used to be a Dominican friar, poor Giordano — and was disrobed and excommunicated because of his pernicious notions. There would have been worse, most likely, had he not run. I doubt he's a zealot of any cause but that of knowledge and free thought — and the conciliation of moderates everywhere. Friends, though, are another matter. Do you truly believe he would betray the trust of your Monsieur de Castelnau?"

And indeed … for all his gossipy ways, Bruno (a friar!) never talked of the Ambassador but with respect and gratitude. The smallest sense of shame stirred under Tom's ribs. Had anyone but Sidney been sitting across the table, he would have conceded the point instead of persisting. "Still, one kindly Ambassador and the Queen of Scots are not the same," he said. "Howard, Throckmorton, Mendoza — they're hardly the moderates he favours: wouldn't he be eager to hinder their efforts?"

A good conclusion, to Tom's ear — but one Sidney was not going to swallow quietly.

"But if Giordano is Fagot — and I do not believe it — if he were, why won't he reveal himself to you?"

Because he doesn't trust me. Because I'm of no consequence. Because… Hadn't that very question — among a thicket of others — kept Tom awake through the night? But this — and his own uneasy answers — he was not going to share with Philip Sidney. Nor Castelnau's little charade after dinner.

And he may be no soldier, but Service men — Sir Francis's men — could square their shoulders and forge on too… "Ah, but the same question holds true of whoever else Fagot may be. And, come to that, of Courcelles himself. I wonder if his courage hasn't failed him…" A most distrustful man, Bruno had called him. Could he be a cowardly one as well?

"Or he is playing some deeper game," Sidney said. "Have you not thought that he himself may be Fagot, feeding us what he wants us to swallow?"

Us. Us — as though he were part of the game. As though he had galloped to and fro these past four years, carrying secrets, and thinking, and studying, and obeying, and uncovering murderers for Sir Francis… *Us*. It was the greatest satisfaction — if a rather sour one — to thrust back. "Oh, I have — but wouldn't he be giving himself away, by growing coy all of a sudden?"

And to this, for once and for a wonder, Philip Sidney had no response, except a sort of sideways tilting of the head, and a spreading of the hands.

"A hit!" he said — smiling with a better grace, if one was honest, than Tom would have had in his place.

And it would have been gracious to stop there — but… *Us*! Tom turned to Sir Francis. "I still think that Bruno could be Fagot, Sir. I wish I could see him and Courcelles together, engaged in speech…" And, come to that, both of them with the absent Fowler…

"Are you so good a judge of character, Walsingham, that you could read their souls by seeing them together at dinner?" Sidney asked — and so even paragons of chivalry didn't like to lose an argument…

And didn't they look like two boys, vying for a favourite schoolmaster's nod? A hot retort was on the tip of Tom's tongue — and a blush creeping up his neck — when Sir Francis held up a hand.

"Children," he said, half-weary, half impatient — the very likeness of that imagined schoolmaster — and so unexpected that Tom barely swallowed a startled laugh. More unexpected still, was to catch a touch of the same rueful startlement on Sidney's face…

"I believe there was much food for thought in this discussion. A hearty breakfast for the mind, would you not say?" Sir Francis rose, and so did Tom and Sidney. "No, Thomas — stay. You barely ate at all. Wat tells me that you are for Southwark?"

Which, though couched in kindly terms, was a dismissal. Tom was left back, while Sir Francis and Sidney went their way — perhaps to discuss between themselves Tom's belligerent report and childish pettiness… Lord save and deliver!

I hope, Thomas, I truly hope that Mr. Secretary's business will keep you well and long…

His mother's voice echoed across thoughts that were less than pleasant.

Tom gave his uneaten herrings a baleful stare, and off he stalked, to Southwark, and to enact the scheme he'd had no chance to explain.

Clad in his shabbiest riding clothes, Tom first crossed the threshold of the Half Moon early enough that the taproom was sparsely attended — but still late enough that morning chores should have been done with.

They were not, and Tom's entrance stopped a step short of the rear end of a woman with a broom. She was sweeping away the filthy sawdust with neither great zeal nor skill — raising a haze around herself that billowed in the slant of morning light.

An especially angry backward jab would have thrust the broomstick right into Tom's stomach, had he not caught it firmly and thrust it aside with a call of, "Have a care!"

The woman yelped, and turned without releasing the broomstick, and indeed raising it in defence.

"A fine welcome you give, eh!" Tom snapped, the slightest hint of an accent woven in his speech. "Do I need a drawn sword to enter?"

All of it as loud and as public as could be — and there were half-hearted chuckles from the half dozen men who sat here and there across the long, low-ceilinged room.

The woman glared at the newcomer. As luck would have it, she was not the same who had showed Tom the way to the Falcon the morning before. This one was younger, taller, with light-chestnut curls bound in a yellowed kerchief, and a round face that might have been pretty when she wasn't scowling at strangers. Was this *the girl* of Skeres's sighs?

"I have a horse to stable, Mistress, if you are done staring. And I wouldn't mind some ale myself."

The prospect of business shook this domestic Amazon out of her fierceness. She took a sharp breath, and lowered her weapon with a hasty curtsey.

"Ay, Master," she mumbled. "Have a seat. I'll have the boy see to the horse…"

She even wiped a corner of her apron across the nearest table, and would have run away if a round-bellied man had not emerged from a door at the long room's far end.

"Agnes!" he called, loud enough for a town-crier as he waddled close, round eyes swivelling back and forth between the servant and the stranger. "What is it, girl?"

Or perhaps she was not quite a servant, for Agnes showed no humility whatever in her answer. "What must it be?" She nodded her chin at Tom. "There's this gentleman as wants drink for himself and his horse."

"So he does." Tom offered his feigned accent for show again. "If he can have it without being ambushed by brigand-women."

The landlord's eyes went rounder still, and he shot a glare at Agnes, at the broom still tight in her grasp. "You must not mind her, Master. She's addled in her wits, these days." Another glare at Agnes. "Off with you, girl! Go and rouse Perkin. I swear, the boy sleeps his days away… Have a seat, Master. Ale, will it be? The finest you ever tasted. Let me… And what say you to some mutton pie to go with it, or maybe…"

Whether the landlord always fussed this breathlessly over each soul that crossed his threshold, or the influence of murder made him fidgety, remained to be seen… Agnes was halfway to the door already, and the lingerers had gone back to their chattering and backgammon, so a pretence of secrecy was easily done.

Now, let the right pair of ears strain to hear…

"Just the ale." Tom lowered his voice as he sat — but not too much. "And a word with Mr. Hurston, if he's about."

Had Tom fired a pistol in the room, the effect on the landlord could not have been greater.

The fellow's fat shoulders rose up to his ears and fell with a sharp exhale.

"Hurston?" he faltered, louder than he meant, surely.

Tom shushed him with an impatient gesture. "Barnaby Hurston. I'm a day late to meet him — but I'm just straight from Dover. Is he about?"

"Ay, you're late, Master. Two days late." With a great sigh, the landlord — Kellett, the constable had called him? — drew out a stool and sat across the table. "Barnaby Hurston is dead."

"Dead!" Tom played the greatest surprise, leaning to grab Kellett's arm. "How dead?"

Kellett looked away, then up again, chewing at his bottom lip, the round eyes sliding this way and that — reckoning, no doubt, what this alarming stranger should be told.

Tom shook the sleeve he gripped, and asked again — lower and sharper: "How dead?"

He could read the making of a decision, clear as day on the fellow's forehead.

"Stabbed, the constables say." Kellett nodded with the grim solemnity of one imparting sad news. The sort of news that, no doubt, could be heard at any fountain by now.

Also, the sort of news the dusty stranger who'd come to meet with a dead man would not take calmly. "*Que diable*, man — stabbed! Who stabbed him? Was it robbers?"

This startled Kellett into more gaping. "Robbers — bless you, no! Or … well, God knows, for the constables do not, for sure. There's all sorts of ruffians passing through here…"

"Here? It was done here? I thought — what with him being a carrier…"

"No, no…" The landlord had the look of one wishing it *had* been robbers on a road. A faraway road. And also the look of one who was not very good at hiding his thoughts. It had been wise on Girault's part to buy Constable Samford's blindness, for the suspicion gathering in Kellett's eyes was there to see for all who looked — until it turned to cunning and then to a mournful shake of the head. "Poor fellow, ay. A good man, was Master Hurston — and you coming all this way for nought…"

Tom sat back, eyes narrowed, as cold as he knew. "Are you not paid enough, Master Kellett, to keep your thoughts to yourself?"

There. One jolt at hearing his own name, one at the hint to the bribe… The poor man began to sputter, then thought better of it, and clamped his mouth shut.

'Tis always better, Thomas, not to ask all your questions at once. Few things undo wariness as relief at not having betrayed a secret.

So Tom just gazed at the landlord for a moment longer — and there it was, the relief when a brace of customers entered from the street, calling loudly for ale and meat… Kellett nearly overturned the stool in his haste to rise, and bustled away with such alacrity that Tom could not help himself.

"What of my ale, Landlord?" he called, earning himself more round-eyed gaping.

Brat! He could hear Tom Watson's laughing voice in his head. But it seemed that brattishness was to be rewarded on this particular day for, just as poor Kellett turned, the other door opened, and who must look in but Nick Skeres.

It did one good to see how the lad strove to look impassive, how he took care not to meet Tom's eyes.

After today, with any luck, there would be no need for secrecy — but meanwhile…

Meanwhile, see how the landlord's eyes scurried from one stranger to another, and see the scowls a few of the drinkers threw Skeres's way… And so much for making friends at the Half Moon…

Agnes, emerging from the tap with three pots, made a great show of not even noticing the poor Minotaur — but, when he withdrew, there was no mistaking how she frowned at the closing door.

She served the two newcomers first, and, when she came to Tom, she found fault with the table, and set to swipe at it with her apron, the way she'd done before, but much more purposefully.

Tom didn't have to wait long.

"Were you friends with Master Barnaby?" she asked in a whisper, eyes lowered on her hands.

"The sort of friends who have business together," he answered, in the same tone. "You know what happened to him?"

She shrugged, mopping and mopping. "Stab him, they did. And threw him in the river."

Girls are fools like that, they fall for a mouth of white teeth… But Agnes looked more upset than bereaved.

"Here at the Half Moon, was it?"

"Master Kellett don't want it said." She plunked Tom's pot on the table. "And 'tis downriver that they found him, by way of the Falcon."

Before she could think to go, Tom made as though to pick up his pot so that he spilled some of it.

Agnes pouted, and went back to her mopping.

"You know who did it, Agnes?"

The girl sniffed at this for the foolish question it was. "I know who found him," she said. "There's a manservant, has been here three days. Waiting for his master, he says. Loitering about, say I. Long hands and a long nose — always sticking them where they don't belong." A little shrug. "Well, in the morning he goes out for a piss, and comes back saying there's a dead man in the river. Just like that! Master Kellett says 'twas him as did it."

Tom had been amused by the girl's description of Skeres — but this sobered him at once. "Murder Hurston? Why?"

Another shrug. "Some people are just wicked. They'll pick quarrels, draw a knife for naught…"

"Wouldn't this man have run, then? If you killed a man in anger, in a place not your own, would you stay or would you run?"

Agnes looked up at last. "I didn't kill no one, did I?" she snapped. "And that one, why should he? He's made up as he just found poor Master Barnaby, and Constable Samford swallowed it whole. Same as you asked: *He didn't run, did he?* Samford is a lack-wit!"

"Is he? Or else he wonders, as I do, if there is anyone who ran instead…"

Agnes straightened with a snort. "Then you lack your wits too, Master. 'Tis an inn, the Moon is. Folks come and go, don't they?"

With that, the girl decided the table was clean enough, and off she went.

And just for whose sake she so eagerly threw the blame on Skeres, was a whole new matter to consider.

There was an alley along the Falcon's courtyard, that led to the bank and the water stairs — an ill-smelling passage, narrow enough to touch both walls at once, had one been so minded — and that's where they convened to talk, right at the mouth, towards the river, like two waiting in the shade rather than the sun.

The Minotaur was indignant when he heard of Agnes's suspicions.

"Just like the other time. 'Ow is it that inn folks always think me a murtherer, eh?" he growled, throwing up a hand.

"Because, Dolius, you go around looking like the villain in a play — and it's twice, not always. Unless there are more murders and more inns that I don't know about?"

Skeres snorted, unassuaged. "And leastaways they were French, the other time — but Agnes…"

Agnes, of course.

"If it consoles you, she doesn't think it. She, and Kellett, and every soul around here — they'd blame the Queen herself, had she been here the other day. You are just the scapegoat, so nobody will think the murder has to do with anything that goes on here."

And there was no time for the lad's bruised heart, so it was a relief when Skeres, instead of grumbling more, took on a thoughtful air, and mused. "Or else they did it themselves."

"Either that — or, more likely, they know who did." Tom paused to shake his head at a hopeful seller of codlings, and waited until the fellow was out of earshot. "I take it that you did not find the books?"

"Find 'em!" The lad spat, in a show of supreme disgust. "I can't move a step without one of them looks askance and follows… I've looked where I could, but…" A shrug. "Was it for the books they killed 'im?"

"It seems very possible, yes."

"And the other fellow too, that cook of yourn?"

"Butler's man," Tom corrected. "But…" But in truth, he did not know. Hurston's death had looked like confirmation of Fowler's claims, at first — half of them, at least — and yet… "If you were to kill two people, Dolius…" He frowned at the river, squinting into the grey shimmer. Not far off in the current, two boats had managed to tangle their rows, and the boatmen were trading abuse, their angry voices carrying over the water. "Would you poison one and stab the other? Would you try to disguise one murder, and then make the other plain as the nose on your face…?"

Skeres hummed in earnest consideration. So earnest, in fact, that…

"I don't want you to do murder, mind," Tom hastened to add. "Not even one — much less two. I was just thinking. What you must do is stay here."

"'Ere?" The lad swept a mournful look at the filthy passage. "What for, 'ere?"

"Anywhere you like, as long as you can keep an eye on the water stairs — both here and there." Tom tilted his head in the direction of the Half Moon, and earned himself a gusty sigh.

"There by the river door, then," Skeres grumbled, eyes raised Heavenward like those of some old martyred saint — if martyred saints groused and swept their hands over the backs of their sweaty necks. "There ain't nowhere else."

"Good. Look idle and, if anyone should come, don't stop him, don't even look at him too much — unless he tries to run."

Oh, the way Skeres brightened at this last scrap of instruction! "Then I trounce 'im?"

"No, you don't! Just stop him. With any luck, he'll be the murderer of Hurston — but, even if he isn't, I'll have a good many questions to ask him."

For his part, Tom resumed his place at the table, where he could keep a good discreet eye on both doors. He called for more ale and that mutton pie he'd been offered, and disposed himself to look grim and wait.

In spite of what he had told Skeres, he wasn't half sure about who was going to pay a visit… Someone would, of this he had little doubt. Someone from Salisbury Court, as soon as the news crossed the river that a stranger from the Continent had turned up asking to meet the dead man. Whether it would be the murderer himself, though… What if Hurston had fought before dying, and the murderer was lying injured somewhere? What if he sent someone else…?

Ah well, one could only hope.

And also hope that, whoever came to inquire, would make some haste, for the sooty taproom seemed to ripen in the growing heat, the air damper and closer, with all the stenches gathering thick from the river, the rotting heap at the back, the unwashed drinkers, the tallow from long-burnt rushlights, the less than fresh mutton in the pie…

Tom pushed his trencher away, and sought Kellett, spotting him across the length of the room. The landlord had been doing his best to steer clear of this particular guest — but a pointed look and a sharp beckoning he could not ignore.

Having approached with all the signs of reluctant displeasure, he stood by the table, much like a hare ready to bolt. Surely no innkeeper since the days of Roman Maccus had ever observed with such relief an untouched pie as Kellett did.

"'Tis not to your liking, Master?" How solicitously he picked up the trencher, ready to bustle away to the safety of the kitchen… "I'll have some cheese brought —"

"I've no stomach to eat." Tom pushed out a stool right in the man's way. "I'd rather have a word or two, Landlord."

And cold imperiousness worked well enough, because Kellett, for all his hare-like manner, did not bolt.

"Master, I have to —" he tried, casting about the all but empty taproom for anything that might require his attention…

"Sit."

Not a hare, no: a half-trained hound, sitting slowly, eyes rolling askance to the man who gives the order. "Now, Master…"

"Where did Hurston keep his carts?" Tom cut right across the protestation.

"I … I don't —"

"Come, come, Master Kellett! And him calling here so often!"

And, wild shot that it was, this struck home, plainly. Kellett looked away, sucking his teeth. "Were I to know the whereabouts of all who come and go…" he tried again, then looked up and away with a wince. "Downriver-way, behind The Beargarden, he always said." Then the wary relief of another thought washed over the flabby face. "Going there, that's what you want —"

"No, I don't want to go there."

There was mournful shaking of the head, and downcast eyes — and then a narrow figure appeared at the street door, black against the glare outside. A step across the threshold revealed him for a round-faced man with a domed forehead and yellow hair, who looked about, squinting in the taproom's gloom. It didn't take long for the yellow eyebrows to raise in recognition.

The man came to stand behind Kellett, who twisted on his stool to see who it was that suddenly held his tormentor's attention. Tom had to wonder, for the landlord did not look like one who knew Sylvanus Scory, for all that he seized his chance and scuttled away, grasping the trencher of uneaten pie like a long lost coffer of gold and rubies.

Scory watched him go, lips curling in a faint smile, and then turned to Tom. "I wondered," he said, head tilted in half-mocking contemplation. "And, a little, I still do."

Devil take Philip Sidney — and also the Bishop's son! Oh, for the Gorgon's gaze, to turn the fool to stone where he stood, so pleased with himself … but throttling him with his own lace collar would have done.

Surely, though, Leicester's man had not slunk here before cockcrow to stab a smuggler to death? Never on his master's orders, surely? What had Hurston known that he should not have? What was Scory's own part in this business — if he played any? And, more importantly, what of Lord Leicester?

Tom pushed this particular breed of questions aside — for the moment — and took a deep breath. It would not do to show how irked he was. "What are you doing here, Scory?" he asked, with reasonable coldness.

'Twas not to be believed how the idiot's smile widened, in a pretence of apple-cheeked innocence. See how he took the stool the landlord had vacated, and even eyed Tom's pot. "Is that any good?"

Skeres's words came to mind. "Ditch water, truly. If I were you, I'd go seek my drink elsewhere."

And was that real mirth in Scory's silly chuckle? "If it's good enough for Mr. Secretary's own blood…" He looked around, a lazy elbow on the table, as though looking for someone to ask.

Tom made himself keep quiet and think. No matter what Anger might hiss, what Suspicion might insinuate of Sidney knowing Tom's own plans, Reason spoke against Lord Leicester having any part in the smuggling, much less in the murders. Scory himself, on the other hand…

"Oh, far from good enough," Tom warned, sitting back against the wall — carelessness being a game that two could play. "I fear you have been sent on a fool's errand."

At this Scory dropped enough of his play-acting to turn, and lower his voice. "But I was not sent, dear fellow. Not at all. I was at Salisbury Court, and happened to catch Monsieur Girault — you know the man — and another servant huddled up in great agitation. Oh, they broke up as soon as I walked in on them, and Girault made a show of making some reprimand or other — but I caught a few words, and the Moon was one of them. Now, it could be your Italian friend's influence, having the whole household marvel at the skies — or else it could be the inn across the river. Can you blame me that I bethought myself to come and see what had Girault in such a dudgeon?"

Tom hummed. "And now that you've come and seen, how will my Lord Leicester like what you have found?"

That, too, amused Scory — if a little ruefully. "Ah, but I don't know that yet. In fact, what *have* I found? Besides Walsingham's man, that is."

A show of ignorance, Thomas, will loosen some men's tongues; a show of knowledge will crumble the walls with others… Therefore, always be wary of both.

"I believe that's all you'll find, Scory. Walsingham's man is here — you can tell that to your master." *And to Philip Sidney* — but this Tom kept to himself.

At last Scory dropped the pretence of idle cheer. High forehead creasing in a mighty frown, he sat upright. "Now, see —"

And he went no farther, for there was a commotion by the door — the inner door that led to the Moon's bowels… Tom whipped around to catch a glimpse of a man's back, disappearing through the door.

Oh, Tartarus take Scory for his distractions… In a trice Tom was on his feet, and giving chase — through the door, into a dark passage with another door on the left hand, and a third at the end that opened outside. Tom caught a blur of movement against the light, and went for it, Scory hard on his heels.

"In there!" Tom called over his shoulder, pointing to the left-hand door, and then barrelled outside onto the riverbank.

Skeres alone peopled the place, sitting on his rear and looking dazed, but not so much that he couldn't point upriver.

"There!" he shouted.

And there was the man, scrambling past the stairs, up the short slope, and around the inn's corner. Tom scrambled after him, unmindful of Skeres's calls, and of a woman screaming at a window… He rounded the corner into a strip of unkempt garden, just in time to see his quarry vault over the fence, and dash across the street, right in front of a large cart. The carter startled, swerved his horses hard enough that the large dray skidded sideways, strewing cabbage leaves all around, and nearly flattened the pursuing Tom. That the fellow jumped off his seat to bellow curses and shake his fist at Tom himself, went to prove the general unfairness of Man's mind. Tom smacked an angry palm against the cart's side, and hastened around, pushing through a gaggle of chattering folk, who'd come out of nowhere to comment on the accident… By the time he emerged, the fleeing man had disappeared.

Tom would have cursed, had he not been so breathless — more from the encounter with the cart than the short chase.

"Oy, Master!" someone called — and there Skeres came puffing and flushed, elbowing his way through the little crowd, with Scory following at a more sedate trot.

"Are you hurt, Master?" the lad asked, quite ferociously.

Tom shook his head, and turned on the still cursing carter. "Enough!" he barked — angrier at himself than the fellow. "You've taken no damage, have you? Then go your way — all of you!"

Women with baskets, urchins, labourers, a peddler, a youth astride an ancient nag, a few apprentices — for there was never a lack of those — some muttered, some laughed, for it was all good sport to them. The carter sulked, with the look of one reckoning Tom's travelling clothes against the gentlemanly arrogance.

"Do I trounce 'im, Master?" Skeres asked, taking a step towards the fellow.

The carter heard and went crimson. How was Tom going to explain it all to Sir Francis? His quarry lost, Leicester's man now alive to trouble, and a brawl in the street for good measure...

"Oy! Make way! What's this now?" called a stentorian voice — and lo! the rumbling subsided, the gaggle swayed and unknotted...

And there stood Constable Pitt himself, sash, cudgel and all — Heaven-sent to nip the mayhem in the bud. Tom could have embraced him. Sweat-soaked and flushed as he was, Pitt looked a good deal more masterly with the Southwark rabble than he had been standing guard over Hurston's corpse, and made short work of sending the carter on his way.

With the principal agitator at last gone, and the crowd thinning away, Pitt doffed his hat, wiped a sleeve over his face, and narrowed his eyes at Tom first, then at Skeres, and then, more uncertainly, at Scory.

Well, there was no explaining now, no asking for assistance — not with Scory about, all eyes and ears, and, in truth, not to

Constable Samford's underman, well-meaning though the underman may be. Besides, by now, the fugitive would be halfway to Calais…

Swallowing his bile, Tom nodded at Pitt. "Thank you, Constable. Most providential."

And see how the fellow beamed! "Glad to be of service, Your Honour. Bit of a nose for trouble, have you?" he said, with a grin.

Oh, Lord impart wit to all constables and watchmen…

But perhaps there was hope that Pitt was not entirely lacking… When Tom covered his grimace under colour of a thin smile, the constable sobered, and nudged them both a few yards away from the others — and, once he had Tom in some semblance of private discourse, leant close enough for earnest whispering.

"I didn't tell Samford, Your Honour…" came on a whiff of garlic and sweat. "Didn't tell a soul."

And so Skeres was right: here was a thankful man, bent on doing — and gaining — favour. And this being the state of things…

"What about Hurston, then?" Tom asked. "What of the coroner?"

"Inquest's tomorrow — but already he calls it wilful murder, seeing as no one turned up to claim self-defence. Just like Your Honour said."

"Did Samford find anything yet?"

"Passing ruffians, he says…" The constable's whole freckled face knotted unhappily. "'Twas no passing ruffians, eh, Your Honour?"

Tom raised a doubtful eyebrow — let the man conceive doubts, do his own thinking. "It may be ruffians that will return, Constable. I'd keep a wary eye on the Half Moon," he said.

Pitt nodded gravely, donned his hat, and went his way, swinging his cudgel like one deep in thought. Whether his thoughts were of Samford's dishonesty, or of Mr. Secretary's favour, though...

With a shake of his head, Tom turned on his heel, and made for the Half Moon's untidy kitchen-garden. Behind him marched Nick Skeres — and...

"*Your Honour* has business with the law here, then..." And Scory, of course — all sing-song mockery and knowingness. "And how was it? *A bit of a nose* —"

The apish tickle-head! Had it not been for him... All charity lost, Tom turned on the man, fierce and low. "Are you content with yourself, you lack-wit? He saw you, and ran!"

"Me!" Scory exclaimed. "He saw *me* and ran! What about you, then? He saw you, too."

"Me and you both — no matter. He took fright, and ran, and now we'll never know!" And look at the fine sight they made, Walsingham's man and Leicester's, squabbling in the street like two fishwives! Tom brushed a hand down his face. He looked up to catch a dour Skeres taking a breath to speak. And what he was about to say took little guessing...

"No, Skeres. Much as I'd like you to, you are not trouncing him." That said, though, there was no reason to let the Bishop's son enjoy the smallest shade of triumph. "But I'm warning you, Scory: stay out of my way."

And, empty threat though it was, it left Sylvanus Scory gaping in outrage — and belike a little doubt — in the middle of the street.

Tom strode for the water stairs at Paris Garden, tugging at his collar to loosen it — the air so thick it stuck to one's skin. He'd gone halfway before he stopped, and Nick Skeres caught up.

Oh, Lord look out for fools — what was he doing? Stalking away in a dudgeon like a thwarted child…

"Did you have a good look at that fellow, Dolius?"

"Did I!" Skeres snorted. "Run right into me, 'e did. Bowled me over. Took me by surprise with that big stick of 'is, or I'd 'ave given 'im what for…" He grunted, underlip jutting.

Tom had seen no stick, and it occurred to him to wonder. For one who spent half his days threatening trouncings, had the Minotaur ever come out of a fight other than battered, since they'd met?

Ah well. "I'm sure you'd have. Had you ever seen him before at the Half Moon?"

The lad considered for a while, before he shook his head with great vigour. "Can't say that I did, no."

Which meant little enough, considering that he'd been at the inn barely three days…

"What did he look like?"

There was no considering this time. "An ugly big fellow, 'e was."

He had not looked very big, but then he'd been running half hunched… "Tall, you mean? Big-shouldered?"

A shrug.

"Did he have a beard or was he shaven?"

"You said not to look at 'im!" Skeres protested, pouting like Innocence offended.

Oh, patience, patience… "Would you know him again?"

"Know 'im!" Skeres drew himself as tall as he knew — which wasn't much. "Knap 'is nose for 'im, I would! Know 'im, 'e says!"

Of course… "You'll do nothing of the sort. Just point him out to me — discreetly."

Wasted breath, most likely, and the general wisdom of bringing the lad to Salisbury Court was debatable. Still, it might come to that, for one thing was sure: the fleet-footed visitor was no innocent… Tom sighed and squinted upwards, where the morning haze had curdled into a boiling of grey clouds. Sir Francis would have to part with more rare books for Skeres to enter the Embassy…

"Maybe they knew 'im. The folks at the Moon…"

"And you think they'd tell us?" Tom snapped — and look if Skeres didn't lower his head, scuffing at the edge of a root with his shoe. The Minotaur meekened. Still, unlikely as it was, could Tom overlook the chance that someone would talk?

"Let's go and find out," he said with another sigh. "And Heaven send we don't find Scory there."

A foolish thing to say, for what could be done, in truth, should the fellow still be at the inn? A foolish thing — and trust Nick Skeres to latch onto it.

"That one!" he huffed, grabbing for his cap when a gust of wind blew at their backs. "All a-gawpin' like a gudgeon at Billingsgate! *Stay out of my way…*" An approving cackle. "Let 'im go cry to 'is master — and, of all 'ands, what do you care where 'e is?"

"I don't, not a whit. I care where he *was*. I care that your big ugly friend saw the both of us together — and if he knows who we are, and whose men, he'll think that half the Privy Council is in this together…" That, with or without Scory, now the smugglers knew themselves found, he kept to himself. Oh, he'd known, in concocting his plan, that he'd be giving himself away…

You may well renounce an advantage, Thomas, to gain a greater one.

But had he? As things were, it seemed that all he'd done was barter the smugglers' ignorance for a view of the back of a running man.

Leicester's nuisance of a man had not returned, after all, to the Half Moon — and that was one scantling relief.

The dinner throng — such as it had been — had dispersed quickly, and the loss of business had put Kellett in a mind to bluster for answers rather than give them. His was not a very robust courage, though, and a few sharp words were enough to cast down his comb. Still, it was little wonder when he denied ever clapping eyes on the fellow who had run — either today or ever in his whole life.

When Tom pointed out that not seeing him this day made it hard to deny having ever seen him, the innkeeper was too flustered to see that he had been caught lying — and just kept shaking his head, in a babble of fervent perjury.

'Tis an aggrieving truth that Cicero's own dialectic will make wreck against stupidity. There's no reasoning with dunces, was how Watson put it — and Kellett of the Half Moon was living proof of that.

But there was no reasoning with stubborn girls, either. Agnes was either less of a fool or less affrighted, and did not fall into philosophical traps by the very simple means of denying she had been there to see the man at all. Minding her chores, she'd been, and with one thing and another, and gentlemen wanting private parlours — and what did he think the Moon was, the Lord Mayor's palace? — and the mistress wanting this and that, she'd had no time to loiter about and see the man coming and going. And having not seen him, how could she know him?

Of the morning idlers, only one elderly man remained, now busy shifting backgammon counters about the board for his solitary entertainment. Oh, he was eager enough to talk, was Master Grene — all toothless smiles and tapping of the nose, full of gossip and of how strangers came and went all the time, but there was this one fellow, who now and then…

It took Tom very little time to see through it. "In your place, Master Grene, I'd ask for better than Kellett's ale, to feed balderdash to strangers."

The old man snorted. "I told him. Told Kellett you're not thick enough to fall for it, I did…" He gave a reedy chuckle. "And look you, lad: God's truth is, I'd half dozed off, and by the time I looked, there was just the door a-shutting…"

And Tom found that he believed old Grene rather more than the whole Half Moon put together.

A good deal more than he believed Bridget Kellett, the landlord's sister and alewife, who also happened to be the one who had pointed Tom towards the Falcon — not that she remembered him. Then again, Mistress Kellett didn't remember where she'd been earlier, either, when all the ado had happened. Oh, but wait — in the kitchen, that's where she'd been. Scouring pots, she'd been, not seeing the man. Lord bless, ay — she'd been the one to scream. Anyone would scream to hear such a burly-hurly! Oh ay, Master — anyone would, especially after the death of poor Master Hurston, what with that bully still loitering about… What bully? Why, but Tom knew him! Mistress Kellett had seen the two of them together, giving chase, and the other gentleman, too… Not that Mistress Kellett meant that they were… Lord save, but she had seen them together, with her very own eyes — and that one…! That one was a sore ruffy, Master — one best warned against. And, if Mistress Kellett's opinion were sought, the very one who did the murder…

"Made no friends at the Half Moon, did you, Dolius?" Tom asked of Skeres, as they hastened towards the stairs at Paris Garden for the second time that day.

While Tom had lost his time being lied to by the inn folk, the sky had lowered and darkened to a greenish hue, like tarnished pewter.

Even Skeres's prodigious snort was half lost in the gusts of dusty wind that blew up the river, smelling of water and the promise of rain. "A pack of liars, that's what they are. Lying through their teeth…"

As likely as not, Tom's mother would have called it unchristian, the amusement her son found in the lad's outraged manner…

"In their place, with all those books hidden away, wouldn't you throw the blame on the first convenient stranger?"

"Teach 'em, that's what I'd do!" Skeres groused. "Stay another day or two, and teach 'em to lay the blame — liars and murtherers all! Why you want me to come away, I'll never know…"

This from the man who had wailed to High Heavens at being left there for three days… Tom sighed. "Little use in staying, now that they know you for my man, is there?" And if their fugitive ever came back, and if the books were still there… Ah well. Would Williams find someone else to put under the Half Moon's roof, or would he grouse that they'd ruined it all? Both, most likely…

The alley by the Falcon's courtyard was already half dark in the thickening gloom. Tom hadn't taken half a dozen strides along it, the grumbling Skeres on his heels, when he heard himself called by name.

"Mr. Walsingham!"

The voice sounded eerie in the narrow confines, and they both turned to see a black figure picking an uneasy way, balancing with a hand against one mouldy wall.

"Young Walsingham, is it?"

Between the two of them, Tom and Skeres filled the width of the passage — and the sight they made must have been menacing enough, for the man stopped and spread his hands with a rueful smile.

"Are ye for Seething Lane?" Archibald Douglas asked, a little out of breath. "We can share a boat to the bridge, I'm thinking."

And no, the smile that creased and knotted his red-bearded cheeks was not rueful at all — and of a sudden a piece clinked into place — a small piece, of still uncertain moment. *Gentlemen wanting private parlours*, Agnes had said…

"Mr. Douglas —" Tom flattered himself that he'd learnt that kind of unsurprised, half-questioning manner, not that it would much impress such an old devil — "have you been long at the Half Moon?"

The Scot's smile never faltered, but amusement gleamed in the deep-set eyes.

"Och, I was wanting to see what Mr. Scory had found across the river to disquiet him so. I didnae think it would be ye…" Douglas looked up, grimaced at the slice of darkening sky above, and brushed something from his shoulder. "Is it raining, ye think? We had better find that boat, eh?"

In truth, the first fat raindrops were in the wind as they emerged from the alley to the water stairs, and secured a wherry to carry them downriver — but, once they had left the bank, the weather seemed to worry Douglas a good deal less. All the way he sat gazing brightly around, as though the traffic on the Thames were a new sight to him — and, when asked about Scory's disquiet, he just replied with a question of his own.

"Hae ye been sitting in Monsieur de Castelnau's gallery? A braw place to see who comes and goes by river…" and then he went back to his observations. To think this fellow was a man of the cloth… But then, so was Fowler. The Kirk of Scotland chose its men strangely.

The wind had picked up by the time they disembarked at the Old Swan Stairs, and the rain was starting in earnest, so they hastened up Pepys Lane, holding their hats — Douglas to his lodgings near St. Margaret in Billingsgate, Tom and Skeres to walk past the bridge and take another wherry.

In Stockfishmonger Row shopkeepers were closing their awnings a little early, and slamming their shutters closed, and women made haste home, their aprons billowing in the wind. Thunder rolled above as they reached St. Magnus, where they were to part ways…

And then an urchin hurled against Tom — a small cutpurse, most likely, whom Skeres caught by a shoulder and shoved away, with a cuff on the head for good measure. And off the child ran, piping curses fit to make a waterman blush…

"You don't have to guard me like a —" Tom began — and stopped short. Three steps away, Douglas stood frozen, gaze riveted to the alley that yawned black between the church and a tavern's back.

Three men stood there — caps lowered over their eyes, two armed with thick cudgels, the third fingering the hilt of a dagger far too long for such a ragged-looking lout…

"Run, Master!" Skeres yelled, drawing his own overlong dagger.

As though Tom would run! He grabbed Douglas instead and shoved him back, before drawing his sword and going to stand by Skeres, just as the three ruffians stepped out of the alley's mouth. With a dull clink, their leader drew in turn.

Wonder of wonders, more steel hissed out of a scabbard, and Douglas was there, shoulder next to Tom's, guard high. Or not such a wonder, after all... Had the man not been party to a few murders in his day...?

The three assailers were spreading wide — but the one on the left, a gap-toothed young bully, threw a glance at his companions, less sure now that he faced three armed men...

"Scared of good steel, are you?" bellowed Skeres over the hiss of the rain. "Come on, you quake-breech!"

Goading a foe into rashness, Thomas, is only a wise move when you can more than meet what he will rashly do.

It was doubtful that Skeres had thought that far — but sure enough the man with the dagger stamped forward and lunged, his cronies running up, brandishing their cudgels... Tom parried easily enough, riposted, and held the fellow at bay. On one side, Douglas was thrusting again and again at his bully's face; on the other, a roar was followed by a yelp as Skeres just ran under his foe's arm, and careened into him.

Tom's opponent, with a sleeve ripped and the arm grazed, stepped back, calling to his fellows. The three retreated down to St. Magnus, and a crowing Skeres would have given chase had Tom not caught him by the jerkin.

"Do you want more of it, you fool?" he scolded, sheathing his sword. "Let's get a boat. Mr. Douglas is coming with us."

The Scot looked grim. "To Mr. Secretary's own door?" he panted.

And a fine time for scruples this was! "If it's you they're after, I'd say it matters little now." For the second time in a row, Tom took hold of Archibald Douglas's sleeve and pushed him less than gently down Fish Street, back towards the bridge and the river.

Off they ran under the rain, down empty alleys that stank of privies and gutted fish, narrow and dark in the shade of the overhanging houses, and all the way they looked over their shoulders at each splash, each step, each call… They spilled out at one of the wharves, among the forest of masts of the moored vessels. Tom had lost track of which wharf it would be, but no matter. They ran into a pair of men — fish sellers, by look and by odour, hastening away from the rain. Tom stood squarely in their way.

"We need a boat," he said.

The two shook their heads. "These ain't wherry stairs, Master — not that gentle-folks ever take notice."

And they would have gone their way, but that Skeres hissed, "Master!"

Shoulders up to his ears, the lad was peering towards the bridge — and Tom took it to mean that their new acquaintances were coming for a second bout, maybe in greater numbers…

He fished into his purse for a sixpence, and handed it to the older of the pair, a squint-eyed fellow with a barrel chest.

"Pretend we're fish," he said. "And pretend quickly."

The two traded looks and shrugs, and the squint-eyed one jerked his head towards a mooring place where three flat-bottomed boats bobbed, dwarfed amidst bigger bows and higher keels.

In a trice they were all piled in the smallest of the three, filthy with fish guts and blood, the two fish-sellers shoving away from the wharf with their rows, making for the open water, just as the pursuers came running on the wharf. There were now five of them.

"Where to then, Master?"

Tom named the Water Gate, and off they went downriver. Through sheets of rain, back on the wharf the thwarted ruffians could be seen. Two ran away, but the others…

"Oy!" one of Tom's rowers cried, stopping his toil to point. "They're a-stealing the boats, the poxy rascals!"

Tom swatted at the pointing arm. "And if they catch us, they'll cut five throats as soon as three. Row!"

And, for a blessing, this piece of exaggeration made the fish-sellers put their back into it, though they did so with the blackest of scowls. They were no doubt cursing their passengers with each push, but they were welcome to curse all they liked, as long as they pushed heartily. And so they did. Squat and flat-keeled, the fish boat had never been built for speed, nor for agility, much less when carrying the weight of five grown men…

Did they weigh more or less than a boatful of fish? Tom wondered idly, eyes fastened on the pursuit… But whatever else they were, the three ruffians in the boat were not the sort who row and steer boats for a living: among the moored vessels, and thinning traffic of the rainy afternoon, there was no mistaking their lubberly manoeuvring, and soon they were lagging well behind.

"'It something big and sink, that'd serve 'em right!" Skeres ground out — and small blame to him.

Douglas sat still and tense, face frozen in a mask of icy loathing, all the smiling malice gone. Had he looked like this, before bursting into the chambers of the Queen of Scots to stab the Italian secretary?

He only shook himself when the boat swerved for the Water Gate.

They were out of it the moment it hit the stairs, just as the rain started again in pounding earnest.

Tom threw another penny at the rowers. "Row on a while, and they won't follow," he called, over the hiss of water. "'Tis just us that they want. Although…" He leant close to whisper to Douglas. "I should have said 'tis *you*, shouldn't I?"

And what the Scot's skew-whiff grimace truly meant — guilt, rue, or an attempt at misused innocence — was for figuring out another time.

"Come!" Tom ordered, and Archibald Douglas, nobleman, murderer and ambassador to queens, followed eagerly enough as they made haste up Water Lane, splashing in the rain-swollen runnel.

They were past Thames Street before they knew they were still being followed — and it was Skeres who noticed. Tom stopped, hand raised to silence the lad — and there it went, the squelch of hurried steps, soon halted.

"De'il take them!" Douglas cursed under his breath. "How did they get here?"

"Landed at one of the quays, then ran here. We help them by tarrying here." Tom made to urge his little troop forward — and stopped. Right ahead the lane made a sharp turn, much like an elbow bent around the bulk of the Bakers' Hall, and one could walk into anything around it… As quietly as he could, he unsheathed his sword.

"Remember those who ran from the Old Swan on foot, Dolius?" he murmured.

And look at the red-faced glee of the lad, as he drew. "These ones I trounce, eh?"

Ah well. "Yes, you trounce them. Or at least, you push past them, and run for Seething Lane. You run with him, Mr. Douglas — and I'll bring up the rear."

Douglas had barely the time to draw before Nick Skeres, with a mighty bellow, threw himself around the corner, brandishing the dagger in one hand, a stick in the other — and where he had found that, Tom didn't know.

He followed, though, walking backwards, guard high, the parrying dagger in his left hand, trusting his Minotaur — and perhaps the Scot as well — to watch his back as he held at bay the three that came running up.

A thrust, a lunge, another… And glory be for long rapiers! The two men with the cudgels now held knives too, but it would be a while before they could step close enough to use them … and glory also be for cock lorels, standing together to fill the width of the lane, crowding Tom, yes — and hindering each other, most of all the fellow with the dagger.

Soon enough, a shout of "Master, run!" came from behind. Good Minotaur…

Tom would have liked to say that he danced out of reach — but it was somewhat less graceful than that, and it cost him a glancing blow on his dagger arm, hurtful enough, for all that the one who dealt it took a much worse cut in return. Still, Tom was soon running past the Bakers' corner — where a bloody-faced man sprawled, moaning — and out into Tower Street.

And why should people crowd there — not many, just a gaggle of boys and blue-capped apprentices, milling at the mouth of Seething Lane, hooting and laughing in spite of the pelting rain… Tom shoved himself and Douglas past them, trusting Skeres to do his own shoving, and slammed into a crimson-clad back.

The soaking wet back of a man in a bright livery-coat and cap, who swung around, brandishing a long oar. "Make room for the Worshipful Company of Watermen!" he roared — a foolish thing, in truth, for he was the very last of a procession that marched up Seething Lane to the sound of a drum…

"What the de'il is this…?" asked Douglas, peering over Tom's shoulder.

And Tom laughed aloud. "I'd forgotten Midsummer, and the Rose… Come!"

They filed on, squeezing between the soggy ranks of watermen and the walls — and thank the rain for it, or the lane would have been packed with cheering idlers, barring the way to Sir Francis's gate…

"What rose? What is this?" Douglas kept asking, loud enough to be heard above the drum, the rain, and the splashing march.

"Were you not here this time last year, Mr. Douglas? They go to the garden over there, and nip a red rose for the Lord Mayor. The fine for a footbridge that some lady of old built without asking… A silly thing, but grand enough and pretty — in dry weather."

And it looked neither grand nor pretty, as watermen with their oars, and guildsmen in their finery, and drummers all marched like so many drenched cats… But still, enough to reach the gate safely. Back at the lane's mouth the pursuers stood in a malcontented bunch, jostled this way and that as the apprentices followed the marching guildsmen in merciless mimicry.

Before he knocked at the gate, Tom could not help himself, and nodded at the ruffians. At his side, Douglas worked his mouth…

"Let's walk on a while if you worry, Mr. Douglas," Tom said — little as it would serve now…

Much to Skeres's grumbling, they followed the procession for a dozen yards up Seething Lane, up to where it turned into the rose garden, like a wet, crimson snake squirming into its nest in clumsy haste.

When Tom looked back again, only the hooting apprentices remained.

There they stood, dripping and shivering in the hall, much to the dismay of the servant who had let them in, whose early candle lit streaks of fire in the small puddles at their feet.

Leaving Skeres to pacify his fellow servant, Tom turned to Douglas.

"'Tis you they followed, Mr. Douglas." Flat-voiced — the stating of a fact, not a question. "You knew you were followed ever since Bankside. That's why you sought my company."

The Scot looked amused, guardedly so — and, if he meant to offer any answer (which Tom very much doubted) he was spared from doing so by the arrival of Wat Williams. Williams came briskly from the office with a candle of his own, ready to voice some displeasure, no doubt — and stopped short at the sight of the unexpected guest.

"Back with us, are you, Mr. Douglas?" he asked, slow and, by the narrow look that went with the words, a good deal less than pleased.

And there was no mistaking the glint of mischief in the Scot's eyes as he replied. "Och, not for any continuation, I hope — although … God knows, now that young Mr. Walsingham dragged me here for all to see."

The shameless lie-teller! A younger Tom would have gaped in outraged disbelief, even sputtered defence… It was a source of some satisfaction that he only smiled in answer to Williams's raised eyebrow.

"Mr. Douglas met with some inconvenience, and attached himself to me hoping to eschew it..."

And if Douglas was irked by this recounting, he didn't show it. He showed nothing, in truth, beyond a nod that might have been avowal — but looked uncomfortably like that of a grown man allowing the last word to a boy.

Williams gave the softest snort — but then, he had suffered Douglas for months...

"Will Sir Francis see me, Wat?" Tom asked — and would have liked to know of Philip Sidney's whereabouts as well, but he would not ask. Not before Williams. Not before Douglas.

A pointed frown was what he had from Williams, though. "Either like this now, or seemly at supper," said the Welshman — for one did not sit at Sir Francis Walsingham's table in mud-spattered riding things. One did not discuss certain urgent things before the Douglases of this world, either. Still, what if Sidney was still there, though? How would Tom excuse himself after pleading urgency? And did he want to miss Douglas's talk at the supper table? So there was nothing for it but to dismiss Skeres and make haste upstairs, two steps at a time and candle-less, leaving Williams to see to the Scot's comforts.

Sidney was not at supper.

The poached salmon, the well stoked fireplace to dissolve the damp chill — all these were also pleasures.

Douglas's presence was not. Tom had vaguely hoped that the Scot would excuse himself to bed after all — but no: there Archibald Douglas sat, in borrowed black garb, eating with well-bred appetite, and drinking for three men — and none the worse for it, although he harped on and on about what he called the day's reeling.

"Had it not been for that procession... A bold thing it was, to send these cut-throats after Mr. Secretary's own kin!" he mused once again, eyes on the pewter cup he turned about and about. "A reet paughty thing we'd call it, back across the Border..."

This was the third time that Douglas ventured that notion. The first two attempts, Sir Francis had politely ignored — and so had Tom, following his lead.

Now, Mr. Secretary smiled, the narrow smile of amused tolerance, and slowly drank a sip of small ale while the servant placed a plate of ripe figs on the table.

"These come from my garden at Barn Elms," he explained. "And are rather fine figs, very sweet — and truly, Mr. Douglas, you do not believe those men were after my cousin."

Douglas carefully chose the bigger, fatter fig, hmming as he fingered the purple skin, and made no word.

"Nor can you think that they were much in the way of throat-cutting. Armed with cudgels, you said, Thomas?"

"Mostly, Sir." Tom sat a little straighter. "Save for one, who carried a long dagger. Also, they had no qualms about striking in daylight."

"Indeed," Sir Francis said, expectant gaze on Douglas.

Never a man had been so absorbed in the skinning of a fig. Only when he had pushed a thumb into the white pith, and opened the fruit in two to reveal the red heart, did the Scot shake his head with a sigh, and return his host's scrutiny.

"There are... There are mischancy things happening at Salisbury Court. Perhaps some are wanting to fright a man who pries into such things?"

"Perhaps." There was that small smile again — Sir Francis being indulgent with the Scot, but not overly so. "And since my cousin wasn't the one seeking safety in numbers, I am inclined to think it's you they want to fright, Mr. Douglas."

And at last, for a wonder, Douglas was discomposed. He dropped his halved fig, and, when he looked up, the light of the candles scored deep shadows in his scowling face. "Mr. Secretary, ye neednae be told how many enemies I made in yer service. And that they were so bold as to pursue me in the company of yer own kinsman —"

All amusement, all tolerance had gone from Sir Francis's manner. "You came to me with plenty of enemies of your own. The Spanish King's ambassador, for one. I doubt Mendoza shares Monsieur de Castelnau's liking of you."

"Aye — the Spaniards." Douglas ran a hand down his coppery beard — and how much older he looked without his usual mask of genteel malice… "And Castelnau's overdressed de'il of a secretary, on behalf of that mistrusting lady in Sheffield… Like Courcelles, the Queen of Scots wishes that Monsieur de Castelnau could be persuaded to mistrust me. And now twa men are deid…"

"Two men." Tom was, truth be told, a little proud of how he covered his sudden thought, and managed to not quite ask…

But Sir Francis seemed to have the very same thought. "You count the stabbing at that inn, then?"

"Count it!" the Scot exclaimed. "With yer cousin there spying about, and the Ambassador's servants all in a fever, and now those ruffians sent to fright me away, should I nae count it?"

He fell silent at last, and sat back, calmer for the stream of words he had released — a little of the mask braced back in place. For a while there was only the rain outside — the angry hiss now gentled to a sigh — and Douglas breathing through his nostrils, whether in fatigue or anger, it was hard to tell.

At length Sir Francis nodded, like one who had heard what he expected. "Will you have Williams fetched, Thomas?" he asked. "Mr. Douglas, I'm sure, will want his rest."

Oh, the bitter smile of Douglas, as Tom stood to obey, and more of that thin silence. And perhaps the Scot was working himself up to say more — but Williams arrived, with a blank face and a candle, to play escort and to show that trust was not in abundance.

The moment the door was shut again, Sir Francis turned to Tom. "So, Thomas?"

"So … not a word of the books."

"Indeed. Did he say how he came to be in Southwark?"

Tom recounted the Scot's explanation, and Scory's part in it, and from there, more and more dejectedly, his own bungling plan. Bungling — and worse. "They had no reason to think that anyone would link the murder at the inn with the Embassy — but now…"

"Well, Mr. Douglas did — as soon as he heard about it. You do not think this Scory can be your murderer? Kin to Bishop Scory, is he?"

"His son, and…" Tom hesitated. "And my Lord Leicester's man."

There. It was said. He watched as the threads knitted themselves behind Sir Francis's dark eyes. It was very quick.

"And he was warned of your presence at the inn, was he?"

"He says…" Tom grasped for the most scrupulous fairness — and was relieved, foolishly relieved, to find Fairness had arguments. "He says he heard the butler talk in great agitation. He seemed surprised to find *me* at the inn."

"I see — and yet…" The longest while of silence — long enough to observe the rain had ceased. "And yet you think of breakfast this morning. Is there anything else that you kept to yourself then, Thomas?"

Oh, was there! Mild as the words had been, the blush flamed up Tom's cheeks, and burnt on as he blurted it all out, with barely a care to shape the whole into an argument… Of the hemlock, he told, and of how poison and stabbing felt like things different hands would wield — and there was a small host involved, if Fagot wasn't lying, so it could well be, but then why counterfeit one death, and not the other…?

Above his steepled fingers, Sir Francis raised an eyebrow. "You are still young enough to believe that reason guides men's actions. You will do well to learn that rashness, fear, and plain stupidity must be taken into account. Besides, here we have a thicket of murderers, have we not?"

"*Prima facie*, yes." And here was the faculty of thought recovered. "Both Hurston and the butler's man had ties to the smuggling. It would be much of a chance that they were killed within days of each other over different matters, I think. And if there's any truth to Fagot's last letter…" Tom stopped short, with a sharp intake of breath. The pieces rearranged themselves in his mind — not in a very orderly way, in truth, but rather as though he'd walked into a wall, shaking the pieces into a different shape. "There have been no more letters, have there, Sir — not since Barbier's death?"

"Not one," Sir Francis said, slow and considering. "No, indeed. It could explain the secrétaire's sudden mistrust —"

And more than that… "Why, Courcelles might have —" Oh dear Lord — interrupting Sir Francis…! "I beg —"

But the lapse was hardly noticed.

"Indeed — indeed, Courcelles might have. Fagot pressed him too much, and when he wrote the letter... That foolish man! I wish..." It was a rare sight, Mr. Secretary's impatience, the knuckles softly hitting the tablecloth. "I wish we had the means to make sure, one way or the other. Surely Wat can discover when Bonetti last visited Salisbury Court."

Oh, curse it — Bonetti! Rocco Bonetti, and Castelnau's plaguey letter... Here was something else that Tom had kept to himself this morning. Another thing to blushingly recount. "And I fear that the letter must still be..."

Sir Francis waved him silent with a sigh. "Oh, there is little need to read it, I'm sure. I never was one to dance, not even in my youth — but I have watched enough of it in my life to tell you, Thomas, that what Monsieur de Castelnau and I do is very much akin to a pavane: polite in the extreme, courtly, just a little solemn — and, when you look at it, pointless for the most part. He is telling me that he knows about Bonetti — who has, on occasion, worked for us ... and he is also letting me know that he knows your presence at Salisbury Court may be less innocent and poetical than we are all willing to acknowledge."

"But then, does he also know of Bonetti's hat?"

"That might depend on whether Monsieur de Castelnau can afford to pay better money than we do — and it may be worth our time to look into Bonetti's loyalties. Yet, would it not be a great waste to uncover a spy and betray this fact to the spy's own masters? Bonetti matters very little in this game — but a knowledge of Fagot could be put to better use than pavane dancing. I trust that you acted very blank when told about the poor ill-used Italian?"

Tom's expressed hope that he had, earned him no more than a distracted nod — Mr. Secretary's mind already fastened on another question.

"I will not say that you know Courcelles, Thomas — but you have met him more than once. Would you reckon him a poisoner?"

Would he, indeed? Claude de Courcelles, with his bright silks and his fan, one moment languid, and all sullen suspicion the next, gaze darting this way and that. The man was mad-eyed, but … bending to tip the deadly poison into a man's cup, peering over his shoulder…?

"Is Douglas right in calling him … how was it — an overdressed devil?"

There went Tom's own thoughts, read like horn-book letters. He smiled at his great cousin, because in truth… "In truth, between Courcelles and Douglas, if I were to choose a poisoning devil, it would not be Courcelles. Or a stabbing one, either."

Sir Francis tilted his head in question. "Because of Queen Mary's murdered Italian? I wonder whether Mr. Douglas would be flattered or offended by your assumption — but he was not of those who stabbed the poor fellow. One of the conspirators, most surely. One of the murderers, just as surely not."

And Tom was saved from the foolishness of finding disappointment in this revelation by a knock at the door. The servants in the Walsingham household knew never to intrude on the gentlemen talking at the table, not even when they tarried unusually long — so it was no wonder that, when Sir Francis called, Williams himself entered.

Parson Douglas, he reported grimly, was well tucked in bed, after demanding a posset for the *coldment* he had caught in the rain. "Not a chill, mind you: a coldment! He does it to aggrieve me, I'll swear!"

Tom was not surprised — nor was, it seemed, Sir Francis.

"Swearing is a bad unchristian habit, Wat — though I will not put some pettiness beneath Mr. Douglas. Do you happen to know a man named Scory … how is it, Thomas?"

"Sylvanus Scory."

"Sylvanus Scory now…" Williams stepped up to lean against the back of a chair as he thought.

"Son to the Bishop of Hereford."

"That one, ay." A contemptuous grunt. "Found him at Castelnau's table, Mr. Thomas? Thick with the French, he is — and with the Spaniards. A soldier in Flanders, says he, *and* the Bishop's son. And Leicester's man, by all accounts — and…"

"And?" Sir Francis prodded.

"And a great friend of Sir Philip Sidney's. Says he."

Tom felt his cousin's gaze on his bent head — and it was hard not to look up, although…

"I see." Sir Francis did not sound put out in the least. "I shall be for Barn Elms and Richmond again, tomorrow, and will not be back for a few days. From now on, Wat, the matter of Fagot, and of the murders, and of all that pertains to Salisbury Court, is in Mr. Thomas's hands. You obey and report to him."

And this time Tom did look up. *In Mr. Thomas's hands… Obey and report to him…* It took some work to listen to what came next.

"Once at Richmond, my Lord Leicester will have to be told — though not in great detail. I expect His Lordship will be much amused to learn that you are once again in the thick of things, Thomas."

Either much amused or much annoyed. Tom's last encounter with the Earl, two years ago, had been more of a brush than anything else, and the Queen's favourite had only half liked Tom's part in it… Petty and ungrateful of the Earl, seeing that Tom had, in the end, cleared the man of some carefully engineered suspicions…

"What if Scory isn't obeying orders?" mused Williams. "Maybe he's got notions above his station. Maybe His Lordship doesn't even know…"

"In that case, I shall hear of it," Sir Francis said. "And so, I expect, will the fellow."

Tom imagined Sylvanus Scory taking the brunt of His Lordship's displeasure — and couldn't find it in himself to be sorry…

"And lastly, Wat, there is the matter of William Fowler."

There was a long-suffering sigh. "What of him?" Williams asked.

Sir Francis turned to Tom — and waited. *It's in Mr. Thomas's hands…*

Pray that he'd not shown the jolt! "I have yet to see him at Salisbury Court," Tom said — and raised a hand to stop Williams when he would speak. "And Monsieur Castelnau himself wonders what became of him. Fowler goes against his orders."

Anger, when masked, will show differently in different men. With Wat Williams, it was a matter of pinched eyes and flaring nostrils.

"Does he, the poxy prating natural! Begging your pardon, Master — but just let me get a hold of him…"

"Yes, yes." Sir Francis rose from his seat. "Just see that you cure him of his timidity, rather than otherwise, will you?"

Williams straightened, and, when bid to advise the servants, bowed stiffly, and stalked away as though the hapless Fowler waited chained in the kitchens to be chastised.

Sir Francis shook his head. "An unmannerly man — but capable and loyal."

Words that sounded like instructions on how to deal with Williams in the days to come… And also a warning that the man's loyalty was to be earned. Did Williams also sigh and mutter at Tom's own name when he was not there?

"Thomas…"

Tom blinked out of his thoughts to find Sir Francis on the threshold.

"You doubt that Sir Philip warned Scory of your plans. Of what he knew of them."

Not a question — and, if it had been, not one Tom could easily have answered in the negative.

"I … I…" Oh Jupiter.

"Do you truly believe that Doctor Bruno may have written Fagot's letters?"

Not truly. Not until Sidney spoke to the contrary… "He may … he may." What a petty, jealous fool… "He may have better reason than most to…"

"I see." Sir Francis sighed. "You and Sir Philip, Thomas, have more in common than you have to divide you. I hope that, in time, you both will come to see it."

And with that, he was gone.

An owl hooted outside in the garden. Left unattended, the fire had burned down, and the room was growing damp.

More in common than you have to divide you… For once in his life, Tom was very much inclined to doubt Sir Francis's words — and even to question them.

CHAPTER 8

Sir Francis left at first light, with Davies and the secretary Wade.

Rousing Douglas and sending him on his way took rather longer, and enough play at civility to set a man's teeth on edge. Some of it, at least, should have fallen to Williams, and it was not in the best spirit that, Douglas at long last gone, Tom went in search of the Welshman.

It took some searching to find him in the stables, and some effort to wait for the dismissal of what looked like a ballad-seller before asking — quite irritably — what Williams had been doing.

"Seeing that an eye's kept on the Half Moon," was the answer. "Have folks coming and going, now that you took Skeres away." Williams's gaze was firm, barely this side of a challenge. "If it please you, Mr. Thomas."

And talk of taking the wind out of one's sails — for it pleased Mr. Thomas quite precisely. Indeed, the watching of the inn was the first order Mr. Thomas had meant to issue, now that the matter was in his hands…

So, what did one do before such a display of efficiency? "Good," was what Tom settled for, together with his new soldierly nod, and a level gaze of his own. "Good — and another thing: Rocco Bonetti."

"The fencer? What of him?"

The fencer! Bonetti's offended glare came vividly to mind. "He'd challenge you for calling him that!"

This drew a snort, and — wonder of wonders — even a small smile. "The master of defence, then. What do you want with him?"

"I have an itch to know more of this hat of his. Such a Canterbury tale — but it's time to find out just who Fagot is, if he's still alive, if he ever was. I don't expect that Bonetti is to be trusted…"

A half laugh. "Trusted? God keep you, no — but he's well paid."

Which was the next best thing, after all, was it not? Any discussion of the point, or of Bonetti himself, was curtailed by the arrival of the porter: a message had come for Mr. Thomas.

The note, it turned out, was from the Embassy: Monsieur de Castelnau would greatly appreciate Mr. Walsingham's company for a soirée.

And, because a liveried page was waiting for an answer, Tom hastened to the office for ink and paper, with Williams following.

"A dance?" inquired Williams, watching as Tom wrote his lines of thankful acceptance, all the time thinking of suitable finery — and wishing he hadn't already worn his brother's ox-blood sleeves at Salisbury Court…

"A dance — Heaven forbid! Like a salon, he says. All the rage in Paris. There is music, and poetry, people reading aloud, sometimes their own work. Fowler calls himself a poet, doesn't he? This should be right up his alley."

"And yours."

"Not really — no." Not content with sprinkling sand on his note, Tom blew softly to dry the ink faster. "Latin poetry is beauty itself. French poetry of the day, on the other hand…" Ah well. Williams would think no better of him for pedantry.

"But I'll even pretend to like Fowler's verse, if it lets me gossip a little with Courcelles." He folded the note, addressed it…

"They wouldn't keep you the night?" Williams asked. "If you were timid of the curfew…"

Ah, to stay the night, and to venture around Salisbury Court in the darkness — but of course…

"His Excellency takes great care in assuring me it will all be finished in time for the closing of the gates. Curse these long summer evenings."

An unsurprised shrug. "Ah well. He would, wouldn't he?"

"Also, 'light will be provided', so I can't even take Skeres with a lantern…"

Williams sniffed like one who had little faith in the Minotaur's use. "You should play the lute. Then he could carry it for you."

That he did play — but very badly — Tom kept to himself. "Yes, yes — I am a useless dolt," he said instead. "Make sure Fowler attends tonight, will you, Wat?"

Williams nodded, and went to see that persuasion was applied, leaving Tom to fold the letter, and to wonder if he had just cut the Welshman's impertinence, or an attempt at a joke.

In the long summer twilight, constellations of candles and torches shone around Castelnau's narrow garden. They lined the flowerbeds and the gravelled paths, and were reflected in the fountain's shallow water, each with its halo of dancing moths.

Right in front of the fountain, four tall branched candelabra lighted a square dais, their flames straight in the soft, heavy air — the scent of beeswax mixing with that of honeysuckle and the river. In that well-lit spot, for the best part of an hour, readers had taken turns declaiming to those who listened, pitching their voices loud against the music of two lutes and a viol half hidden among a group of pyramid-shaped laurels.

Chairs had been set in groups all through the garden, and servants went about pouring sweetened wine for the guests — perhaps a score of them.

Was Henry Fagot among them? None of these transient visitors — but one of the household? Or was he dead already, one and the same with the Frenchman Barbier, betrayed to the Ambassador by Bonetti? But then, even if the fencing master had sold his knowledge, why kill an uncovered spy…?

"Do you miss Paris, Mr. Walsingham?"

Tom turned from what he hoped looked like a survey of the garden to find Diane de Bochetel lowering herself into a chair at his side. And see how the candlelight made her creamy skin glow, see how it painted on her lovely mouth the curve of a faint smile…

"Paris, Madame?" Tom shot to his feet, bowing and holding the chair for her — too late, and what a witless answer!

She moved a white hand on her lap, not quite motioning at what lay all around. "*Monsieur mon cousin* says that you lived there for a long time. All this must remind you of it a little, surely?"

"Well…" *I once was at the Tuiléries gardens when… Not that we do not have this kind of thing in England… The gardens at Placentia… I did not much attend… I'm just a lowly courier…* "I haven't been away long enough to miss it properly, perhaps. Do you?"

The black, black eyes lowered for a heartbeat, before catching Tom's gaze again. "Country mice like myself scarcely know Paris at all, Monsieur. Not enough to miss it. It must seem strange to you, who are used to great cities…"

"You live in a very great city now…" Tom began, and stopped, because as likely as not Diane de Bochetel saw very little of London beyond the confines of Salisbury Court... Before he could think of some clever turn of conversation, someone stepped up behind him, drawing Diane's attention.

"Monsieur Claude," she said, and lowered her eyes. She said it in the strangest manner, with no inflection, so that it was hard to tell whether she spoke in greeting, in surprise or in displeasure.

Claude de Courcelles, all sea-green silks and huge ruffle and oiled curls, chose to take it as an invitation — and, with a bow of flowery condescension, sat on Tom's other side in a cloud of perfume.

"Are you enjoying yourself, Monsieur Walsn'am?" he asked in that languoring manner of his. "It seemed to His Excellency that it must please you to delectate in some French company again..."

And whether they truly thought that after tasting the joys of Paris an Englishman should languish away from it, or it was the one manner of conversation that occurred to one and all, Tom had wondered before — but Courcelles asking it, Courcelles asking anything, Courcelles even seeking Tom's company at all...!

And another wonder was in store: a little laugh from Madame de Bochetel, like a crystalline gurgle breaking the immobility of a pool. A deep, dark, mysterious pool...

"Poor Monsieur Walsingham!" she said, with a smile. "I wonder if a soul under this roof has not asked him, does he miss Paris?"

Well, well, a night of miracles, Tom would have called it — but that the fair Diane's delightful smile did not reach her eyes, and that the secrétaire looked less than pleased at the fair Diane's words, mild as they were... An awkward silence descended on the three of them, Tom casting about for something, anything to say, thankful when, on the dais, the current reader came to an affected halt, bowed to polite applause, and retired.

"I had no inkling that there were this many French poets in London..." Tom said. "They must all be here, surely?"

Courcelles raised both eyebrows in the manner of one enduring much. "Oh, they are not all French, Monsieur — and, most certainly, they are not all poets." He tilted his head at the next reader, who took his place among the candelabra, clutching a sheaf of papers, his yellow head swivelling this way and that — and who must it be but William Fowler returned.

From the first row of chairs, where he sat in the company of a lady in rose-pink silk, Monsieur de Castelnau gestured. "Begin, *mon cher*," he cheerfully called.

Had the Ambassador bid him to ascend the scaffold, Fowler could not have looked more dismayed. He cleared his throat once, twice, announced three roundels on the subject of Virtue, and then, voice reedy and flat, began to read.

Before he had gone three words, Courcelles clicked his tongue in contempt.

"Poor Monsieur Fowler." Madame de Bochetel shook her head. "Monsieur Claude never liked him, nor his poems — but Monsieur Jauffray says that he does much better in his own tongue."

"Fowler is a Scot," said Courcelles. "Proper English isn't even his tongue." And, with another click of the tongue, he dismissed either Fowler's Scottishness, or Monsieur Jauffray's opinion, or both.

Tom turned to Diane, who was listening to Fowler's efforts with the pitying frown that they deserved.

"I don't think that I've met a Monsieur Jauffray..."

"No, perhaps you have not..." she murmured. "He keeps much to himself... But look, there he is, with le Docteur Bruno, by the plum trees."

The light had begun to dim by then, and it took Tom some squinting to see that, with Bruno by the plum trees, stood the noble-faced fellow who disliked Douglas so much. And who apparently did not dislike Bruno, for he nodded now and then at the Italian's whispered conversation, although he seemed much taken with the music...

So here was another dweller of Salisbury Court, one Tom had not had a chance to observe yet. Another Frenchman, by his name — and just what language did he use in conversing with Bruno? But Jauffray would have to wait, Courcelles's extraordinary friendliness clamouring for precedence.

Extraordinary, and rather ill-judged. Even supposing he had swallowed whatever qualms he held, did he mean to signal this amidst a crowd, and right in front of the Ambassador's own cousin? What had changed in two days...?

Ask questions to draw a man on, Thomas. Pick it out of him piecemeal...

"I am very glad to see you in better spirits, Monsieur," Tom whispered, under the patter of applause that met the end of one of Fowler's roundels. "Has the rain restored you since the other day?"

"You are most kind, Monsieur." For want of a fan, Courcelles flapped both hands in front of him. "The heat has abated, as you promised — but the damp, the damp..."

And yet, under the long lashes the gaze was sharp...

"You should promenade yourself. Out of the city walls there are many pleasant places to take the air... Do you know Spitalfields?"

And curse the fellow, there he went, stiff with suspicion again, almost squint-eyed in his disapproval. "I misdoubt there is a corner of this island where the air is wholesome, Monsieur — within or without your walls."

Lord give strength! What did Claude de Courcelles expect — what did he think he was doing? Tom turned away so he didn't glower at the mistrustful dunce — and, as he did so, caught Bruno and the stern fellow, Jauffray, watching him. They had moved away from the trees, close enough to the candelabra to see that Bruno looked amused. Jauffray, on the other hand, did not, and looked away the moment he caught Tom's eye.

Had Courcelles seen too? Was that why he went on about how he'd heard such places were the hunting ground of pursepickers and worse?

"No more than other parts of London," Tom murmured, "or Paris."

Oh, for the hundred eyes of Argus, at times…! For, when he turned to see what Madame de Bochetel made of the conversation, she had recovered her alabastrine indifference, but for a look of mild expectation fixed on Monsieur de Castelnau.

The Ambassador was rising to his feet, applauding poor Fowler with such eagerness that all joined him, much to the bashful flustering of the poet. The flustering froze to dismay when Castelnau went to stand by the poor Duckling, and, a hand on his shoulder, addressed the company.

"And since, as Monsieur Fowler has put so eloquently to us, Beauty and Virtue are one, I would show you all something of beauty, if you but follow me to the gallery."

"Oh yes, His Excellency's surprise!"

Was it relief in Courcelles's manner, as he excused himself and made haste towards the house? Not for a minute did Tom believe that he remembered some neglected task. See how he scurried for the porch-like door under the gallery — where pricks of light were blossoming behind the leaded glass. See how Jauffray's gaze followed him from under a furrowed brow… And again this would have to wait, as Castelnau offered his arm to the lady in rose-pink, and led the way towards the house.

By the time the Ambassador's flock entered it in a small procession, the gallery was brightly lit. There were exclamations of astonished pleasure — and they were well-earned. An abundance of fine wax candles burnt in candelabra and sconces, their flames reflected in the four glazed windows. Seen from the garden — and even more from the river — it must have looked like a prodigious lantern, held aloof by a giant's hand. Under Girault's watchful gaze, a handful of servants hovered, ready to trim the wicks as need arose, while at the far end three men stood with the air of having just retired there. None of them, it was worth noting, was Claude de Courcelles. Tom recognised the scribe Laurent, a tall stranger and, more surprisingly, Archibald Douglas. Had he been ensconced here all evening, watching them all from above? *A braw place to see who comes and goes*, he'd called it… That he had worked with Feron seemed unlikely, and surely he stood aloof, and showed much less interest in surveying the arrangements than the other two did…

The arrangements consisted of three sideboards, arrayed between the windows and draped with wine-coloured cloth, each carrying three pictures of some sort, each picture set so to catch the best of the light.

"Fine and rare prints," Monsieur de Castelnau beamed at Tom, with the delight of all collectors — half child with a toy, half prey-laden hunter. "Come and admire my find, Monsieur Walsingham. It cannot but be to your taste."

And indeed, it was. Little as Tom knew of printing and pictures, he was astonished at the fine, intricate workmanship, at the rich detail bringing the scene to vivid life. See how the minute leaves sprouted from Daphne's fleeing limbs, her plaited hair coming undone in her flight… "These are exquisite, Excellency. Even to as untrained an eye as mine." He glanced at the next print: Andromeda chained to the rock, the sea serpent rearing its head above the waves. "Are they all from Ovid?"

Castelnau beamed — and truly, truly, could this be the man who had spies poisoned in his own kitchen?

"But yes, the Metamorphoses!" he explained. "The work of Virgil Solis — the original work, etched by his own hand. Exquisite, as you say. There are many more, but so hard to find now! It was a great chance and a great work to find the nine you see."

"Do not despair, Signor Ambasciatore," a new voice said in Italian, and Tom turned to find Bruno at his shoulder, and Jauffray with him.

This mysterious fellow, clad in the soberest drab, had shed his earlier scowl in favour of mildness, in perfect counterpoint to the Italian's animation — Calm and Liveliness from an old-fashioned play. *He used to be a Dominican friar*, Sidney had said of Bruno. Just as sharp-witted, no doubt — but had he been this bright, in the Dominican black and white?

"We were just discussing, were we not, Signor Jauffray? Of what a miracle it is that your Sauldane found even what he found."

Jauffray smiled indulgently — and so he must be one of those who understood Italian, although he answered in French.

"I don't know that I would call it a miracle," he said, soft-voiced. "But a very fine enterprise, for sure. If more can be found, then Monsieur Sauldane will."

He spoke the French of an educated man, though without the ornate courtliness of Castelnau or Courcelles. Tom studied the sagging profile, melancholy even as he leant close to marvel at Solis's skilful Andromeda. The hollow cheeks, the stooping shoulders, the greying temples, all made him look to be well past his fortieth year…

He straightened when Tom echoed his words: "Monsieur Sauldane?"

"Oh yes." Jauffray looked over his shoulder, this way and that, until he found the tall stranger conversing with Feron. "Over there with our Laurent, you see? Crispin Sauldane, a most cunning Flemish merchant, with a fine eye for works of art, His Excellency says."

He said this as of a great authority, and hastened away with an apology when His Excellency, who had proceeded along the row of prints with the lady in rose pink on his arm, turned to call for them to join the flock. "But do come, Messieurs, come and see the rest. Here is the Battle of the Centaurs…"

Tom stood back to let Jauffray pass, and Bruno with Madame de Bochetel. He would have followed, but from the corner of his eye he caught Fowler, released by the Ambassador and hovering at the edge of the little crowd, darting sideways glances in a manner that, no doubt, he thought subtle.

Swallowing a sigh, Tom let another man pass, another one of Castelnau's poets, and tarried by the third print. He had barely the time to observe the subject — a distraught Apollo holding the lifeless Hyacinth in his arms — before Fowler sidled up.

"Mr. Walsingham —"

Oh Lord guard all fools — and those who had to do with them! "One would be well advised to give Apollo a wide berth, don't you think?"

"Eh?" Fowler startled. "I must have a —"

"Daphne there, changed into a bush, and poor Hyacinth here… One should be wary of certain dealings…"

"Aye — aye, but Williams said —"

"My name is Thomas Walsingham. I heard you read your verse earlier, but did not catch your name, I fear…"

"I … oh. Oh." The Duckling's Adam's apple bobbed up and down as the poor fellow grasped for a hold of himself. "William Fowler at your service, Sir," he blurted at last, and bowed a good deal lower than Tom's rank warranted. "You must tell Mr. —"

"No, Mr. Fowler, I insist. A most ingenious set of rhymes." And in a much lower tone: "Up. And smile."

And the Scot straightened, at last, lips stretched into a creditable smile.

"Have you ever written on this matter of gods and mortals?" Tom gestured at the figure of the dying prince. "He must have wished that he'd stayed well away, poor lad."

Again as he had before Sir Francis at Seething Lane, Fowler seemed to gather his wits all at once.

"Aye — but belike he would have," he said, smile turning grim. "Only … a man can find himself in a deadly position through nae choice of his own."

Tom shook his head. The Duckling must see, surely, that they could not talk? Not there, not in the middle of a crowd, where anyone might be listening… He moved to the next picture, and then the next. No use: Fowler trailed after him most duckling-wise…

Ah well, then… "Hero and Leander, would you think?" A lady was pictured throwing herself over a man's dead body. "Such a cheerful fellow, Ovid…!"

"No, ye see?" Fowler leant to peer at the closely printed legend. "Halcyone and Ceix…"

"Who is this Crispin Sauldane?" Tom murmured under his breath.

Fowler stiffened but, to his credit, didn't startle or draw back. "Sauldane? A … a Fleming. Works for one named Courtois or Cortez — but —"

"A Spaniard?"

"I think…"

"And Jauffray?"

"The chaplain…" Fowler began — and stopped when a shadow fell across the sideboard.

"Oh, right you are!" Tom laughed. "Hero and Leander are in the Heroides, are they not?"

Fowler blinked a little. "The Heroides, aye…"

Both turned to face Castelnau himself, with Courcelles, and the Fleming — Sauldane.

"Will one of you gentlemen settle this for us? Are Hero and Leander in Ovid's Heroides?" Tom asked in French, smoothly enough, he hoped, to cover the flash of recognition. For Crispin Sauldane, tall, lean, and fox-faced, was one of the men he'd met the other day, leaving through the garden door.

"But yes…" Courcelles tapped a knuckle to his lips in thought. "The Seventh Epistula…?"

"Eighteenth, I believe," Castelnau corrected, with gleeful erudite zeal. "The Eighteenth and Nineteenth Epistle, in fact, because Leander has the courtesy to write back. Or rather, he writes first, eh?"

Sauldane shook his head. "I do not know of these things," he said, speaking to Tom and Fowler rather than the Ambassador — but, if he had recognised Tom in turn, he showed no sign, unless it was in the hint of a smile that curved his moustached mouth.

It lasted less than a moment, before Castelnau laughed. "Do not be modest, Sauldane!" he exclaimed, patting the man's shoulder. "It is to him that I owe the finding of these prints, and many others besides. He does know of these things!"

Sauldane's smile creased deeper, without widening, as he took a small bow — and of what else this man knew, Tom wondered very much. A pity that the Fleming was left behind, in person as in subject, as Castelnau took Tom by the arm and steered him away. "But you barely saw the half of my new treasure, Monsieur Walsingham. Let me show you…"

And, thank the Fates, Fowler had the sense to stay behind too.

It was a while before Tom could disengage himself. A while so merrily filled with the merits of Ovid and Solis, that one had to wonder. The Ambassador's enjoyment was too keen, too well informed to be less than sincere. What else it covered, though, was another matter…

With this in mind Tom brought the discourse on the merits, also, of a French edition of the Metamorphoses that Sir Francis possessed. It carried, he said, pictures by Leroy. The book *had* pictures, this was sure, and remarkably fine ones. Whose work they were, in truth Tom had no idea — but it did not matter greatly, nor did his knowledge of such things, beyond what let him launch himself into raptures of comparison when it transpired that Castelnau had never seen the book.

"Mr. Secretary would be happy for Your Excellency to see it, and peruse it at leisure," Tom promised. "I could have it sent. Tomorrow, perhaps?"

Sent — or brought, and carried by a servant, of course…

"Oh, this is most kind of you, my young friend!" the Ambassador exclaimed. "I would like it of all things — and I will, though not tomorrow. Nor the day after that, I fear, as I will be joining Her Highness's court at Richmond, tomorrow. I shall meet Mr. Secretary, there, I expect — and I will have much to commend of you."

And on he moved, with his small cortège about him — but Tom was suffered to lag behind, which he did feeling a little light-headed. Monsieur de Castelnau's laughing warmth was such to always leave a sort of void behind him. This time, though — this time… Had there been a hint of dismissal in the Ambassador's manner? Had Tom brought it about, by showing himself too eager…?

But surely not? Surely it was this perfumed, airless heat, that muffled all reasoning? Oh, for a cup of that sweetened wine now … but there were no servants to be seen.

For all its length, the gallery was low-ceilinged, and the number of people and burning candles made the air thick under its dark beams, close enough to prove Courcelles right. Since one did not loosen lace collars in such company, Tom made for the nearest window, whose iron casement stood ajar, easing it open, and he leaned against the sill for a lungful of the evening air. Down in the garden, the musicians had ceased their toils, and servants went about, snuffing torches and candles. A full moon had risen, and sailed low in the sky, the colour of straw, its light strong enough to redden the few flames that still remained, and to reflect on the fountain's water. Beyond the garden's far wall lay a stretch of neglected land, its wild bushes black in the moonlight — and beyond that the river gleamed dully. Seen from above, on the other side of the wall, Water Lane was a black fissure, and the river stairs invisible. *A braw place to see who comes and goes*, Douglas had said… A lie, or at least an omission: even in daylight he could not have seen Scory coming back across the river, unless the man had come back to Salisbury Court through the garden door. Also, was this how Fagot had seen Lord Howard and Throckmorton arrive for their midnight visits? How he'd seen them, perhaps, but not how he'd known of them in the first place — for no one could be recognised in the dark at this distance. So Fagot must have had this from Castelnau himself, or from Courcelles…

Courcelles, indeed. Was it worth pursuing the fellow's conversation right now? There he stood, alone by Apollo and Hyacinth…

"Monsieur, please…" someone called softly from behind, and Tom turned to find the clerk, Laurent, watching him with mild disapproval.

"Please, Monsieur, this damp air is noxious to paper. If Monsieur would allow me…"

"Of course — thoughtless of me." Tom stepped back between the draped sideboards, nearly dislodging one of the prints with a clumsy elbow.

"Careful, Monsieur," warned Laurent.

The man had a soft rumble of a voice, and was large enough that he had to slide sideways between the boards, which he did nimbly enough in spite of his great frame.

"Now, you will think me too forward, Monsieur, but…" he began, as he worked the window shut, stopping to push and grunt when the casement resisted.

"Not at all," Tom said. "This is especially precious paper — and entrusted to your care, I suppose?"

Still occupied with the window, the clerk half turned to nod over his shoulder — and was that a smile, half hidden in the leonine beard?

"Indeed, like many other papers, you could say —"

He stopped, frowning at something beyond Tom's shoulder. Diane de Bochetel, bearing down on them and back from a smiling converser to the stern housekeeper.

"This is hardly your work, Maître Feron," she said — in that colourless manner that was so hard to read.

Easier to see, if not to fathom, was Laurent Feron's struggle. Fists bunching at his sides, he made to speak, and held the lady's gaze for a moment before lowering his own.

"Madame."

A little imperious… The servants do not love her, had been Bruno's words — and Laurent Feron was not quite a servant — but there was turmoil in his manner towards Madame Diane — and see if there was not some sort of ripple in her obsidian eyes, gone as soon as it had come.

"I am to blame, Madame, I fear," Tom interceded, "for thoughtlessly opening the window. Maître Feron's care was all for his master's prints."

Whatever had discomposed Diane was gone or covered. "No one is to blame, Monsieur. I make no reproach — but the wine is being neglected, and Girault is not to be seen. If Maître Feron would be so kind…"

The clerk wasn't half as good at masking his mind. He stiffly bowed and hastened away, disappearing down the stairs — and what it all had been about, Tom was not alone in wondering: half across the gallery, minor satellites in the group that revolved around their host, Bruno and Jauffray watched, still standing side by side as they had in the garden — one amused, and the other frowning… The Ambassador's own chaplain, if Fowler was to be believed. But yes: the noble, aloof manner, the simple clothes, the friendship with the former friar… It could very well be.

Alone by the next window, Crispin Sauldane was also observing, his fox-like face intent.

None of it had escaped Madame de Bochetel. Her gaze lingered on the Fleming, before it travelled to Bruno and the solemn Jauffray, and then to Fowler himself, fidgeting at the periphery of a small group of ladies.

"I thought that you and Monsieur Fowler had never met," she said suddenly, with that equally sudden hint of a smile. It was as though an invisible Pygmalion had kissed her back to life.

Of course. Of course their conversation had been noticed… "But we had not — until tonight." Tom risked a rueful smile. "It seemed discourteous not to laud his verse, and we came to talk of Paris, for he was there too. He mentioned some acquaintances in Paris, one or two of which are also mine. Henry Neville, the Throckmorton brothers…"

A reckless thing to say, a whim of the moment — but if Diane de Bochetel saw the name for the bait it was, she didn't bite. Or at least not on the morsel Tom was dangling, for she frowned a little and said, "Then he must know more about you than you do about him…"

And this could just be a woman's aversion, or else the Ambassador's cousin, trying her hand at this game of chess that England and France played at the Embassy… And a sign of the suspicion that followed Fowler's steps at Salisbury Court — and as for himself…

"Oh, every soul here knows and worries that I left Paris lately," he said, sheltering behind his most innocent manner. "But I suspect Doctor Bruno on this particular account."

Which was less than true, but plausible enough to bring back the smile — or to bring up a new one that made a small dimple in Diane's perfect cheek. A delightful, girlish dimple that changed her as though by magic, that made one wish there were more in this world to make her smile —

"Yes, Monsieur Bruno talks," she said. "He talks of the skies, and of the ways of men, general and particular… Perplexing things, sometimes… *Monsieur mon cousin* says that there is no true heresy in them — but all the same he begged le Docteur Bruno to refrain tonight from talking of such things as how the sun does not move around us. And he — only half in jest, he says he cannot help himself under a starry sky!"

"He cannot help himself under a moulded ceiling!" Tom laughed. "He told me of the sun the very first day at dinner, while we discussed the poetry of Horace…"

Madame Diane shook her head, the dimple fading — and Tom wondered if he had put the little Italian in the suds. He also wondered at himself. He was Sir Francis Walsingham's man, by Jupiter — not one who made unguarded talk in summer gardens… He threw a sideways glance at the woman beside him, tranquil and composed, but for the hands tightly joined at her waist, as she surveyed the servants bringing more wine for the guests. Diane de Bochetel struck him suddenly as a dangerous creature.

For all that, it was not late when the company moved from the gallery down the stairs and to the hall, where the air, by contrast, felt cool enough to clear a man's head. Footmen with torches were provided for the departing guests, to light their way in the purple twilight. A very civil custom, the way of a gracious host — or a wary one…

There was much exclamation on the wonders of the evening, much extolling of the Ambassador's hospitality, and much taking of leave. Fowler made a great show of greeting each and all, until he reached Tom.

They bid each other good night, smiling like the best of acquaintances — but the fear was plain in the Scot's round eyes.

"I must talk to ye, Mr. Walsingham," he hissed, and Fates send that nobody was watching too closely his effort at a forged smile. "Talk truly, and not in riddles."

"Williams —"

"No, no, no!" Fowler stopped brusquely to turn and bow in the French manner to a lady passing by, and then, still smiling after her, muttered out of the corner of his mouth: "Williams doesnae listen, but I hae things —"

Things! "Tomorrow, then." Tom had a fair notion of what Fowler's *things* would be — but then he had questions of his own to ask. "I'll come to your lodgings in the afternoon."

"But…" And see how the Duckling stiffened, wide-eyed for anyone to see…

Never had Tom believed he would be thankful for Girault — and yet he was, when the butler called:

"Messieurs, if you please…" By the great door that was thrown wide open on the warm night, showing a small swarm of torches in the court, Girault stood tall and ponderous, sorting men, sedan chairs, horses, and guests like an ugly Thyrsis with an unruly flock.

Tom obeyed the summons, the Duckling trotting at his elbow.

A small procession of a half dozen mounted gentlemen and two lady's chairs was headed for Ludgate and the City — with two light-men at head and foot — and this Tom was to join, a groom holding his horse ready for him.

Fowler, headed Holborn-way on foot, together with a couple of others and a single torch, dithered in spite of the butler's impatience…

"Good night to you, then, Mr. Fowler," Tom called. "And I'll stand by what I said."

They exchanged nods, and then the poor fellow had no recourse but to let himself be shepherded away.

Oh Lord…

"What did ye say, young Thomas, that ye'll stand by? Never that ye like his poetry?"

Tom turned to find Douglas on the threshold. How long he'd been within earshot, and what he had heard, though…

"He asked," Tom sighed. "Asked most anxiously. What was I to say?"

And though Archibald Douglas sniffed, there was a spark of mischief in the deep-set eyes.

"Aye, what indeed," he said. "Some would wonder whether ye're far too kind or a verra good liar — but I'm thinking that the twa often gang together."

How did one respond to this, but with a laugh?

Tom was the last to mount in the saddle, and Girault came to pat the first sedan's side, to set the group in motion.

Douglas stepped back. "Good night to ye, then," he called.

"Are you not joining us, Mr. Douglas?"

The Scot shook his head. "I'm an auld man, not fit for riding about at night. His Excellency was so good as to offer hospitality."

Of course. Of course, damn him — although… The evening gloom made it hard to read the cast of the man's features, whether he looked gloating or apprehensive…

And yet the fine voice held a shade of mockery. "Hae a safe walk hame, lad. Safer than we had last time, eh?"

"Thank you, Mr. Douglas. I trust that it will be," Tom said — and this seemed to grimly amuse the Scot.

The man knows no shame, Jauffray had once said of Douglas. Perhaps, though, he was beginning to know fear for his life… The fear Fowler knew well already, and perhaps Fagot too, hidden in the folds of the Ambassador's household…

Ah well.

Off the small train went, chatting and well lit, all cheerful with the good wine and the company. At a very sedate pace, they crossed the court and entered the lane to Fleet Street… A narrow lane, it was, dark but for the ruddiness of the two crackling torches — and the temptation was great… Tom let his horse fall back, stopped, and bent to fiddle with a stirrup. Back across the court, the house loomed in the moonlight. What if he were to lag back, slip into the shadow of Water Lane, and see whether some midnight visitor came by way of the garden —

"Master?" The liveried light-man waited, torch held high, head tilted.

Tom waved to him. "Go ahead, I'll join you."

But no, of course. The officious fellow must shake his head, come to plant himself where he could shed light on Tom's perfectly good stirrup… "I'm waiting for you, Master. Monsieur Girault don't want us to leave the guests alone."

No, he wouldn't, would he? And he would know if Mr. Secretary's man slipped away — a foolish thing to try in the first place…

"There." Swallowing a sigh, Tom straightened in the saddle and nudged the horse ahead, taking his place in the small cortège again, with the contented light-man at his back. And all the time he turned in his mind the nature of Castelnau's courtesy — to those who left and those who stayed the night at Salisbury Court.

Still, it seemed wasteful not to seek a chance — and the chance showed itself at Ludgate, where, once inside the City proper, the gentlemen began to protest that there was no further need to proceed in one group, and do the round of each guest's door like a Passion play of old... The footmen protested in turn that they had orders — but lost all their qualms when they were vailed and were sent off to light the way for the two ladies in the chairs and their escorts.

Tom joined a pair of young men — one French, one English — headed Tower-wards and impatient to continue the night in pursuits that had little to do with poetry. Indeed, so impatient they were that they barely took notice when, once in Saint Paul's churchyard, their invitation to join them at the Boar's Head tavern was refused. They went their merry way with nary another thought for their unsociable road-fellow, who, as soon as they were out of view, turned his horse and hastened back to the gate.

Back to the Queen's own work, dangerous and urgent, unlike those who spent their nights in aimless idleness...

A bolstering thought — and shamefully immodest, Tom's mother would call it, not to mention foolish: for all he knew, those two might well be arch-conspirators, or at least likely to inform Castelnau of his detour...

What if they did? What if this one act of rashness were to undo all the careful work of months, and leave Salisbury Court unobserved just when it mattered most? Neither man had looked very sharp-witted — but then neither did William Fowler... Still, there was the way the guests had been shepherded away, and Girault's zeal in seeing them gone...

Sedit qui timuit... He who fears to fail, sits still, as Horace had it...

Tom did not sit still. He reached Ludgate just as the guards were closing the heavy gate, but a look at Guildford's finery, and a groat to share among them, were all it took. In a trice Tom was out of the City walls.

By day Fleet Street was always filled with crowds in and out of London. It was quieter in the warm, moonlit night — and yet far from deserted. The closing of the gate brought out a different humanity. Men, women and children still went about — few of them bent on honest pursuits. They talked aloud, and laughed, and strutted — all with a manner of swaggering menace, half fighting-cocks, half prowling wolves. Some of those wolves, male and female, had hooded, glittering looks of consideration for the well-dressed man on horseback, who cantered down the paved slope of Fleet Street. Tom was well armed, and the Watch was likely to intervene here, if not elsewhere in the Ward — but still it would not do to tempt the wolves too much...

Soon after crossing Fleet Bridge, Tom reined in at the George Inn, still well alive with custom, and dismounted in the yard. A yawning ostler took the horse to stable, and shook his head when the rider's high-crowned hat came with it — although without the brooch.

"Too fair-'eaded for a moon night, Master!" he pronounced, clicking his tongue in disapproval. "Wait 'ere."

A moment later he was back with a dark cap, a broad grin, and a ready palm. A ha'penny changed hands with the smoothness of usual business.

Better not wonder who had worn the cap before, better not dwell on what may live in it… Tom donned it low over his eyes, and hitched his sword well in sight, wishing for simpler clothes… On second thoughts, he turned his short cape inside out so that the darker lining showed. With any luck, in the dark he'd look like a ruffian wearing someone else's cast-offs… A good thing that he hadn't far to go. With the ostler's knowing wink for a blessing, he plunged into Fleet Street again, past the conduit, and then into the shadows at the gaping mouth of Water Lane.

Black as iron-gall it was, all the blacker for the sliver of moonlight down at the river end — and darkness feigned the slope steeper to the foot. A few steps down, Tom flattened himself again the wall, partly to let his eyes adjust, partly to make sure no one followed him with ill intentions. He waited — the air thick with the stench of piss and rotting — until he was able to tell ground from wall, and then began to creep ahead, a hand trailing along the damp bricks, towards the garden door of Salisbury Court. Once or twice dark things scurried out of his way, and the clay squelched underfoot — or belike it wasn't clay at all, and Tom didn't even want to think of his shoes… He stumbled when the wall fell away of a sudden: a rough passage yawned there, like a crook-toothed maw, ready to swallow the unwary…

And wasn't he six kinds of fanciful idiot! There was nothing preternatural in the burst of coarse laughter that wafted out from the passage, nor in the angry hissing of the cat who shot out of the blackness … and no need to be short of breath — none at all!

Another half-dozen wary steps, and Tom stopped. A few yards ahead something showed dimly in the wall opposite — the wicket door, surely? He huddled in the blackest of the shadows and considered the joints and flexures of the matter.

Item: there was no knowing for certain that Howard or Throckmorton would visit on this particular night;

Item: it was unlikely that, if anyone did visit, anything of import could be gleaned — not even the visitor's identity;

Then again…

Item: no honest soul would visit the French Ambassador in the secret of night;

Item: there had *been a suspicious whiff to Castelnau's solicitous farewell. More than a whiff, in truth;*

And, most of all:

Item: one of those visits would go a long way to proving Fagot trustworthy…

Ergo, the chance was worth waiting.

They never come except at night, Fagot had written. Tom squinted up at the slice of night sky above, trying to gauge the hour, but it was no use. The moon was not in sight, and yet luminous enough to paint the night in that silvery blue that swallows the stars.

Ah well.

Selene might well lead the dance of the nymphs in the skies above; down in the filth of Water Lane, darkness led to a very different tune — one of screeches, and squelches, and scurrying, and distant shouts of abuse, and barking, and…

And a drawing of bolts.

Tom tensed, straining his ears.

It was soft, but he'd heard it before, this whisper of greased irons. Heard it — and thought of nightly ill-doings … and here they were.

It was too dark to see the door opening, but a bulky shape leant out into the alley, the blackest black against the faint luminescence down at the river end. It stood there for a few heartbeats, and then retreated. There were words murmured, then another shadow, a good deal smaller, stepped out. This second man was less wary.

"Yes, yes," he hissed. "I heard your master well!"

Could this be the voice of Francis Throckmorton? There had been bouts at the *salle d'armes*, and some tavern-going, though never much of it … very, very hard to tell. Certainly Throckmorton was no large man, just like this mysterious fellow — and like a good half of London…

More murmuring came from the door and, with no more than an aggrieved sigh, the man who could be Francis Throckmorton stepped away, and down, towards the river. It was easy to imagine him, one hand on the hilt, the other feeling the wall, ears straining for the softest hint of a threat. Down to a waiting boat, no doubt, braving the risks of the river at night.

So that was it.

There *were* secret visitors at Salisbury Court. Fagot had not lied about this, at least.

With a quiet sigh, Tom shifted his weight, and…

Truly, he did nothing worse: a quiet sigh, and the smallest shift — so it was rank unfairness that a rat should take offence, and break into a squeaking fury as it skittered between Tom's feet… Tartarus take all vermin!

"*Qui est là?*"

There was no mistaking Girault's thick voice, or the steps running down the alley. The visitor was fleeing, but the butler had other notions.

Even before the feet of two men scrambled into the lane, Tom was leaping for the dark passage. He threw himself inside it just ahead of the scouring beam from a lantern.

Water Lane had been near silent, a moment ago. Now it was alive with hissing and squeaking, and chattering, and the angry whispers of two men.

"'Tis just the rats!" one voice snarled — Foulques?

"Someone was there." This from Girault, with more approaching steps, and the lantern's yellow fingers searching, searching…

Tom retreated deeper into the alley. The darkness, the stench, the dampness were thick enough to make Water Lane seem like a garden by comparison, and there was nothing in the way of shelter, once Girault shone his light past the mouth. A few steps further, a narrow black opening showed, and Tom only hesitated long enough to unsheathe his knife. It was a passage, leading to a scantling court where a rushlight shone at a window — a greenish, greasy pinprick of light, guttering in the close air.

A shutter banged overhead, and a woman's voice shouted: "Back already, Peterkin?" rousing an echo of hoots, and laughing abuse that came from everywhere.

Squeezing into the darkest corner, listening for his pursuers, Tom caught his breath, cursed to himself, and thought. He could find safety from Girault and his crony by venturing deeper into this straggle of sagging, crooked houses… A ribbon of blackness at the court's far end promised another alley — why, a maze of them, belike. But this was the old White Friars, where one got lost, and sometimes never emerged again. Only a stone's throw from the French Ambassador's stately house, here festered a burrow of ill-meaning ruffians of all sexes and ages. It was the way of

London — but not one to experience alone — much less at night…

A burst of furious barking from the alley jolted him. There were voices, too — French voices and English, raised in argument over the unseen dog's baying…

And then four or five bullies came running from the passage on the court's other side. Shouting with ferocious glee at the prospect of a tussle with the French, they made for the alley, eager to join the commotion there…

"'Tis the Frogs!"

"Teach 'em!"

"Away with the mounseers!"

Here was a chance! Tom drew the cape closer around him, and joined the gaggle, shouting with the others, safe enough in the dark and the mayhem, as long as he looked out for knives and cudgels … but here, also, was a conundrum: was he going to let these cut-throats murder the two Frenchmen? Little as he liked the fellows, he could not leave Girault and Foulques to be slaughtered…

Oh, curse it!

So now see Thomas Walsingham to the rescue! Mr. Secretary's own man, elbowing his way through a drunken, mad-eyed White Friars rabble, to stand shoulder to shoulder with two French ruffians who, in his place, would no doubt shrug and look the other way… Let Sir Francis never know what a lackwit he has for a cousin!

But perhaps Fate was looking out for conscientious lackwits. When, after some jostling and shouting, he found himself in the alley, the Embassy men were in flight, the halo of their lantern bouncing up and down blackened walls, two large four-legged shadows snapping at their heels. For the second time, Tom joined the pursuit — in the hope that nobody would take much notice of him before they were out of the White Friars… They spilt out of the alley and into Water Lane just in time to hear the wicket door slam closed. Someone had brought a torch, and by its light the two huge mongrels could be seen, growling and scratching at the door… A few of the bullies ran there, and, when their kicks proved useless against the sturdy wood, they lowered their breeches to piss on the threshold. Their friends hooted, and sneered, and whistled, and called the French every name that could be thought — and, as a last insult, the man with the torch hurled it past the wall, into the garden, together with a few stones.

And Lord be thanked, at last, for the sudden darkness. Tom took his chance and slipped away towards Fleet Street and the moonlight — with, of all things in this world, Diane's roses in his mind. Surely the Embassy folk would go and quench the fire, wouldn't they? And would Monsieur de Castelnau complain to the Council for the indignity of having his home assaulted in such a way?

As luck would have it, the same ostler let Tom in at the door of the George's yard, raising an eyebrow at the sight of his breathless and battered state. Not all that battered, in truth, beside a tear in the cape and the half-ruined shoes — but the cap was gone, lost in some dark corner of the White Friars, and had to be paid for, before Tom could obtain a pallet in an already crowded room. It was noisy, and stifling hot, and less than clean by touch and smell, and besides, Tom's elbow hurt, and, at Seething Lane, Williams would be wondering, if not worrying…

All of it of little import, when gauged against the certainty that, at least when it came to Castelnau's nightly visitors, Fagot was no liar.

Tom fell asleep, and dreamt of Henry Fagot: a dark, hunched figure, dimly seen from behind as he threw a torn cape, again and again, at a bush of burning roses.

CHAPTER 9

At Seething Lane, the house was on the verge of uproar by the time Tom was back — just in time to stop the messenger who was to inform Sir Francis that his cousin was missing.

"They're murderers, there!" Williams groused, with all the ill-temper of relief. "How was I to know they hadn't sent you to the pot?"

The shortest telling of the night's fruit pacified him somewhat — but he was still malcontented when Tom summoned him to the empty kitchen parlour.

As Tom sat at the table with a bowl of water and a roll of bandages, washing and dressing his scraped elbow, the Welshman leaned against the doorjamb, arms crossed, legs crossed at the ankles, much in the way of one who expected nothing good.

Tom could have told him that he expected no better himself. Left to do as he liked, he would have sorted his thoughts in the solitude of his own head — but now…

Now Sir Francis had put him in charge of this matter, and also had given him Williams — and through him Fowler and Douglas. And Williams was trusty and had much experience, and knew the two Scots well… It would be witless arrogance to disregard the man's knowledge, and his soldier's level head. On the other hand, there he stood, a doubtful eyebrow cocked, thinking of poor Guildford no doubt, sniffing wolf-wise for weakness — and secure in the trust of Sir Francis…

But then, so was Tom, was he not? He took a good breath and let it out. "So now we know that Fagot is in earnest. Or was, for I am wondering… Have you found Rocco Bonetti yet?"

"You think that man that died, Barbier, was Fagot?"

"I think we haven't had a letter since he died, have we? But much depends on whether and when Bonetti went to Salisbury Court."

"He'll turn up. What help he'll be, though…"

A protégé of mine, Castelnau had called the Venetian… "He's as close to Fagot as we've come, so far — and now Fagot is either dead, or alive and in danger. I want to find out."

"Using Bonetti's hat!" Williams snorted.

"Yes, rather fantastical — but then, Fagot's whole charade is not the work of a plain mind…"

"The mind of the under-butler?"

And if it was meant as a challenge, Tom ignored it, for the question was fair.

"There you have me, Wat." He winced as he dabbed at his elbow with a damp cloth. "I hardly know what Clement Barbier's mind was like. A servant may eavesdrop a good many things, but he'd need to be sharp-witted and to cover it well…"

"Still, he needn't be Fagot to be killed — if you are sure that he was killed."

"Coxcombs are sure, all the more when they don't see the body for themselves — and no, he needn't be Fagot."

"I'll lay you a wager he was in on the matter of the books. The other fellow was."

"Hurston? Yes, but…" But how to explain this was just why Tom doubted — and all because of what he had observed of one other murderer… "Yes, he was — for all that Hurston was stabbed in anger, and Barbier poisoned with hemlock."

"Hemlock … the devil!"

"So it seems. Is it that hard to find, you think?"

Williams laughed without mirth. "Not that hard, no — a crooked apothecary, a wise-woman... Only, they'll never tell."

"I wouldn't, in their place — but no matter. Wherever the hemlock came from, someone fed it to Barbier because he was Fagot, or because there was a falling out among the smugglers, or else he never was one of them but found out."

"Ay, that could well be." Williams was losing some of his doubtful manner. "There must be heaps of money in that, and most of all, a traffic of papist books is not such a trifling matter..."

"No, indeed. Nor is..." The pieces shifted in Tom's mind, rearranging themselves. "Nor is it spying on the Ambassador of France. Wat, what if..." Tom rose, paced to the window and back. "What if Barbier was never Fagot? What if he found out who Fagot is, though — and what he is doing? And Courcelles, too. A good man would go to Castelnau, denounce them."

"But Barbier was not a good man."

Lady Ursula's salve smelt of comfrey and stung like the devil. Tom hissed through his teeth as he daubed it over the raw scrape. "Barbier was both greedy and a fool. He was the sort who goes to taunt his quarry, who tries to sell his silence..."

"And Fagot makes a show of buying, then finds himself some hemlock — and there goes the butler's man."

"Fagot, or Claude de Courcelles."

A shrug from Williams. "You are the one who reckoned that Fagot could be him."

"But I reckoned wrong. Imagine: Barbier goes to Courcelles, tells him he knows he's turned traitor, and he'll speak unless his palm is greased. If Courcelles has made up Fagot and the whole riddle to leak false letters to us, what does he do?"

Williams hummed, tapping his chin. "He laughs in Barbier's face."

"But he did not, did he? Either he or Fagot resorted to poison. 'Tis the action of one who has much to hide — and much to lose."

"And the same goes for stabbing the other fellow, and for sending that rabble after Parson Douglas," Williams conceded. Then he pushed himself away from the doorjamb, and asked: "And who is Fagot, then?"

Ah, this now… Tom began to roll the bandage around his elbow, thinking as he talked. "One who lives at Salisbury Court. One who is either privy to the Ambassador's doings, or in a position to watch covertly and eavesdrop. He can make friends with Courcelles, if the fellow can be said to have friends —" Which, in truth, should have ruled out Barbier from the beginning… *I have made the Ambassador's secrétaire so much my friend*… What had Tom been thinking?

"So?"

"So…" And it was a little disheartening that all of this still left a long list. "So it could be the chaplain — for Adam Jauffray says Mass for Castelnau, it seems. Or the clerk Feron. Laurent Feron: do you know anything of him?"

"That he writes Castelnau's letters. A fair hand, they say, but maybe not… Wait."

Williams disappeared briefly — leaving Tom to curse at the awkwardness of binding his own arm — and reappeared with young Toby Chandler in tow, red-eared and apprehensive.

"You mind the letters from the French Ambassador, Toby?"

The lad shifted his weight, and nodded laboriously. "Ay, the letters. There was one yesterday, was there?"

"You said something to me of those letters. Now tell Mr. Thomas."

There was more nodding, and Toby chewed his lip, frowning as he recollected his own words. "Ay, well. The fellow that writes them — he's a fair hand enough, but I don't reckon he was trained as a scrivener."

"How so?"

"He's not precise. The way he writes his letters, it changes, like he is in haste sometimes, and then he is less careful, he goes all large and sprawly. When you begin to train properly, one thing they cane into you, is to make your letters always the same."

Once Toby was thanked and dismissed, Williams closed the door behind him, and turned to Tom with a shrug. "For what it's worth."

"Make some inquiries about this Feron, will you? And if he's not Fagot, there is Diane de Bochetel, the Ambassador's cousin."

Williams pulled a face. "A woman spy…"

"Why not? A most intelligent and secretive lady. But in fair truth, if I were to lay you a wager, it would be on none of them. I'd say Giordano Bruno."

Again Williams looked unconvinced. "The Italian?"

In fair truth — yes. Tom had not been sure when debating with Sidney, but the more he thought of it, the more likely it seemed.

"He has lived there since the time the letters started, more or less. He has the Ambassador's trust. He is not French. He speaks the tongue, I'm sure, but he won't — not to me. He knows everything of everyone, and has no qualms in sharing his knowledge. Also, he has little love for zealous Catholics. He may like to throw a spoke in the Duke of Guise's wheels."

"Ay — but he's talked to you, hasn't he? And many times…"

"They all have — and none revealed themselves. Perhaps Fagot fears discovery. He — or she — has nothing to do with the murder, and in fact, like Fowler, fears to have been the intended victim — and cannot leave Salisbury Court for lack of means…"

"Or he changed his mind, eh?"

And yes, there was that… "Or he changed his mind — and then there's all the more need to make fast friends with the secrétaire — for all that he may well be a murderer."

"God's shirt!" Williams stalked close, and snatched the loose end of the bandage from Tom's hand. "Let me," he grumbled. He tore it into two strips, and began to fasten it. "'Tis like walking round and round in a damn tangle of brambles. What are you going to do with it all?"

And there it went again, the doubt, the challenge — under colour of asking for instructions… What was Tom going to do, indeed? He flexed his newly bound elbow, and thought. It had been easier to chase murderers in France… Harder and easier — running around on borrowed time, with a good chance of ending up dead himself, and with no one to turn to, no one to give orders, advice, correction or approval…

And he had made it, had he not? Stumbled through the maze, making his own moves until he'd uncovered the joints and flexures of the affair. He'd done it to the satisfaction of Sir Francis — enough that he was now expected to do it again…

Tom rose, unrolling his sleeve over the bandages. "Not quite round and round, Wat. It's brambly — yes, but we are going somewhere. You are to seek out Bonetti for one thing, and for another, to find out about Laurent Feron. I, instead, am going back to Salisbury Court — and taking Nick Skeres."

He went to the door. In the huge kitchen three servants were busy scouring, cleaning, tending the fire, and Tom sent one to fetch the lad.

"And what if he knows the man from the Half Moon again?" Williams asked from behind, as he came to stand at Tom's shoulder. "How will that help you with Fagot?"

Another fair question, in its way, and one to which Tom only had the haziest of answers himself. Hazy — and yet of a most nagging import…

"One thing with brambles…" he began, slowly shaping the argument in his head as he spoke. "One thing with brambles is that they tangle and coil together. Fagot's last letter, the death of Barbier, and that of Hurston… I was so certain it could be no chance! Well, chance it may be after all — and still all one snarl, though not from the same root. I must find out why Hurston was killed. Let me cut away that vine, and the rest will unravel…"

A reasonable argument — but just as well that he had not to defend it further, when a sweaty Skeres came trotting up the kitchen, crimson-cheeked and odorous, jostling a shoulder against the doorjamb in his eagerness. Whatever chore he'd been snatched from, it must have been loathsome…

"'Ere, Master," he announced — as though his arrival might have gone unheeded. "They 'aven't made lard of you, then, eh?"

Here, indeed. "No, they haven't — and you're coming to Salisbury Court with me."

Yes, a truly loathsome chore it must have been — for look how the lad lit up… "To find 'im as ran away?"

"Him, and whoever else you may have seen at the Half Moon — and one other thing." Tom turned to Williams. "One who takes sufferance money will grow suddenly wealthier than he was, won't he?"

"If he was paid at all — other than in hemlock."

"Even if he was not, he'd have expected to be…" *A greedy braggart*, young Rowley had called him. "You'll gossip with the servants, Dolius. Say you heard one of them has died. See what they tell you — most of all, if he bragged of some windfall of late…"

"Ay — but mind you, Skeres…" warned Williams — and small blame to him, in truth, if he doubted the lad's subtlety…

Skeres, of course, sulked. "Ay, ay, I can mind all you like, though 'ow you want me to gossip with them as don't speak God's own English, I don't know."

The wonder was that Williams came to the rescue. "You think ambassadors bring their scullions from France?" he snapped. "Some will be English, some French, but born here. Gossip along — just see that you don't throw Mr. Thomas's name around."

"And much less Mr. Secretary's," Tom added, for it never paid to take things for granted with Nick Skeres. "Now go and make yourself decorous. And do wash!"

Off marched the Minotaur — and Tom swallowed a sigh as he closed the door and leant against it to find Williams cocking his cursed eyebrows.

"I know, I know." Tom raised a hand to forestall objection. "But I want him to see the people there — and how many does it take to carry one box?"

It was something, Tom supposed, that Williams hummed in acknowledgment, if not in agreement. "But will they receive you like this, uninvited?"

"I said that I'd bring the book." And, in truth, was as good as told not to… "And besides, Castelnau left for Court this morning. He could decline to see me, or dismiss me in a trice — but Courcelles, Girault, Madame Diane… They can hardly show me the door, can they?" Or so it was to be hoped.

More unreadable humming. "But will they keep you long enough for Skeres to make friends in the kitchen?"

Ah, that now … that was the crux. Tom shrugged away from the door, picked up his doublet, and threw it over his shoulder. "I'll go look for the book. Find me a box, will you, Wat? A large one. And see to Bonetti and Feron. And…" A sudden thought flashed to life. A narrow, fox-like face; a small, intent smile. "Do you know of a merchant named Courtois, or Cortez?"

"Philippe Courtois? Friend of Mendoza's, if he's the one you mean."

"Most likely, yes: his man was at the Court last night. A Fleming — if he's that — named Crispin Sauldane. And again just the other day — attending on another I thought his master at the time. A dark-complexioned, pock-marked fellow."

"Courtois himself, I'll wager."

Not much of a surprise, but… "Well, now one thing we know: when Mendoza woos Anjou for his Infanta, Castelnau listens, at the very least."

Sir Francis wasn't going to like this.

There was no mistaking that Girault would very much have liked to leave Tom on the threshold. If nothing else, the man must have known by now, from his mysterious crony, of the masquerade at the Half Moon… He had little reason to welcome this particular visitor. Unlike the absent porter, though, he did not venture, or did not find it politic, to refuse the entry. He did inform Monsieur Walsn'am, though, that he could not be received.

Tom smiled, as wide and guileless as he knew. "Oh, but I know His Excellency is at Court — no matter, I wouldn't want to bother your master even if he were here — but he will be glad to see what I bring, at his convenience. Meanwhile, Monsieur de Courcelles will do very well."

Girault looked at Tom, then at Skeres behind him, ruminating — it was clear as daylight — the chances of lying, of saying that Monsieur Claude was away too… Tom held the disapproving gaze until, with the frown of a displeased bishop, Girault left the unwelcome visitors in the hall, and went to fetch the secrétaire himself.

Cerberus passed, then.

Nick Skeres, sweating in his decorous attire, and holding the box the way he would an armful of logs for the fire, leant in to whisper in Tom's ear — one of those thunderous whispers that would be well heard all across the hall: "'Im I never saw."

Tom had barely the time to shush him, and to bid him keep the box properly, before Claude de Courcelles appeared on the gallery, looking not a whit more pleased than Girault had.

"Monsieur Walsingham," he called, and pointedly stopped at the head of the stairs, square in the middle of the last step, like a Yeoman of the Guard barring passage — in spite of his bejewelled fan, and of the wilting manner. "Monsieur l'Ambassadeur —"

"Monsieur l'Ambassadeur is at Court, I know. He told me himself just yesterday. But…" Trusting that Girault would shepherd the stranded servant to the kitchen, Tom took the box from Skeres and started up the stairs without being invited. "But he expressed much eagerness to see a book, you'll remember. Well, I brought it."

Did they teach that sort of smile to French diplomats and their men, a smile like a closed gate?

"Most kind, I'm sure — but you would have done better to wait for His Excellency's return, Monsieur. He will be much disappointed that he was not here to meet you..."

"I am expecting to return to Paris any day now. I did not want to go without bringing the book."

"You should not have troubled yourself so, Monsieur..."

"Oh, no trouble, no trouble at all — and it would weigh on my conscience not to show my gratitude for His Excellency's great kindness to me..."

And all through this word-fencing, Tom never wavered in his smile or in his ascent, until he stood in front of the secrétaire who, after the shortest struggle, seemed to decide that, as Tom's mother said, the way through was the shortest. With the greatest dignity and condescension, the Frenchman stepped back.

"Come with me then, Monsieur." He motioned a languid hand towards the door at the gallery's far end. "His Excellency will be most glad of such a thoughtful gift."

A gift! Tartarus seize the fellow, so he was bent on making Tom pay for the bother, was he? Tom hoped Sir Francis did not care too much for the book. One of several books of Ovid — and most of it pictures, fine as they were, with little of the poetry left. Costly, no doubt — but then again... *Knowledge is never too costly, Thomas...*

Covering his grimace under a smile, and the hesitation with a half bow, Tom let himself be ushered ahead. The door, as he remembered, led to the parlour next to Castelnau's own study, the small green room with the lion-footed tables. At one of these, near the window, stood the clerk Feron, busily copying titles from a pile of books. Feron, who, after a small bow, made no move to leave, nor was he dismissed. Feron, who perhaps was Fagot, and perhaps was not — so that there would be no way to talk to Courcelles…

Not that Courcelles looked as if he wished for conversation. He motioned to another of the leonine tables as a good place for Tom to leave his burden. It was the same where he had laid the illuminated Horace… Much more of this, and he would decimate his cousin's books.

"I'm sure, Monsieur Walsingham, that I speak for His Excellency in expressing the deepest gratitude —"

"I rather fear that I made a mistake last night. I said that the etchings were the work of Leroy, while they are that of Bernard Salomon. Still a Frenchman, though…" As if the secrétaire had not spoken, Tom proceeded to unclasp the box, take out the book, leaf through it — and all the time he talked, and talked. Tom's oldest sister Barbara, long married now, always had her way by only hearing what she chose to hear, by keeping to the path of her own intentions with no pause for breath. Of course, she did so with her younger siblings (and now with her husband), never with French diplomats, never having to pretend she knew about foreign etchers… "And you will point out Andromeda in particular to His Excellency, won't you, Monsieur? So much like that of Solis, and yet so unlike…"

"Yes, yes, Monsieur, I will, most particularly." And if Courcelles had ever truly meant what he'd promised to Fagot, no trace of it showed in his bored impatience.

Tom forged on. "Why, we discussed Andromeda with Doctor Bruno, how the Greeks explained their stars… I would very much like to hear what he makes of this one depiction."

"You will have to wait for that. A long time, I'm afraid, if you are for Paris soon…"

And whether this was meant to discourage further conversation, or as some manner of warning… "Oh. Has he left Salisbury Court?"

Courcelles then did something Tom had never seen him do. Two things, in truth. For one, he laughed. Not much of a laugh — a creaky, breathy thing, as though the man were little used to the exercise, matched with a toothless smile. "But no, no — he accompanies His Excellency at Court. Monsieur l'Ambassadeur often brings him as his *gentiluomo*."

And for another, as he spoke, the secretary caught a friendly but firm hold of Tom's elbow. "I very much fear, Monsieur, that they will not be back from Court before your departure. They will both regret it, I am sure. When you are in London again, surely?"

Or otherwise, in plain English, keep well away until you are sent for.

The languid waving of the fan, the darting eyes, the firm clasp steering Tom towards the door… *Are you so good a judge of character?* Sidney had mocked — but yes, Tom prided himself on some keenness in reading men, and yet he could not read Claude de Courcelles, could not tell anger from fear, or plain impatience, in the fellow's restless manner. Not that it changed the fact that Mr. Secretary's own kinsman was, after all, being shown the door.

And he let himself be steered, blathering assurances of friendship and gratitude to be conveyed, *et cetera* — for truly, how did one resist this false courtesy short of…

Ah, well.

Pray that no one ever heard of it — not at Seething Lane, not at home, not in Paris — a most foolish prayer, and yet it filled Tom's mind as he stopped his babbling to raise a hand to his forehead.

"Oh..." he sighed. "I do not..." He swayed just on the threshold, made a show of catching himself against the jamb...

"Monsieur!"

It would have been diverting, the round-eyed dismay of Courcelles, faced with a languishing Englishman. It would have been diverting — but for the discountenance of it, the awkwardness of the pretended weakness... Did one flush so when swooning of the heat?

Thank the Fates that you needn't earn your living on the stage, Tityrus! Watson's amused voice echoed in Tom's mind, adding to his confusion.

"Monsieur...!" Courcelles, having dropped Tom's elbow like a burning coal, stepped away. What did he take it for, the plague?

"The heat..." Tom panted, still drooping against the door. "I beg your..." And damn Courcelles for a dunce! What if it were a calenture or such? Would he leave the Ambassador's guest to die on the threshold? It took a most pathetic sigh — almost a groan — to jolt the man.

To jolt him away, as it turned out, calling for Laurent with recovered firmness.

Under his lashes, Tom saw Feron hasten close, with more calls of "Monsieur!"

"'Tis nothing... The heat..."

At last Feron offered an arm, and led Tom to a chair. "Rest here, Monsieur. A sip of watered wine, and you will be well."

"This dreadful air!" exclaimed a well recovered Courcelles. "Send for the wine, Laurent. And shall we fetch your servant, Monsieur Walsingham?"

Save and deliver! "No..." All this ado to buy Skeres some more time in the kitchen... "No, thank you — he's a most useless fellow. Just let me..." Tom straightened himself in the chair, in a show of recovery. "Just let me take my breath. I beg a thousand pardons. I never… You must think me a disgrace, Monsieur."

Courcelles likely did — both a disgrace and a nuisance — but the ruse worked well enough. The secrétaire clucked, and Feron hovered about, and the watered wine was brought, and Tom dosed with it, and still the clerk hovered, until Courcelles took notice.

"You can go back to your work, Laurent," he said. "Monsieur Walsingham is restored now." And, because the man seemed to dither, he added in a sharper voice, "The letters are done, I trust?"

It was a strange sight, a man of Feron's age and manner flustered — but fluster he did as he retreated. "Nearly, Monsieur. Nearly done…"

And Courcelles was displeased, and…

Oh Good Lord — the letters!

The pieces in Tom's head gathered in a new shape: such a clear, logical shape, he could have laughed aloud — or slapped himself. What a blind idiot! *He writes Castelnau's letters*, had been Williams's description of Laurent Feron. A clerk, yes — a scrivener, but also a keeper of secrets, was he not?

Tom turned to the man with a smile. "Indeed, I am restored. Thank you, Maître Feron — and you will forgive me. I see now that I have not made your work any easier."

There were bows, and murmurs of apology, and a hint of a wavering smile, and a scudding retreat — and there, without a shade of doubt, there went Fagot's *sécretaire*, the seller of secrets, all that Claude de Courcelles was not.

After that, there was no way to loiter any further — nor, in fact, did Tom want to. He hoped that Skeres had made good use of his time, but even if he hadn't… Hunting for hare and coming home with deer, had been a saying of Turley's back at home.

How small, how paltry did the gallery look by day, deserted and empty, with the pictures gone, the naked sideboards, and each crack, each blue-green shadow of mould glaring in the merciless daylight. Courcelles saw the guest downstairs in person, all the way lamenting the English climate. To think of all the times Tom had tried to draw him out, to sound him, thinking him Fagot's friend…

Down in the hall, Girault waited, together with Nick Skeres, by the cavern of the empty fireplace.

The butler was instructed to see Tom out through the garden, and to have a boat ready at the stairs for him.

"For Monsieur Walsingham is not well."

Girault's solicitude was less than warm, but ready enough.

"And so we part, Monsieur," was Courcelles's valediction. "His Excellency will no doubt inquire after your health, and will ask for the pleasure of your company when you return to London." And if there was a plainer way to shut the door in a man's face, Tom didn't know it. Just out of contrariness, and because the fellow looked so pleased, he rattled out all the most flowery leave-taking pleasantries he could think of — and at length let Girault escort him to the garden, with Skeres trotting at his heels like an eager terrier.

For a wonder, though, the lad did not try to speak in Girault's presence. Could it be, oh Fates, that Nick Skeres was at last learning some good sense? In fact, he kept quiet enough until they were out in the garden, where they found two women in straw hats inspecting the plum trees down by the wall. One was, of course, Diane de Bochetel.

"Monsieur Walsingham," she greeted, walking to meet the guest with that pleasantness so devoid of warmth. "I did not know that you were here." What friendliness she had shown last night had faded with the candlelight — for all that being outside had put some colour in her perfect cheeks. Still, when the greetings were exchanged, she clicked her tongue on hearing from Girault of Tom's indisposition…

"Do you have the boat ready, Girault? Wait. Margot!" She called to her companion. "Is Rowley here? Have a boat fetched for Monsieur."

Margot had been busying herself with the still green plums. The moment she turned, Skeres stiffened at Tom's side. She was a pretty young woman, Margot, even with the reddened eyes and wan cheeks. Without a word, she wiped her hands in her apron, dropped a hasty curtsey, and ran away toward the garden's end.

Skeres was all but jiggling at Tom's elbow — but had the wit to keep his thoughts to himself while Madame Diane informed herself of Tom's health.

"Oh, 'twas nothing," he assured her, cursing the flush that crept up his neck — and so much for no one ever knowing. "Nothing at all. I was a little overcome by the heat… Nothing, truly."

"How unpleasant," she murmured, and then Margot was back to announce that her husband was fetching the boat… And see if she didn't startle a little at the sight of Nick Skeres — the briefest widening of the eyes, before she curtsied herself away again, scurrying not back to the trees, but toward the house. And before she went, Tom caught sight of a wrist, mottled with black bruises under the sleeve.

So the girl Margot knew Skeres in turn — and had been beaten…

If Madame Diane had noticed, she did not show it, but … had Girault's sempiternal scowl deepened?

Before urgency got the better of Nick Skeres, Tom took his leave of the lady, and followed Girault to the door and into Water Lane. The butler would have escorted them to the stairs, but Tom assured him that there was no need for that, he being attended, and feeling much better now.

And a good thing it was, because they had not gone a dozen steps before Skeres exploded into one of his stertorous whispers.

"It's 'er!" he exclaimed, and only shook his head when Tom would quieten him. "The girl — it's 'er!"

This now… "Are you out of your mind, Dolius? That little Margot threw you and ran?"

A snort and a dismissive wave. "That was a man, and 'im I didn't see — but *'er*! Margery, they call 'er at the Moon, and she was there the day before 'Arrison died —"

And with that they emerged at the stairs, and, wonder of wonders, Nick Skeres fell silent. Not only that, but he kept his head down, though Tom could see his jaws working, and the balled fists…

"'Tis 'im!" the lad rumbled, under cover of rubbing at his mouth.

At the stairs a man stood, spitting French-coloured abuse at two equally bristly wherrymen. A bearded fellow, it was, the Castelnau livery straining across big, ungainly shoulders… Tom knew him even before the man turned away from his querelle.

Foulques, or Foxe or Renard, or whatever he called himself. Castelnau's porter, a smuggler of forbidden books — *the worst of the lot* — and Margot's nasty husband, and now possibly a murderer…

"The barque," Foulques said with the grace of one wishing the boat would sink and drown all that she carried. One eye was blackened and swollen … so Skeres *had* given as good as he took…

It seemed wrong to tip this man — a lout who quite likely had done murder, and, even if he hadn't, beat his pretty wife — and all the time, as they boarded the wherry, Skeres gritted his teeth, shoulders up to his ears.

The boatmen began to push out into the current, when running steps were heard, and a shrill call of, "Mr. Thomas!"

A boy spilled out of the lane, skidding to a perilous halt a yard from the bank — so that Foulques reached to grab him.

"What do you think you're doing, you little runt?" the porter barked in French.

The boy — young Tib from the stables at Seething Lane — looked at him blankly, before freeing himself and waving for Tom. Tom rose, making the little boat rock as he clambered back to the stairs.

"What is it, Tib?"

Panting, the boy rummaged inside his jerkin. "Nearly missed you, Master! They said at the house you were gone this way… Here!" He triumphantly produced a crumpled note bound with a piece of twine. "Mr. Williams was going to skin me alive…"

Wondering always a little at the awe Williams inspired in the servants — with the exception of Skeres — Tom took the note.

There were barely a dozen words of it, hasty and smudged, as though there had been no time to dry the ink…

Be at the Black Friars, it said. *Ask for the old ordinary.*

The Black Friars now… Tom would have much liked to visit the Half Moon before Foulques got there — but there was Bonetti, too… He thrust the note in his sleeve.

"Very well, Tib. You take the boat home, and…" Tempting as it was to send Skeres with the boy… "And you come with me."

The servants changed places — Tib once more narrowly avoiding a plunge in the Thames in his eagerness — and, with a last nod to the scowling Foulques, Tom hastened back up Water Lane.

For all of Skeres's boasts of knowing London like the back of his own hand, it took some asking before they found there was another Water Lane within walls, across the Fleet, right by the old Black Friars, and there they directed their steps.

This — and what he called Tom's untrusting ways — the lad would have been inclined to lament at length, but that Tom nipped the laments in the bud to ask instead of the kitchen folk at Salisbury Court.

"I hope you put the time you had to good use, Dolius," he said, as they made their way into the press that always curdled around Ludgate, and all city gates.

Trotting and puffing at Tom's heels, Skeres threw him a suspicious glance. "Those bladder-puffed fellows said that you were unwell…"

"Never mind that — the kitchen."

The kitchen itself, it turned out, had not been open for the visitor to see — and this was no surprise — but he had been suffered to wait in the kitchen parlour.

"And all a-bustle, with people coming and going like Leadenhall Market, and the butler lording it out, until your lady came, and told 'im 'is own like it was 'er business."

"Madame is not *my* lady," Tom said with great severity. "And she's the housekeeper, so it *is* her business. You didn't catch what it was about, did you?"

Skeres shrugged. "She speaks French, your Madame does. But there's a kitchen maid as calls 'er a bandog, and they're at odds, 'er and the butler."

No great wonder — but… "What about?"

Another shrug. "Things, you know. Sugar, and candles, and spices, and physicks, and whatnot — and, between 'em, Lord 'elp you if you get yourself a lick of sugar…"

This last said with such knowing bitterness, it had to come from life at Seething Lane. Some further prodding brought Skeres back on track, and to having spied no known faces in the kitchen — a pardonable lack, considering Foulques and his wife.

"And you are sure of the porter?"

"Sure!" In his indignation, the lad stopped dead in his tracks, causing a seller of codlings to slam into him.

"Sure, 'e says!" Skeres stood mid-street, oblivious to the codling-man's curses, firm in the middle of the swirling crowd like a Scylla-less Charybdis. "'E ran out of nothing, bowled me over when I tried to stop 'im —"

"The cheek of him!" bawled the peddler, appealing to Tom. "*I* bowled him over! I ask you, Master — I was going my way, and this chub stops, he does, and —"

There was nothing for it but to silence the fellow with a coin, and to grab Skeres and drag him past the small, laughing audience they had gathered.

"So you are sure. And of the wife, also?"

"Ay. She was there with Agnes — the girl, you know…" A pouting shrug.

"The day before Hurston died, you said."

"Ay — and the same day, too. Out of 'er wits, she was, when she 'eard they'd fished 'im out of the river…"

"Was she, now…?" Poor Margot *had* looked grieved and fearful earlier in the garden, and that bruised wrist, and her husband… The pieces were moving again in Tom's head, to make a different picture. Two pictures, perhaps… "And they call her Margery at the inn?"

"Ay — and why a comely lass like that must go and wed a Frenchman, and one as beats 'er… 'Ave you seen 'er arm?"

Foulques's English wife — and, quite possibly, also young Rowley's sister. *Wed to one of them*, the boy had said. "I think here is, at last, one strand that we can cut — for, after all, Douglas was wrong. When we are through the gate, Nick, you go back home."

And oh, the betrayed look! "Couldn't I go back by water with Tib?"

"A little walk won't kill you. Tell Mr. Williams what you said to me. And also…" Tom leant close to whisper. "Also tell him this: not Courcelles, but Feron."

"'Tis 'ot as a furnace, all the way there…" the lad protested.

And wouldn't one think he'd been raised an earl's heir, at times? "Then get yourself a sculler, if you must — but first, attend: not Courcelles, but Feron. Repeat it to me."

It took a few attempts before the names sounded like something Williams would recognise. Oh, for Tom's friend Phelippes, and his satchel of writing things always at hand … but the little cypherer was far away in Paris, and if Williams made his inquiries about Feron, he would be better off knowing of Tom's new discovery.

They had to wait at the gate — one always did — and Tom, ignoring both his servant's grumblings of dinner time gone and past, and the prisoners bawling for bread from the looming gatehouse, occupied himself with considering his new discovery. Not Courcelles, but Feron. For all the stifling heat, it made him shiver to think how close he had got to betraying himself, and Fagot, to the wrong man, and undoing all of the careful net Sir Francis had woven around Salisbury Court. And besides … Feron! How was he ever going to deal with Feron? Once at the Ambassador's house, it would be easy and natural enough to cross paths with Claude de Courcelles — but with the clerk…?

There was a shout, and then another, and a wave rippled through the crowd. Not the sort that violence moves, though, and soon it became clear that this was no riot. By the gate, a clutch of women fussed around a reclining girl.

A woman braced herself against Tom's shoulder to better see, craning her neck. "She's a-fainted, poor chuck, the air's that close —" she cooed, in the gossipy way that will always come among strangers around an accident.

"'Ot as a furnace," Skeres repeated, funereal and knowing. "Not a day to leg it about."

Then the press cleared, and they were through the gate, just as Saint Paul's bells overhead started to chime noon, answered by the smaller churches all around. Soon the air was full of it, tense and clanging — enough to make a man light-headed.

As soon as they were inside, Tom ordered Skeres off. The lad made to go — but stopped, forefinger held up.

"Forgot to tell you," he bellowed in Tom's ear, to make himself heard above the bells. "There's this scullion-boy, 'e said your dead man 'ad an 'eavy purse of late. A-boasting as 'e'd go 'cross the river, and buy 'imself two Winchester Geese for a whole night!"

An idea Nick Skeres approved of, judging by his knowing wink. Tom waved him away with instructions to tell Williams that as well.

If Barbier had been selling his uncertain silence, if Feron was indeed Fagot's friend, then Feron had a reason for poisoning Barbier — and so had Fagot, whoever he may be.

Now let Rocco Bonetti be of some help.

The old ordinary at Blackfriars, it turned out, was reached via a passage that led to a suite of huge, dark rooms with boarded windows. In truth there was no ordinary there, and there hadn't been in a long time, but Tom had no need for it. In the second of these caverns, a hall paved with flagstones, he found Rocco Bonetti.

The Italian was pacing around, in and out of the bright patches of sunlight that filtered around the tall, ill-boarded windows. Not just pacing, though. He held a sword in his right hand. Wielding that, he stamped, and lunged, and dancingly retreated, only to lunge again, not in and out of the light, no — but around it. And all of this, there was no denying, he did with great elegance.

He startled when Tom clapped his hands.

Or perhaps startled was not the right word — no more than pacing had been. What the Venetian did was gather himself in coiled stillness between one heartbeat and the next, the sword held in an open guard, the other hand up to shadow his eyes.

"Duelling with the sun, Mastro Bonetti?" called Tom — and it was enough.

Bonetti's guard loosened into an airy salute. "Signor Walsingham. Your Williams was most insistent."

"I have questions for you."

"Then I hope I have answers." The Italian gestured around with his blade. "This used to be a fencing school, did you know?"

"A mere school? Not like your college, then?"

Bonetti clicked his tongue in great disgust. "They don't begin to compare, your English masters! My *collegio* was a very elegant place, to begin with. The finest weapons for the students to use if they so liked, and also a table with fine paper, pens and ink..."

"For those who should feel inclined to pen verse between one bout and the next?" Tom asked.

"You jest, Signore. You jest — but Bonetti's *collegio* was a place for gentlemen, you know."

"And you would build it again in here?"

"It would look good, do you not think?" The Italian looked around, sighing wistfully, before holding up his sword again. "Would you care for a bout? Just to hear how blades would ring under this ceiling? I'd welcome you as a pupil."

And wouldn't he wish! Tom laughed. "I can't afford you, I'm afraid. And no, no bout. Answers."

"It depends on your questions, do you not think? If I am able to answer..."

"Oh, you will be. The first question is this: how did you come to be in possession of the letters that you brought to Seething Lane?"

"Ah yes — the letters." With a sigh, Bonetti sheathed his rapier, went to one of the benches, and dusted it with a kerchief. He must have done it before, because his hat sat at one end — but still he put great care into it. "I told your Signor Williams about that..."

"And now you will tell me."

"The letters, then." The Italian sat and ran a hand down his small beard, frowning into the gloomy distance. Making up his mind or concocting a lie... "Three letters ... no: four, were there? And all of them I found in my hat."

"How?"

A shrug. "How does a man find a letter in his hat? When I went to take it back, the letter was tucked into the lining. Addressed to me on the outside — and I'll tell you…" A little laugh. "So neatly folded, so dainty… The first one, I took it for the message of a lady."

"A disappointment, I am sure." Tom went to stand before Bonetti, arms crossed. "Still, back to your hat. Why did you leave it lying around? And where exactly?"

"Ah, Signore…" Skeres would have been jealous of the Italian's white-toothed smile. "I did not spend all my time in conversation with the Signor Castelnau, you know. My hat, at times, I would leave in that passage by the kitchen, you know the one? I'd put it on a bench, and there it remained until I needed it again."

And if all of the fellow's hats were like the high-crowned, plumed, beribboned affair that lay on the bench, there would be no mistaking it, even in the dark.

"The passage by the kitchen… Would someone who is not a servant be noticed lurking there?"

"Ah." Bonetti nibbled at his underlip, black eyebrows knitting in consideration. "I see why you ask… The truth is, I don't know. But belike not: the passage also goes from the hall to the garden, so … I, for one, was never challenged in there."

"So anyone in the household could slip the note in your hat, and no one would be the wiser." Which was a good deal less than useful.

"Apart from the Signor Castelnau himself, yes. Him, I'm sure, they would mark."

And that was even less helpful.

"And it never occurred to you to find out who it was?"

A foolish question, in truth — and Bonetti must have thought the same, judging by the way he spread his hands.

"But, Signor Walsingham, even if it did, what could I do? Hide in the shadows and watch my hat? That they would also mark, I'm sure."

Of course they would — and all the more in such a household. "And if you bribed a servant to do it, there would be questions asked."

"Well…" Bonetti leant back against the worm-eaten wainscoting, smiling at the dance of dust motes in the nearest beam of light. A most knowing smile. "There is this servant girl, you see. A pretty creature, prettier than she is sharp — and fond of a penny or two. I thought of telling her that someone was playing jokes on me…"

"But if she thought it a joke, she'd see no reason to keep it a secret. And if she knew it for a secret, then…"

"Indeed, Signore, indeed." Bonetti gloomily shook his head. "Is it not sad that the nature of Man — and Woman — is what it is?"

And this from the fellow who made a living by selling secrets to Sir Francis — and most likely to Castelnau as well… Not Fagot's name, though — not yet, at least — because certainly it had not been Barbier. And on the other hand, if Henry Fagot was only a cog in some French machination to feed false papers to the English … well then, no great harm would come of uncovering Courcelles's ruse, would it?

Tom sat by Bonetti — the bench creaking under their joint weight.

"How long since you last visited Salisbury Court?"

There was a little humming. "Not since Sunday last, when you saw me there." The shortest pause. "And there was no letter then."

"I dare say not, Signor Bonetti — or we would have it, by now, would we not? I wonder, though… Your mysterious friend — would he pick up a letter if he found it in the hat?"

The Italian went utterly still. "It was never tried…"

"No, it wasn't."

And sometimes, Thomas, 'tis most of all a matter of letting a man talk.

Bonetti was no fool. Tom could see the thoughts racing behind the narrowed eyes. "Would he search the hat, though, if he has nothing to deliver?"

He — or she, for the notion of Diane de Bochetel in the dark passage, a folded note hidden in her basket, to be slipped in the abandoned hat as she went by, was easy to credit…

"But if you were to give some sign…"

"Some sign!" The fencing-master sat up straight. "What if I give some sign to the wrong man, and give myself away?"

"If the wrong man knows, there is no harm done. If he does not, then he won't know the sign for what it is."

"And how do you think that I will find the right man? Or do you think that fencing masters eat at the high table?"

And, Tom found, this was where his willingness to trust Rocco Bonetti had its bounds — Feron's name and Fagot's peril lying firmly outside of them.

"Where do they eat, then? At the servants' table?"

"There is a halfway table of sorts. The clerks eat there, and sometimes the woman who attends la Signora Diana. The butler, too, I think — when he is done serving upstairs."

The clerks. Tom hummed, taking great care to look indifferently pleased. "It will have to do. Name your hat at dinner, and if Fagot eats there, well and good. If he does not, I'll wager your conversation will find its way to the right ears."

Bonetti sprang to his feet, pacing nervously away. "Or the wrong ones! What if…"

Let him steam for a while — and meanwhile Tom studied the hall with great attention. The tall ceiling, the black cobwebs festooning the beams, the heaps of dirt on the paved floor…

"'Tis hard to believe that this cavern could ever look fine…" he observed idly.

A stop, a dancer-like turn on the heel… "And how would I even get there? Do fencing masters knock on a great house's door and ask for dinner?"

"They solicit a kindness. They beg for an audience. They loiter until dinner time."

"What sort of kindness?"

And there he was, hooked and ready… "Why don't you secure a lease on this place, Bonetti? Is it the money?"

The Italian blew out his cheeks, and gave a mirthless smile. "Even if I had it … the place belongs to Sir William More. There's a suit in court over the lease — and the Earl of Oxford has an interest in it."

"And…?"

"And His Lordship has no love for me."

And there was a story that, someday, Tom would like to hear — what the fencing master had done to Oxford, although, by all accounts, it took very little to fall foul of that particularly unreasonable and wayward nobleman. "Both the Earl and More could listen to Monsieur de Castelnau."

"Would they?"

"I do not think they would, no. Especially the Earl." Tom smiled at the befuddled Italian. "But you are not to know this, are you?"

"But…"

"On the other hand, I think that Mr. Secretary's word would carry some weight."

Rocco Bonetti looked away. He looked all around, as though seeing the hall full of light, and of well-dressed gentlemen, the walls decorated with racks and racks of fine swords and rapiers, the air ringing with the clang of blades, the shouts of the fencers — and in a corner a fine writing table, with the best paper, the best quills…

And at that point it was just a matter of rising, and patting the Italian's shoulder. "I'll let you have the note, Signor Bonetti. Be prepared."

There was, of course, the fact that it all would have to wait until the return of Bruno to Salisbury Court… Oh, it would have been much easier to approach the Italian in conversation and ask him — but after the near disaster with Courcelles, Tom found himself wary.

He also found himself empty-stomached, the time for dinner having long come and gone, and since, by Williams's direction, Fowler lived by the Mitre Tavern, there was no reason why the Duckling's *things* could not be discussed over a pot of ale and a piece of pie.

Holborn it was, then. And, little taste as Tom had for a walk under the afternoon sun, he reckoned that, for once, the way would be shorter on foot. He'd already repented it by the time he crossed Holborn Bridge, with the stenches wafting up from the Fleet, his shirt soaked under his doublet, and the sky one great pale glare…

A good thing that by then he had not long to go down Holborn Street — and even better that Fowler needed no finding, after all. The man must have been lying in wait, for he darted out of the Mitre's door as Tom approached it, grabbed him by the arm, and dragged him inside, with a grim, secretive manner to make the angels weep.

"At times, Fowler, I wonder what possessed you to choose this particular calling in life," Tom groused under his breath — and then wished he hadn't, when the words broke some inner cataract in the fellow's restraint.

"But I didnae!" he hissed. "I never did! I went to Monsieur de Castelnau over a debt the Queen owes to my father — the Queen of Scots, I mean — and before I knew it —"

Which was nothing to discuss on the threshold of a public tavern, for anyone to hear, so Tom threaded his arm through Fowler's, and cheerfully asked: "You think they'll have fresh oysters here? I haven't had my dinner yet."

They did, it turned out. And a promise of good, cool ale — and, wonder of wonders, a garden. A true garden, too, with trees enough to make a pleasant shade. With a sigh Tom sat at an empty table, and soon they were sharing ale, and bread and oysters — for all that Fowler had dined not two hours since. Ah well, whatever fear affected in the balance of the Scot's humours, it was nothing to do with the stomach.

The Mitre's garden was far from deserted, and even at this time of the day drinkers and card players sat in twos and threes at the shaded tables, some in the company of young women, all far enough away, and noisy enough that they would not overhear a quiet conversation.

"A good place, this," Tom smiled at the Duckling. "The oysters are fresher than most. Now, you said…"

And if he had meant to offer reassurance, he had clearly failed — because, before he could go any further, Fowler half leant across the table, a sleeve dragging across the empty shells before him.

"Ye must tell him!" he whispered, harsh and breathless. "Ye must tell His Honour to let me get oot of Salisbury Court. They tried to kill me —"

Oh, this again! "No. They did not."

"But —"

"Why did you leave the sweetmeats?"

It was no great surprise that Fowler gaped. "Why did I…?"

"At supper, the night Barbier died. You did not eat the sweetmeats."

The bulge-eyed look of disbelieving puzzlement did Fowler no favours. "'Twas frangipani," he said. "I hae nae taste for almonds. Never had, even as a bairn —"

"Not because it smelt or tasted foul?"

"Foul?"

"Like cat's piss?"

More gaping — but also a flicker of understanding then, and a shake of the head. "It smelt of almonds."

"And there you have it. Barbier was killed with hemlock, and almonds would not mask the stench of hemlock. Ergo, no one tried to kill you." And, having solved this one riddle to his satisfaction, Tom went back to his dinner.

"Are ye…" Relief battled with wariness in Fowler's voice. "Are ye sure it was hemlock?"

Not sure, no… "Yes. So you see there's no reason to leave Salisbury Court — and if this is all you had to tell —"

A furious shaking of the yellow head, and, "My mother is verra vexed," blurted Fowler.

His mother. His mother — of all things! "Yes, well —"

"All my friends in Scotland think I'm an apostate, a papist convert, a traitor…"

"I would hope so," Tom said, around a mouthful of oysters — and look how the fellow paled. "Unpleasant, I'll grant you — but most useful when it comes to proving yourself to Castelnau. And keep your voice down."

A timely instruction, that last, for Fowler, after gaping soundlessly a couple of times, started to squawk: "My m—" Only to put a tighter rein on himself. "My mother thinks that I'm keeping with papists and intriguers. That they corrupt me. That I'm imperilling my soul…"

"She will be happy to learn that this is not the case — in time. For now, I'd call it an excellent result, if they also thought you an apostate at Salisbury Court — but do they? Fagot writes that you dissimulate in your religion. What do they think you, Fowler? A fake Protestant, or a pretend Catholic?"

He saw his mistake the moment Fowler turned green around the gills — so he rushed in before a new stream of lamentations could pour forth.

"Were you ever asked to attend Mass at Salisbury Court?"

This was, Tom was learning, the way with William Fowler: once asked for facts, for earnest consideration, the man was able to put to use what he possessed in the way of a mind.

"Only once, months ago. I hadnae been long visiting with His Excellency."

"And who said Mass? Jauffray?"

"Aye. He doesnae like me much, Adam Jauffray."

Was there anyone, beside Castelnau himself, who liked the poor Duckling at the Court? As for the chaplain's wariness… "You must not have made a very convincing papist."

Fowler shrugged, eyes lowered, twiddling the shells with ink-stained fingers. "His Excellency thinks I'm some sort of Huguenot. He said so once to a French visitor who took exception to me… A Huguenot, and a most faithful servant of the Queen of Scots."

But what of those last reports, then — filled with nothing much? *The Ambassador told me this, and said that* — and most of it inanities… Above, swallows and seagulls keened as they flew this way and that in long arcs, and a warm breath of air — the first in days — brushed through the branches of the apple trees, and for a moment Tom was seized by a memory of the cherries he had shared with his sister at the kitchen table at Scadbury, the soft country air whispering through the open window… A most foolish melancholy, for then Mary had been her sharp-tongued self, and Scadbury was barely three hours' trot away on a day like this… How much worse must it be for Fowler, a kingdom and a half away from home, where his people thought ill of him…

But then, it was not Tom's work to console homesick intelligencers, was it? "A most faithful servant — and yet now Castelnau doesn't trust you anymore, does he? And you fear to be killed… What have you done, of late, to give yourself away?"

"Naething!" Fowler sat up, straight and stiff. "Naething, I've done! One day His Excellency was showing me the letters he wrote to the Queen of Scots, and whispering of French invasion, and the next…" A spreading of the hands. "The next, he tells me the Queen wishes to go to Buxton and take the waters — *the waters*! That's all I know."

Was it truly? Tom sat back, sipping his ale and studying the little Scot through narrowed eyes.

"You know, it would be easy to find out whether your father was repaid." And whether this was true, Tom had no idea — but he much doubted that Fowler knew, either…

And who'd have thought the man was the sort to grunt in derision? "Repaid! Had he been repaid, I'd be back hame, by now. His Excellency makes promises, he writes to the Queen, and naething ever comes of it!"

Nor ever would, most likely — but Fowler needn't hear it. "Should you not want to remain at Salisbury Court all the more, then?"

"Not if it costs —" The Duckling quietened under Tom's glare, and swallowed hard. "Ye say that naebody tried to kill me there — but do ye know why they killed Barbier?"

Having a notion or two — but none that he'd discuss with Fowler, and none that Fowler would find reassuring if he did — Tom just tilted his head.

"See?" An eager duck-like nod. "For all I know, 'tis my father's money against my life. And now that someone cracked my credit with Monsieur de Castelnau…"

And this could very well be — although… "Why go to the trouble, if they mean to murder you?"

"They begin with slanders — to make me gang away. And then, if I dinnae…" A grim click of the tongue. "Belike it was your Fagot. He did slander me to Mr. Secretary, didn't he? He and Courcelles." He threw himself back, sagging on the bench and clawing at his collar. "I wish I'd never come to London!" he moaned.

Courcelles — because Fowler didn't know of Feron… But Feron had warned Fagot, and therefore Sir Francis. Why warn the Ambassador as well? Or had he?

Or had he?

Because, of course, if he had heard someone casting doubt on Fowler, Feron had also heard Castelnau defending him — and the doubt-monger could not know that what Feron heard would go through to Seething Lane.

"Fowler, attend: have you made enemies at Salisbury Court —"

Voices erupted among the trees. Two men, half across the garden, had come to words. One leapt to his feet, sweating and raging, and ready for worse than words. He shoved the other when he would have risen too, and insults flew, and just as the cornered man reached for his knife, the landlord and a pair of sturdy youths rushed to quell the mayhem. Fowler sat still, eyes intent on the fight, brow knotted, one hand clawing and unclawing around the table's edge. Wishing that he could shout, and shove, and even knife someone…? Better not know, most likely.

With a sigh, Tom rose and fished a few coins from his purse. Fowler had lost interest in the now subdued brawlers. He flinched when the coins clinked on the table before him, but never looked up, a fingertip smearing the wet rings his pot had left.

"Douglas," he muttered. "Ye ask if I made enemies… I … I warned Mr. Secretary against Douglas. Said that he knows cyphering, nae matter what he says. And I discovered him when he had a secret meeting that he shouldnae, with a man of the Duke of Lennox."

Lennox — one dangerous tie between King James and France… "And he knows that?"

"He's a bluidy and revengeful man."

Did Fowler also believe Archibald Douglas had done murder with his own hands? But yes — Douglas: here was the one who had discredited the Duckling to Castelnau — leaving himself Sir Francis's one pair of eyes at Salisbury Court. Only he hadn't reckoned with Fagot: a misstep in this dance. Hardly a pavane, though. Something far rougher, with Douglas in the midst of it, scheming, and whispering, and lying, and meeting men in secret that he should not. A visit was in order, no doubt — but before that…

"One more thing: did anyone leave Salisbury Court of late?"

"Leave…" Fowler blinked. "Oh. I … I havenae been there much, of late…"

A fine excuse, that! "No, not half as much as you should have. But you're familiar with the household. Have you noticed someone missing — besides Barbier, that is? Some new face in place of another?"

And see how the Duckling frowned, and stroked his chin, and shook his head to himself — surely thinking to mask his confusion as deep consideration. "I … I… No, I dinnae think… Nae. Not that I'd ken all the servants, mind ye… But… But…"

Oh Lord. Either a most cunning player, or Innocence itself. "No use indeed, are you?"

There was no trace of cunning in the way the Duckling lit up in hope. "Will ye say so to His Honour? And that I havenae betrayed him? Ye believe me, don't ye? And ye have His Honour's ear… Will ye tell him that Courcelles lies?"

Well, not Courcelles — but better not name Feron, in case Fowler was the cunning player after all.

"I may," Tom said in his sternest manner, "if I'm convinced of your good faith. And I won't be if you desert your place at Salisbury Court."

And with this he left — hoping that William Fowler would scratch the fear of murder from the catalogue of his woes.

As for himself, he now had a longer list of questions for Archibald Douglas.

Only, Archibald Douglas was absent from his rooms by the church of St. Magnus. Neither the widowed landlady nor the boy who waited upon him knew where he was, nor when he would repair there again. The boy only shook his head, in what Tom suspected was a play at being very dull-witted. The widow, a very proper matron, looked disapprovingly on the visitor, and observed that it was no wonder Mr. Douglas spent so much of his time from home, poor gentleman, seeing how strangers plagued him at his — and her — own door…

Tom doubted that the good woman knew what sort of poor gentleman her lodger was — and, after entertaining briefly the notion of whispering to her of intrigues and bloody murders — he resigned himself to having chased wild geese…

As a last attempt, he loitered for a while in a barber's shop, perched on the sill of a window that let him see the widow's door… But there was neither hide nor hair of the Scot, and at length, Tom gave up, and hied himself towards Seething Lane, wondering where Archibald Douglas spent his days when the French Ambassador was away at Court.

CHAPTER 10

Sent ahead in exploration, Nick Skeres was told that Mr. Douglas — poor gentleman — was not in his rooms. Where he was then, the Widow Morris professed not to be her place to tell. Whether he had been there at all since yesterday, Skeres had not thought to ask.

"You didn't tell me to ask!" he groused, as he trotted after Tom on their way to the river. "You said to ask was 'e there. Did you say to ask if 'e'd been in?"

Tom hadn't. That it was a most sensible thing to ask, he swallowed together with most of his ill humour — for, in truth, to expect sense from the Minotaur… Nor did one want the Minotaur to venture down questioning paths of his own.

"Next time I'll make you an array of questions," Tom ground out — and off they went to find a boat and cross to Southwark.

Once they disembarked at the stairs of Paris Garden, Skeres was dispatched to find Constable Pitt in a haste. He looked crestfallen, for he must have had hopes of seeing the girl Agnes again, and off he marched with an air of Virtue mistreated that would have sent Fowler into versifying raptures.

Now let him be quick at his task — while Tom made his way to the Half Moon. He did not go by the street, but reached the riverside door. Not a soul was there and, from the narrow passage that smelt of burnt fat and mould, little could be heard that sounded like custom in the taproom. Small wonder Kellett resorted to smuggling to hold his inn afloat… Wat's latest pair of eyes, a beggar who wasn't perhaps as pitifully gnarled as he seemed, had reported no strange doings. It didn't mean that the books must still be there — but, with any luck, it would matter very little by the day's end…

Tom slipped into the kitchen, and into the aftermath of domestic catastrophe. The stench he'd smelt in the passage was stronger here, a greasy bitterness that made clouds in the morning light. Her back to the door, and both hands wrapped in rags, Mistress Kellett held the source of the odour — a blackened pan from whose mouth the black smoke erupted in gulps and billows. A female Vulcanus waving a miniature Aetna at the two girls who knelt on the ground, scrubbing at the stained flagstones.

"Wantwits!" the Vulcanus whispered furiously. "Wretches, and rapscallions, and drossels! And wait until my brother hears… Don't kneel in it, you slattern!"

This last to the scullion, a thin thing of twelve or so, who scuttled back on her knees, sniffing and sobbing all the time.

Agnes was less meekened.

"Ay well, and where were you then, Mistress?" she challenged, kneeling up, and sucking fingers from a reddened hand — and that's when she caught sight of Tom leaning against the doorjamb.

She stifled an exclamation, startling the other women, so that Tom found himself the object of three stares — none of them filled with great friendship.

Bridget Kellett was the first to find her voice to say: "I remember you." She narrowed her pale eyes in recognition. "You came to ask questions the day…"

Tom held up a hand to stop her when she took breath. "No, don't call your brother, Mistress Kellett. I would have a word with you and Agnes."

Vulcanus took a bellicose step, clutching her Aetna. "I don't reckon —"

"But I do." Tom looked pointedly at the scullion, who still knelt on the floor, gaping and wiping a hand over her runny nose.

The landlady looked away — though she did so under colour of bustling the girl out of the room. When she was gone, Tom motioned for the two women to sit at the table.

Mrs Kellett did so, plunking her burnt pan in the middle of it, amidst a shambles of onion skins and spilt fat. Agnes pushed to her feet, wiping her hands in her apron, and came to stand behind her mistress's chair. She gave Tom a long, guarded look.

"If it's about —" she began, and yelped when the landlady twisted around to pinch her arm.

"Quiet, you goose!"

"Don't fret, Mrs Kellett. 'Tis not about the books."

And look at them, both turned to breathless stone, one gawping, the other working her jaw in the effort to give nothing away…

If you will bring down your foe's guard, Thomas, disconcert him — and then hit quickly.

"Tell me rather of Margery Foulques. Or Renard. Or Rowley."

There was a release of breath, and an exchanged look, then Agnes shrugged and crossed her arms.

"Margery, ay. She's my God-sister. What of her?"

Tom hummed. "She comes here often?"

Another shrug. "Enough."

"To see you?"

"Ay, to see me. What of it?" the girl blustered — the thought plain as day in her eyes that if she played it bold perhaps…

"I met your Margery yesterday." Tom tilted his head towards the window, the river, and Salisbury Court across it. "She was much bruised."

An angry look passed between the women, and Bridget Kellett clicked her tongue. "'Tis that husband of hers —"

"John Foxe is a pig!" Agnes came around the table's corner, uncrossing her arms, ready for a fight. "A filthy lout of a pig!"

"Agnes, girl…" There was more warning than reproach in the landlady's voice.

Tom leant against the table — greasy and sticky under his palm. "A rabid pig who beats his wife, is he?" he asked. "And so she comes here to find … consolation?"

"She says…" Bridget Kellett leant forward, gossipy all of a sudden. "She says, poor child, there is a lady at the Court. Madame Diane. A good lady, who takes care of her as much as she can, sees to her hurt."

And Tom was warmed to hear this — Diane protecting the poor, ill-treated young woman — but not so much that he missed the landlady's attempt at evasion. "So 'tis no shelter that she seeks here. Or that she sought, I think — until poor Hurston died."

It was like seeing a castle preparing for a siege — the portcullis slammed, the bridge drawn up… These silly geese! What did they think? The husband knew already — most evidently…

Bridget Kellett rose to her feet, and reached for her ruined pan. "Now we have work to do, Master…"

At her side, Agnes jutted out her chin.

Oh, Lord save him from heather-headed fools! And save him from his conscience, too — for playing on a man's fears was bad enough, but on those of a woman! And yet what of poor Margery with her sad eyes and bruised arms? What of Hurston

— a smuggler and a conspirator, but still murdered cruelly? Tom squared his shoulders.

"I see," he said. "Or perhaps I don't — because you say Foxe beats her, but what if it was Barnaby Hurston? And so Foxe just saved his wife. Or not Foxe, no. But Margery has a brother, has she not? Who knows, did Constable Samford think to —"

"No!" Agnes shook herself free from the landlady's restraining arm. "It wasn't Rowley as did it!"

"Agnes!"

The girl turned on her mistress like a small harpy. "Samford's too stupid to pick it up for himself — but once he sees a way to blame Rowley…?"

So that was the way of things, was it? Poor Nick Skeres… "They hang men for wilful murder," murmured Tom.

"Hang…" Bridget Kellett twisted her hands and looked torn.

"Tell me this first, Mistress: who was the man who came the other day, saw me — and ran away?"

As the landlady hesitated, there was a shuffling from the passage. Now just let it be Pitt…

Agnes must have heard, too — and seen who it was — for she raised her voice to rail at her mistress. "Well, if you won't, I'll tell him — and throw me on the street if you like. I'm not letting Rowley hang for something that John Foxe did! 'Twas Foxe as came the other day, and I'll swear to God 'twas him as rowed himself Sunday last early, and —"

"Shut up, you little bitch!" Kellett barged in, shoving Tom aside, grabbed the girl by the wrist, and slapped her across the mouth.

Tom moved to stop the man — or he would have, but was thrust aside again.

The amorous Minotaur to the rescue.

"Don't you touch 'er!" Skeres bellowed, and shoved the host against the fireplace. Kellett caught himself against the mantel, upturning a row of tin cups and glazed pots that rained to the floor in a clanging, shattering ruin.

"Enough, Skeres!" Tom snapped, when the lad would have charged again. "Not that you didn't deserve it, Master Kellett. Hitting a woman like that!"

If he was blessed with no other gift, the halfpenny wretch was very quick in changing tacks. "But she's a liar!" he wailed, chins trembling, a stubbed finger pointed at the scowling Agnes. "The blackest of lie-tellers. Since a child we brought her up, and still strive to cure her of it, out of Christian —"

"Right Christian — ay!" Agnes sprang forward. "A liar, am I?"

Kellett shouted, and his sister seized the pan again, and there would have been more mayhem, but Skeres caught the girl around the waist — looking none too displeased.

"Quiet — all of you!" Tom roared — pleased when all fell silent. "I'd leave you to cut each other's throats to your liking — but a man was murdered. This is a matter for the law. Is it not, Constable?"

Which was much like a play — or so Tom hoped, for there had been no time to make sure Skeres had indeed fetched Pitt… But yes: perfection! Down to the manner in which Kellett's round face lit in malicious relief — and then fell, when not Samford, but young Pitt appeared on the threshold.

And then, alas, it all went awry when Pitt entered, and Chief Constable Samford after him.

Kellett's smile returned, and Skeres shrugged at Tom's glare of reproach. The women had gone silent.

"Ay," Samford announced, puffing his chest. "A matter for the law, indeed."

Another clown — but truly Southwark was a den of these! Ah well, then — there was nothing for it but…

"Do you know who I am, Constable Samford?" It was not often that Tom used the full force of his name — and he never stopped marvelling at the effect it had. "My name is Thomas Walsingham — and this girl is now under Mr. Secretary's protection."

Samford had gone the colour of jaundice. "But she —"

"Constable Pitt will convey her to the house of an alderman of his choosing, and there she will remain until the next assizes."

"But I —"

"You may choose to ignore her testimony, yes. I will go across the river, now. I'll have the ward of Farringdon Without raise the hue-and-cry for John Foxe, or Foulques, the suspected murderer of Barnaby Hurston. You'll do the same here at Paris Manor, if you are wise."

Which was something of a gamble — for there was no saying who else among the Liberty's men was in Girault's pay… But no: with every word Tom spoke, Pitt looked taller, and see how Samford wilted!

He didn't move a muscle when Tom led the way to the passage and outside, with Skeres steering Agnes, and Pitt as rearguard. Even as they went, they could hear the Kelletts squabbling.

Pitt chuckled and shook his head. "Well, well, Yer Honour — that was well done."

Good fellow, Pitt. He'd be a credit to the Liberty, and a useful friend to have, once he stepped into Samford's shoes. "There will be an alderman or two, I take it, who won't be displeased to take Samford down a peg?"

The chuckle grew into a full-bellied laugh. "Down the whole ladder, they'll throw him!"

"Good. And, Pitt…" Tom leant close to whisper. "I'd have another good search of the Half Moon, if I were you."

Pitt grinned. "Oh, that I will, Yer Honour. That I will. Come now, Agnes."

He caught the girl by the arm, not unkindly — but of course Agnes had to make a fuss. Her hair all in disorder, a bruise already purpling on her cheek, she tried to free herself.

Pitt was not discomposed. "Come, come, girl. Mistress Parton will be glad of having you."

The girl squirmed some more. "But I —"

"But you will do as you are told," Tom told her firmly. "Or do you think they'd leave you alone? Go with the constable, and you'll be safe. And so will Rowley and Margery, once Foxe is out of the way."

This was it. Agnes of the Half Moon gave a grim nod, and let Pitt lead her away.

Skeres watched her go, all spaniel-eyed.

Tom patted the lad's thick shoulder. "Come on, now, Dolius. You went to her rescue like a true knight."

"Ay — and she never 'ad a look for me." A gusty sigh — and then a chuckle. "'Twas well done, though — eh, Master? *D'you know who I am, Constable Samford?* Now 'e'll 'ang, that filthy scoundrel Foxe!"

Which, in truth, was less than sure… "If he doesn't walk out of it."

"Why, because 'e's French?"

"Because he's the Ambassador's man." Would Castelnau abandon his countryman and servant to English justice — and the gallows? Tom thought of the smiling, saturnine face — and was displeased to find that he couldn't begin to tell. But then…

"Cheer up, Nick Skeres. One way or the other, the Half Moon's smuggling days are over. At the very least, Girault will need to find another hiding hole."

The notion of Girault discomfited diverted the lad very much — and, in fair truth, Tom shared the amusement thoroughly.

So this was one vine of the brambles cut and done. Now for the rest. For Billingsgate, and Archibald Douglas.

Tom sent Skeres back to Seething Lane with a note for Williams, to have a request prepared for the constables of Farringdon Without. Not that they could go and drag a servant out of the French Ambassador's house — but there would be enough ado to clip the smugglers' wings…

And then he went to Billingsgate again — and the Widow Morris, dragoness that she was, must have had instructions, for she grudgingly let the visitor in and upstairs, to a spacious room, filled with painted cloths, and embroidered cushions, and painted boxes, and candlesticks, and trinkets of all hues. The Widow's taste, surely — never the lodger's…?

In the middle of it all, Douglas rose from the writing table with a chuckle of half bitterness and half delight.

"Young Mr. Walsingham!" he greeted. "Ye left nae name, but I was half thinking it would be ye. I even sent to the Old Swan for some wine, in expectation of your visit." He ceremoniously thanked the Widow, who retreated with one last disapproving glare at Tom.

Douglas's own gaze held a spark of mischief. "Pay nae mind to Mistress Morris," he explained. "She's taken a liking to me. She thinks I'm threatened."

"You must have given that impression, yes. She never names you but as her poor gentleman…"

"Och, that's what I am, lad. That's what I am." He motioned for Tom to sit on a very old fashioned armchair, with a high back carved with a pattern of diamonds and leaves, and a cushion of figured velvet. "A poor foreigner in this great city, a penniless exile, a pawn in the games of greater men, mistrusted by all — and, if I but try to forward my own poor interests, the object of all manners of suspicion…"

All this he said with that smile that creased his red beard and the lines at the corners of his eyes into a mask, like a sad devil. Add to it the velvety, wistful voice — and what hope had the Widow Morris to resist?

Tom was made, he hoped, of sterner stuff. "Is this why you went nosing at the Half Moon, Mr. Douglas? And why you discredited that poor Fowler? To further your interests?"

There is that sound, that *iphm* — half snort, half grunt — that Scots will use to signify an endless array of meanings. Douglas now *iphmed* in the greatest contempt. "My jaunt across the river was to inquire into the killing, and ye saw what came of it. As for that daft Fowler…" A bitter shake of the head. "Monsieur l'Ambassadeur shouldnae mind such a meddling gowk!"

"So you took it upon yourself to correct his mind?"

A shrug. "Courcelles — ye've seen how he is, that one — was suspicious of him already. He asked me… What was I to do, compromise myself?"

The cheek of the man! "Oh, never! His Excellency, though, has a trusting heart…"

"Aye. Not a fortnight ago, with Courcelles warning him, and even Mendoza's Fleming, he still had good words of all the lad does for Queen Mary's cause…"

And here was what Feron must have heard — and whispered to Fagot… "But the smallest doubt was enough, and when

Fowler lost Castelnau's trust, he also lost his use for Mr. Secretary. Exit William Fowler, without your hand showing — and yours is the one voice Sir Francis hears."

This time the laugh sounded genuine. "Sir Francis taught ye well, young Thomas! But then ye also see that if I hae the French doubt Fowler, they'll trust me all the more for it!"

The utter, shameless cheek! "And you did all this in Mr. Secretary's best interest, surely? You'd never dream of courting favour with the Queen of Scots — or the King of France, even…?"

Anger flamed in the grey eyes — either true or well feigned — and the fine voice dropped to a hiss. "If you believe —"

There was a rapping knock on the door. In a moment, all anger had gone, replaced by the sad smile, and it was the most charming of voices that called: "Come in, Mistress Morris."

The Widow entered, and pointedly went to whisper something to her lodger. If she expected that Douglas would dismiss Tom, though, she was disappointed. After some frowning, and some tapping of the chin, the Scot begged Mrs Morris to let the gentleman in — and, once she was gone, went to open another door. It led to a small bedchamber, with more colourful embroidery at bed and windows, and Tom stepped in, much curious about what Douglas wanted him to hear.

The door remained ajar, and almost directly the entrance of another man was heard — if not seen. One whose voice Tom had heard before… Greetings were exchanged, and there was mild surprise in Douglas's manner.

"Mr. Scory, to what do I owe…?"

Scory! Scory come to visit … whom? What mask did Douglas wear to Lord Leicester's man?

Scory took a deep breath. "I have a notion, Mr. Douglas, that you may find interest in something I just heard."

There was a beat of silence — and it was easy to imagine the two men watching each other, seeking a sign of the other's mind…

"I'm all ears, Mr. Scory," Douglas said at length — and must have gestured, for the armchair creaked.

Then Scory again, in softer tones. "Do you remember a Fleming, a fellow called Crispin Sauldane?"

Douglas hummed. "I'm nae sure…" The liar!

Scory must have thought the same, for his voice rose. "Come, come, Mr. Douglas — you do. A man of business from Flanders. You met him at the Embassy."

"I must have, aye. A Fleming, ye say?"

"Yes — and now he is dead."

"Deid!"

Had Scory observed how the Scottish colour grew thicker in Douglas's speech when he was caught unawares? Then again, Leicester's man sounded rather discomposed himself — and well he might, for … Sauldane! Fox-like, keen-eyed, watchful Sauldane…

The chair creaked again, and so did the wooden floor under a few agitated paces. "They found a body in the Fleet yesterday morning — and it took a full day before someone turned up who knew him. It was Crispin Sauldane."

A silence, then Douglas — slow and considering. "And ye reckon…"

An oath from Scory. "I reckon, Mr. Douglas, that a man who enjoyed some measure of trust with Monsieur de Castelnau died on his way from the Embassy. I wasn't there that night — unlike yourself…"

"And because of some happenings in my past, ye decide that I must be privy to what happened — nay, even a party to it?"

There were protesting noises from Scory, and steps, and Tom had barely the time to move away from the door before it was thrown open.

"Ye heard that well, Mr. Walsingham?" Douglas asked.

He would have made a good play-maker, the old Scottish devil!

Tom stepped over the threshold to face a satisfyingly dumbfounded Sylvanus Scory, who gaped for a moment, before his domed forehead creased in anger.

"This I call most devious, Mr. Douglas. And pointless, I'll wager, for…" He turned on Tom. "You had no need to hear of the Fleming, had you? What is your master thinking?"

Well now, this…! Tom found himself laughing at the sheer stupidity of it. "You don't imagine, Scory, that Mr. Secretary has brigands ridding him of Mendoza's ants?"

Scory was one of those who, be it shame or anger, blushed in red blotches — and looked no better for it. "I never said —"

"Come, come! If not Mendoza's man, then he was Philippe Courtois's — who is Mendoza's. And, again: you don't imagine that we had anything to do with it?"

"Then who…?"

Tom shrugged. He wasn't going to discuss the matter with Lord Leicester's man — but the question was a very, very good one: who, indeed?

"You said he was found in the Fleet. Drowned?"

"How would I know? Why do you ask?"

The prating fool! "Because falling in the river after drinking one cup too many is one thing, and being thrown in there is quite another."

Scory exhaled like one exerting great patience. "They say…" He waved a hand. "The constables believe that it was common robbers, for he had no purse…"

"And was he wounded?"

"Much bruised, they say. Like one cudgelled… But why do you ask? What's that to you?"

"As much as it is to you, I reckon." Tom uncrossed his arms, and took a step into the room. "You know so much about it, you must have asked questions of your own."

Scory's eyes lit with malice. "Why, so have you. A servant dies at Salisbury Court, and you appear. That fellow dies across the river — and there you are. And now this Sauldane… You were at the soirée too, I'll wager?" He turned to their host. "If I were you, Mr. Douglas, I'd be more chary of Mr. Walsingham here." And with that, he bowed to the Scot, and was gone, ignoring Tom altogether.

Crispin Sauldane dead. Murdered on his way from the Embassy, quite likely while Tom hid in the shadows of Water Lane. What might have happened, had Girault and Foulques not been chased away…?

Scory's angry steps clattered on the stairs, all the way down before Douglas shook his head with a sigh. "I'm moving in my mind, young Thomas, this poor man's death. Cudgelled by ruffians in a deserted street… Does it nae remind ye of our own misadventure?"

And in fact it did. Uncomfortably so. "Yours, Mr. Douglas. *Your* misadventure. Only of a deadlier turn … but then, you are no Flemish merchant of little account."

"Nor a kitchen servant, either."

"Nor a kitchen servant," Tom agreed, and then there was another knock at the door, much too shy to be announcing the Widow Morris, and the servant boy appeared carrying a covered jug. Yesterday Tom had suspected this youth of playing slow-witted; now he saw that things were very different: the servant was dumb, but not a whit less sharp for it. With no other direction than a nod from his master, he neatly arranged the jug and two pewter cups on the table, poured the wine, and disappeared. It must be unchristian, Tom supposed, to wonder whether a deaf servant was proof of a charitable bent in Douglas, or a valuable and discreet tool to such a born intriguer…

Not until they had taken their seats again, and tasted the wine — a not too bad Rhenish — did Douglas return to the dropped conversation.

"And for once I think that Scory is right," he said, as smoothly as though they'd never dropped it at all. "Not that ye've done murder — but I'm thinking that you must have come to Salisbury Court to look into the kitchen servant's death…"

Ah well. There seemed to be little point in denying this — and yet … how many men had lived to regret being open to Archibald Douglas? After a short consideration, about Clement Barbier's death he disclosed two things: that he suspected poison, and that the dead man had been boasting of some windfall or other.

"I believe that he was selling his silence," he concluded — and waited to see what the Scot would make of it.

Douglas nodded slowly. "Aye. We have a word for it in Scotland: the black rent. The reivers will take money fra' ye, and not lay yer place to waste… 'Tis much the same: pay, and naething unpleasant will happen. The trick's in never doing it to the wrong man."

"Black rent. Interesting name. You seem very sure that Barbier chose the wrong man — and Sauldane as well, I take it? I only have one question: why would the wrong man want you frightened off? Were you black-renting him as well?"

Douglas sat straighter to plunk his cup on the table. "That, Mr. Walsingham, I resent."

Tom should have apologised. Instead he only smiled. Was it the Rhenish going to his head, making him so bold to a man of the cloth, twice his age and, disgraced as he was, better born? "Well, something you must have done," he heard himself say. "Or seen. Did someone take objection to your fondness for the Ambassador's gallery? One must see — and hear — a good deal, from there?"

Douglas held his gaze for a while, with a hard one of his own. Tom never wavered. He was Sir Francis Walsingham's man, by God — sifting through the joints and flexures of murder…

"Because otherwise I don't see why you should suffer an assault…"

It came as a small rush of surprised triumph when the Scot looked away with a huff of great irritation. "I wouldnae hae myself set upon, would I?" he groused, and glared at Tom askance before throwing up both hands. "But aye, ye think I would. Dafter than I took ye for!"

"Well." Tom took a sip of his wine. Douglas would think he was enjoying his petty victory too well — but in fact, the pieces were shifting in his head, painting the Scot not as a dancer, but a caller of tunes… He made himself smile, as if half in jest. "You would, if you were the wrong man yourself. Make Fowler useless, poison that black-renting Barbier, then make us believe that the murderer was after you as well, and then Sauldane must have suspected something, and…"

There was a bark of laughter. "What, I didnae kill the fellow at the inn?"

"Not that one, no. That was another matter."

"Why, thank ye, young Thomas!" Douglas raised his cup in a mock toast. "There is some ill in this world, then, of which I'm innocent!"

Tom returned the gesture. "Must I be glad the wine was poured before I made my suspicions known?"

And look if he wasn't amused, the unchancy Scottish devil! Leaning back in his chair, peering at Tom over the rim of his cup… "Aye, what think ye, lad — must ye?"

Oh, but there was more than jest to this. It would be easy to make certain whether Douglas had supped at the Ambassador's table on the night of Barbier's death. As for Sauldane… That Douglas had remained at Salisbury Court after the soirée meant little enough. If he had hired a parcel of ruffians to make himself look imperilled, the same men would have been sent to kill Sauldane. There was no doubt that Archibald Douglas could have done it all… The question remained: why?

Tom drained his cup, and rose to set it on the table. "Let us not wander, though. The assault. If you didn't arrange it, someone else must have — and for a reason. Was it anything you saw from the Ambassador's gallery?"

From where he sat, the Scot was forced to frown upward. Whatever he was turning in his mind, he hid with great care.

"The other night, at Seething Lane, you made a list of your enemies," Tom pressed. "The Spaniards, now, I think we can leave out. You also named Courcelles, and any agent of the Queen of Scots…" The name of Throckmorton almost escaped Tom's lips — but no. There was a chance that Mary Stewart's people still ignored that Throckmorton was under suspicion. On the other hand… "Agents like Lord Howard?"

"Aye!" Douglas rubbed a hand down his beard. "Aye, my Lord Howard. Not that I saw him frae the gallery. He always comes at night, that one — but I hae a fine ear… And so has Mr. Secretary, eh? Hearing things all the way frae Seething Lane! He'll know of the other one, then. A young man called Throckmorton…"

"Throckmorton." Tom doubted he hid his surprise very well. No matter. Let the Scot think they hadn't known. The marvel was that he should name Throckmorton at all, if he was party to what was being brewed…

"Aye." Douglas shook his head. "Surely they all mislike that I have Castelnau's ear…"

"So they thought they'd make it uncomfortable for you. And before that, the butler's man must have found out, and thought he'd made his fortune."

"Servants have ears also," was the glum reply.

Quaestio, then: what of Sauldane? But this one he kept to himself. Instead…

"Were you going to tell Mr. Secretary of this?"

A long look, more searching than hard. "Sit, lad. 'Tis unmannerly to loom over a man like this." And when Tom had complied, "Monsieur de Castelnau, ye see…" he began in slow reluctance, rubbing a fingertip along the rim of his cup. "I would have spoken if I thought there were true danger. But…"

This now! Tom swallowed a snort of derision, but not the look of disbelief. "But you wanted to spare Castelnau?"

As when Tom had asked about the black-rent, anger flickered in the grey eyes. "Aye, aye — I know what my reputation is, and all of my own doing. Never mistake me for a wronged soul. Naebody trusts me — and why should they? Yet when I find someone who does… Do ye understand this?"

As though understanding and believing were one and the same… "I'm not sure that I do. I would have thought…"

"That I'd milk the trusting fool for all he's worth? Och, so would I, young Thomas. So would I."

And there it went again, the sad devil's face, the soft voice full of bitterness, of regret. It must have been hard to live in ruthless deceit for so long, and one day find himself stranded beyond human trust and compassion…

Oh, what a fool! How many had swallowed some play like this, only to regret it? Tom made himself raise an eyebrow in doubting coldness. "Well, if I'm to take you at your word on this, then you see that I cannot trust you on anything to do with Salisbury Court."

"Yer cousin's own flesh and blood, eh?" Douglas gave a thin, worn chuckle. "But aye, there's the de'il of it."

"Then I won't ask who informs the Ambassador of things in Scotland."

"Not I, that's for sure. All mistrusting souls, are my countrymen… I think I'm in favour with Gowrie and his party — and find that I'm not. I write to those I called friends, and they believe I've turned papist. I hae all the good offices of Monsieur de Castelnau, and still Queen Mary wishes me ill… Who would inform *me* of the things of Scotland?"

"They believe you've turned papist…" The second of Castelnau's Scots to say so in as many days. "I wonder who would report this in Scotland… Do you hear Mass at Salisbury Court?"

There was that Scottish *iphm* again. "Ye know who willnae believe me an apostate? The chaplain, there — that tristy-faced fellow. I'm sure Adam Jauffray speaks ill of me — but His Excellency, God keep him, will neither listen nor care."

"He doesn't care that you're no Catholic?"

And was it genuine fondness that showed in the old devil's eyes? "'Tis in my mind, young Thomas — it has been for some time — that if men like Michel de Castelnau ruled it, this world would be a place of greater fairness. Of less strife when it comes to God's will."

And here were Bruno's notions again — coming from the most unlikely quarter… "Strange notions for a man of the Kirk…"

"They are Monsieur de Castelnau's notions, not mine. Unlike many of us, he has a generous, broad-minded disposition…"

So … was Castelnau more open to Bruno's conciliation than he cared to show? But then…

"And he has a turn for intrigue, and a will to see the Queen of Scots on the English throne!"

"Och, you mistake him for his lady wife. *She* is the intriguer. *She* is the friend of Howard, of Queen Mary, of the Duke of Guise, and of Throckmorton. And in this Courcelles is more her man than her husband's."

Back in Paris, even at the English Embassy, Madame de Castelnau's fame had been well known. "A most zealous lady, they say."

"Fervent. There will be more Masses than soirées, when she comes." He poured more wine for both himself and Tom. "And we'll both be kicked out, lad — ye and I."

And so would Fowler, and Scory, quite likely, and for sure Giordano Bruno, with his bold notions on skies and men and his talk of conciliation… But would Douglas be, in truth? "When is she expected?"

"By the end of summer, His Excellency says."

Which, even if Gowrie didn't fall before, left a month or little more to secure Fagot's position and Feron's willingness — and to learn all that could be learnt, before whatever plot was afoot began in earnest, and the plotters betrayed themselves… Was the murderer protecting them until then — or himself? And was Douglas the next victim, or the slaughterer? Because one of the two he must be, surely?

A doubt that, it occurred to Tom, had its own solution in itself. "By summer's end … supposing that we are still all alive by then." He laid down his half-full cup, and rose. "You are not safe here, Mr. Douglas. And much less you'd be at Salisbury Court."

"They wouldnae dare, ye said so yerself."

"That was before I learnt of Sauldane's death. He was Mendoza's man — and yet they killed him. You'll be much safer at Seething Lane."

Some nervousness crept into Douglas's protests. "But I know naething that I didnae know when we were set upon!"

Tom shook his head. "We do not know what Sauldane knew — and they do not know what you don't. Mr. Secretary would never forgive himself, were you to come to harm in his service."

There was little chance that Douglas would take a direct order from one who was not Sir Francis himself — but on the other hand … innocent, he would not refuse an offer of shelter; guilty, he could not refuse it lest he arouse — or confirm — suspicion…

Tom allowed himself a small sigh of relief when the Scot went to the door, and bid the Widow send up the servant boy.

That he must see through the charade, mattered little — as long as, murderer or imperilled victim, he was out of the way and under Williams's watchful eye.

Wat Williams barged in on Tom with barely a knock, finding him half-undressed and washing in haste.

"Never be done with Parson Douglas, shall I?" was the grouchy salutation — so truculent that Tom paused in the act of rubbing his wet hair.

"You're in your cups, Wat?" he demanded sternly.

Wonder of wonders, Williams looked sheepish. His fondness for beer, wine, and women was no secret. As a rule, he kept a tight rein on himself in Seething Lane — but with Sir Francis away…

"Takes strength, it does." A shrug. "With Parson Douglas underfoot…"

"Yes, well…" Tom went back to his ablutions. "It struck me that he may be our murderer — and therefore better kept on a short leash."

There was a low whistle. "Are you sure?"

Wouldn't it have been good to be! But… "In fair truth, no. I have good reasons to suspect him, though."

And, half because he wanted to see what it sounded like when spoken aloud, Tom sat on his trunk, and put his discoveries in the form of an argument, beginning with the nightly visits, and ending with Crispin Sauldane's death.

It sounded almost good enough.

Good enough to draw a grudging grunt and a nod from Wat Williams. "And it has to be Lord Howard's plot, hasn't it? No reputation left, has Parson Douglas…"

"Certainly none worth killing for. When it comes to a matter for the gallows, though…"

"True enough." Williams leant against the door, arms crossed, sucking his teeth and studying Tom with narrowed eyes. "True enough — so, why are you not convinced?"

And devil seize the fellow — drunk or sober! "'Tis not that…" But then, convinced Tom was not, and the doubt had been nagging him. "Why did he have to name Throckmorton?

I'd given him Lord Howard already. Every soul in the kingdom knows Howard favours the Queen of Scots. Naming Howard was more than enough for his tale, and no harm done … but Throckmorton?"

"And because of this, you'll believe him?"

"I disbelieve Archibald Douglas on principle — but … for all he knows, of Francis Throckmorton we may never have heard."

Williams shrugged. "So maybe he's not Howard's crony, and then you did well by taking him out of harm's way. Or else, he knows we have our eye on young Throckmorton, and you've brought home a murderer, Mr. Thomas — and he'll kill us all in our sleep."

Tom huffed in laughter — though there was little enough mirth to it — and went to rummage in the clothes press for his good riding Venetians and a leather doublet. "Hemlock smells like cat's piss — keep that in mind. And have a horse saddled for me, will you? Also, some bread and cheese would not go amiss."

"Why, where are you going, at this hour?"

Tom's small square window was thrown open to look on the yard downstairs and, above, the rust-coloured roofs against a slice of hazy sky, pale and light in the beginning of a long, full summer evening. Plenty of time to ride out to Barn Elms.

"If this truly has to do with Howard's conspiracy —" shirt, plain collar, doublet — "then there is something to it that they'll kill to protect — to keep it even from Mendoza and Spain. I think that Mr. Secretary should know, before we take any other step."

Williams pushed himself off the door. "It will be something to tell him — seeing as you still don't know who Fagot is — nor, it seems to me, who did most of the murders."

In vino veritas, indeed! And in beer too, it seemed — and impudence as well as truth! Had the man been wrong, at least…! "Yes, well. I only tied it all to a plot against the Queen. Small work, I know…" Tom tugged on a recalcitrant sleeve so savagely that the point broke in two. "Curse and damn it!"

There was an unimpressed sniff from the door — and the long-suffering look of the veteran for the favoured recruit. "Since you are going, you can take the packet. If courier work isn't too low for you these days."

And that was enough, by God! A hook tore as Tom untrussed the sleeve and thrust it onto the bed. Enough. "Look, Walter Williams, I know what you think of me, what you all think — that I'm only here for being Sir Francis's kin. You all think it downstairs — but understand once and for ever: you're all dead wrong!"

"No."

No? Tom stopped dead in his tirade — struck dumb with disbelief. To his own face… "*No?*"

Williams shrugged. "No, we do not all think it. Some do, I'll say. Did so myself, in the beginning. An arrogant pup with little between his ears, who thinks to order us all about because of the name he bears… Ay, well. You *are* a pup — but one who learns, at least. Also, you're not a complete lackwit."

Well, now… "Why — my most heartfelt thanks!"

"Can't be, if Master reckons you're worth keeping."

"Good of you to —"

"Your brother's his kin. Didn't stay long, did he?"

I didn't do too well with Mr. Secretary, you see… Poor Guildford. And of course they had expected him to be the same…

Tom sat down with a sigh. "Good to know that I'm redeeming my branch of the family," he murmured.

And lo and behold! Wat Williams gave what passed for a smile with him: a thin-lipped raise of the mouth's corner, of the eyebrow. "For that you've got a while to go yet, Mr. Thomas. But Master puts the Service before all: cousin or no, he'd have sent you packing, if you weren't worth the trouble." He nodded his chin at the wrecked sleeve. "See to that, and I'll have your horse and packet ready — and bread and cheese."

And he was gone, and it warmed Tom's heart past all reason that Wat Williams, soldier and veteran of the Service, and Sir Francis's trusty servant, should not think too ill of him — even though he still knew little of the murders, and nothing at all of Henry Fagot.

By the time Tom trotted into the stable yard at Barn Elms, the western sky still glowed in bands of dusty orange and grey clouds, but the twilight was closing in, and the yard itself was a pool of purple shadow.

He was well known to the stablemen and to the servant who met him with a lantern — and the news that Mr. Secretary was at Court, and expected home on the morrow.

Too late now to ride to Richmond, and in all honesty, Tom carried no news that could not wait until morning. Wat Williams's words had kept him company all the way — those that said he had precious little progress to report...

It was with a heavy heart that Tom entered the darkened house. Her Ladyship had the migraine, and Mistress Frances had retired already, Gawton announced in his old, reedy voice. Tom said not to disturb them, and would have gone to bed on the nearest pallet, but that the old man insisted that Mr. Thomas should have a proper bed readied for him, and something to eat besides.

So Tom was left in the cavernous hall, stranded in his candle's island of yellow light amidst the whispering grey shadows. Beautiful as Barn Elms was in daylight, there was a wintry glumness to the place after darkness at the best of times. Right now, with dismal thoughts clinging to him like cobwebs, Tom sat on a windowsill, and wished he'd stayed in London — for, in truth... *Look into Barbier's death*, Sir Francis had bid him. *Find Henry Fagot. Gauge the standing of both Douglas and Fowler.* And of all this, what had he accomplished? Nothing — or little better. A most useless Hercules, he was. What if he failed in his task, and proved himself not worth the trouble...?

"Is that you, Tom?"

He was startled out of his thoughts at the sudden voice, the joyful surprise. Up in the gallery, atop the ornate staircase, stood little Frances, a dove-hued loose gown over her nightdress.

"Mistress Poppet," he greeted, as she ran down the stairs, the flame of her candle hissing green and gold.

"Careful, you'll set yourself afire..."

The warning went unheeded as she ran up to him, all smiles. "*Signor Cugino, quando siete arrivato?*" she asked, Italian conversation being their latest game.

"*Appena adesso*," he said, and bowed over her hand in his courtliest manner.

At sixteen, Frances was more and more her father's living likeness: dark of hair, sallow of complexion, narrow of cheekbones. She would never possess the clear loveliness of a Diane de Bochetel — but in the elfin face the large, dark-grey eyes were full of intelligence.

"Did Gawton abandon you here all alone?" she asked.

Tom tweaked at the arm-thick, glossy braid that hung over her shoulder. "He's gone to find me some supper. I didn't mean to bother anyone…"

"You don't. Gawton is fond of you — and I'm so glad you have come! When I heard voices I thought it could be Father. We don't expect them before tomorrow, but sometimes…" She threaded an arm through his. "Come, let's see where Gawton has lost his way. Poor Gawton, he's getting old…"

Much as when Frances had been a child, Tom allowed himself be led. There was comfort in his little cousin's affectionate ways — and something in what she had said. "You expect *them*. Not just Sir Francis, then?"

"Father and Sir Philip," said the girl, leaning in as if to impart a secret.

Sidney. Sidney underfoot again… And he must be far too transparent — or Frances must be very much her father's daughter — for her smile dimmed, and she stopped to watch him well in the face.

"You do not like Sir Philip, Tom?" she asked. "I so wish that you could be friends, because…" She looked down a little, then rose on tiptoe to whisper in his ear. "'Tis a great secret yet — but I'm to be married to him. Very soon."

Married to him.

Mother and Mary would have exchanged knowing looks, if they could have seen the blow it was — and misunderstood. Never, never had he dreamt of marrying Frances himself. He loved her the way he'd love a little sister, liked her better than his own sisters in truth, and knew she was meant to marry very high. It was good of Sir Francis to choose a young man he liked and admired. A man he regarded as the son he'd never had, as his heir and successor. A man who also thought Tom an upstart with no merit beyond the Walsingham name…

"You dislike him so very much?" Frances's voice had gone small.

Tom shook himself into some semblance of a smile. "Why, no… You take me by surprise, is all. I wish you all the happiness, my Lady Poppet…"

"Silly!" she laughed. "But mind: the greatest secret —"

And she said no more, for old Gawton reappeared, followed by a servant carrying candles and a trencher for Tom's supper. What appetite he'd had was gone, but it would be petty now to refuse, so he ate bread and cold meat, and between bites told stories of Paris for Frances and the old butler, and smiled until his cheeks ached, and all the time wondered why this marriage must be kept a secret. Did Sidney's family disapprove — or, much worse, did the Queen? No matter, though, for Sir Francis Walsingham was not one to be thwarted — and only a churlish, selfish ingrate would wish that, for once, he could be…

At length Tom was suffered to go to bed, with the burning stomach and heavy heart of a man whose prospects had taken a very grim turn.

CHAPTER 11

After a windy night, the day rose clouded. The sky lowered, bilious, shivering now and then with distant thunder.

Of Sir Francis there was no trace.

Lady Ursula, recovered from her migraine, was equally as welcoming as her daughter — if less loquacious on the matter of discreet nuptials — and said that they couldn't expect Sir Francis for hours yet, provided he managed to tear himself from the Queen at all…

She said so with that wry glint in her eyes, and chattered about the summer, and buttered manchets — but it wasn't long before Tom knew his impatience had been seen through.

When he said he'd ride on to Richmond, Frances clicked her tongue.

"You leave already!" she exclaimed.

Lady Ursula tutted. "Tom isn't here to visit, child. I'm sure he carries urgent tidings for your father. Although, if he's in conference with Her Highness…"

Indeed, no urgency would be suffered to interrupt then, and between the packet and his own tatters of news and speculation, Tom carried very little that was urgent — or even truly tidings…

Still he left as soon as they would saddle him a horse in the huge stables, where several dozen mounts were kept for Mr. Secretary's men, and he was on the road as the pickers of cherries began their work in the orchards.

It was not four miles to Richmond — one of the advantages of Barn Elms — and Tom was soon in sight of the great turreted palace, sitting like a bristly creature, russet and many-eyed. All around, even under the swollen sky, the countryside lay in all the green and golden glory of summer — a most pleasant sight for any man who did not ride to Court with all the uncertainties in this world weighing upon him…

Once he was admitted to the Messengers' Antechamber, a stiff-necked usher informed Tom that, as Lady Ursula had foreseen, Mr. Secretary and the whole Privy Council were sitting with Her Majesty, and would be for quite some time.

"A note could be brought in, for Mr. Secretary to see later," the man offered, tilting his head back to give a most forbidding stare. "*If* it is a matter of great import."

And think of a red-liveried servant silently gliding inside some great painted chamber at the first interruption, to slide a note before Mr. Secretary — a note saying what? That one of his messengers was here — and Mr. Secretary perhaps even excusing himself, thinking of some pressing, weighty matter, only to find…

"No, no — thank you." It just bore no thinking. "I'll wait."

You could ask for Sir Philip Sidney, Tom's traitorous mind sneered. *Since this is going to be the way of things…* But no. Even if it was to be, it wasn't yet, and Sidney was still only Leicester's nephew, and little Frances had only whispered in great secret, and most of all, what would be the use in telling Sidney what Sir Francis must hear?

"I'll wait," Tom said again, more firmly — which met with a measure of austere approval from the usher.

And wait he did, for more than an hour, in the antechamber. He paced up and down, watching the sky change hues through the tall leaded windows, and moving about in his mind the pieces of what he knew and what he didn't, and aimlessly counting those who came, and went, and waited in turn — and wishing that, in leaving London, he'd thought to pack finer clothes.

More than an hour, it was — nigh on two. Then he found the disdainful usher, and informed him that he was leaving, but there was no need to trouble Mr. Secretary about his coming.

"I'll be at Barn Elms when he returns there." It was hard to match the haughtiness of one who, for all occupation, practised his own all day — but much worse it would be if a messenger arrived then disappeared with no word…

The usher raised both eyebrows. *Arrogant churl,* these eyebrows said. *Ignorant of the ways of Court, and mistakenly swollen with his own importance…* Oh, let him think what he liked, and hope his blatherings never reached Sir Francis's ears… Bribing his red-sashed kind into discretion was well beyond Tom's purse, and foolish to boot.

Half an hour more of waiting in the stables — where at least no one knew of the pointlessness of his visit — and Tom was on his way back to Barn Elms under the first fat drops of a summer squall, wishing he hadn't gone to Richmond at all.

It turned to pouring before he was halfway, and the first hailstones caught him on the carriage path to the house.

From Lady Ursula herself, down to the groom who stabled Tom's horse, all at Barn Elms reckoned that Sir Francis would never put himself on the road in such foul weather…

A most sensible and truthful opinion it proved to be, and Tom spent a long day trying to stay out of the way, watching the walled garden being shred and drowned by the storm, and gnawing at the same questions, again and again…

Item: who was Henry Fagot?

Item: would the murderers of Barbier and the Fleming kill him next?

Item: what would Feron do with Fagot dead or frightened into silence?

Item: what did the Ambassador know of what went on under his roof?

Item: why had Douglas brought up Throckmorton's name…?

He'd driven himself half out of his wits before it occurred to him to inquire if other messengers had come. They had — from Scotland, from Paris and from Antwerp, but none from London. Which meant that no one else had died (a very good thing), and no Fagot had turned up (a disappointing thing), and Douglas continued without great events at Seething Lane (a thoroughly unhelpful thing).

So Tom was at leisure to resume his whorling cogitations until, about supper time, Sir Francis and Sidney arrived.

What with the late arrival, and the other messengers to be seen to, it wasn't until after supper that Sir Francis begged the ladies' pardon and sequestered himself with Tom and Philip Sidney in his study, where a fire had been lit against the cooler air the storm had brought.

Courcelles in London would be glad of the change, no doubt…

Sir Francis lowered himself into the chair nearest to the fire with the packet from London. Only those who knew him well would see, through the unfathomable appearance, the fatigue and the aches that plagued him lately, and always grew worse in bad weather, and when he had to ride…

Did Philip Sidney see?

An uncharitable thought, quite likely — and one Tom had no leisure to pursue, when Sir Francis, after quickly sifting through the packet and setting the letters aside, rested both elbows on the chair's arms, and asked: "Well, Thomas?"

There had been a whole night and a day to rehearse the arguments, and Tom began smoothly enough with what he had discovered about Hurston's death, and the measures he had taken.

Sir Francis nodded. "Yes. Yes, well done — and a branch of this tangle well out of the way."

Branches and brambles — just as Tom himself imagined the matter. A pity that the rest of the story was still so badly entangled. A pity that Henry Fagot was still nameless and still silent — but there was at least the discovery of Laurent Feron. Not the secretary — but the clerk…

"Either Fagot looked to mislead, or between French and English he used the word in a broader sense — but I have no doubt that our mole is Laurent Feron."

"A good thing, then, that you never ventured too far with the secretary. As for Fagot… Can you be sure, then, that he was not the victim of the first murder?"

And this was the crux, was it not? The thorniest, tightest branch of all…

"I very much doubt it, Sir. And all the more because there has been a third murder."

Sidney sat straighter, with a huff of disbelief. "A murder — did you keep it for pudding?"

The arrogant…!

Before Tom could snap back, Sir Francis held up a hand.

"'Tis Thomas's method, I find, to weed away what is resolved, and so expose what still is not. Go on, Thomas."

Tom took a good, deep breath, and began. Sauldane's death, first, and then backwards, through his own nightly adventures, and the assault on Douglas, and all the way to Barbier, the hemlock, and what Douglas called black-rent.

"And since the secret visitors are no Canterbury tale, whether the murderer is Mr. Douglas, or one who is threatened by him, there is a good chance that it all ties to whatever Howard is plotting on behalf of the Queen of Scots.

Something that involves Monsieur de Castelnau — or Madame his wife and Claude de Courcelles at least."

"So..." Sidney again. "Douglas had all the ways and all the reasons to murder those two men — and still you doubt that he did?"

What was it with this man, that a sheer itch to contradict him made Tom pursue paths that he himself judged dubious? Warily he explained that Douglas had named Throckmorton without need. "And it could just mean that he knows we are watching Throckmorton, but..."

For a great and blessed wonder, Sidney did not scoff. Instead he nodded, in slow consideration. "Yes. Yes, I see — and yet ... if Douglas didn't do these murders, then who did?"

Tom had had the whole day to muse on this. "Courcelles," he said. "Or any other agent of the Queen of Scots at Salisbury Court. Or else Fagot — whoever Fagot is."

"And what of that Fowler of yours?"

Oh yes — Fowler. "Why would he cry murder, then, when all believed Barbier had died a natural death? All he had to do was to keep quiet."

Sidney sighed. "So we can rule out Fowler — who also can't be Fagot, can he?"

And this was safer ground. "He'd hardly discredit himself the way Fagot did. Besides, Fagot's letters kept coming well after Fowler lost Castelnau's trust, early in June."

"But they have stopped now. What if Fagot has left Salisbury Court?"

"I've thought of that — but I know of no one who has."

"Then he has grown wary — and rightly so, for if Fagot is still there..."

Indeed — indeed. "...Then he — or she — is either the murderer or in great danger."

"She?" Sir Francis frowned. "You have formed an idea of Fagot, I take it?"

There was, after all, something to be said for having many long hours to sift and hone one's arguments… "By my reckoning, Fagot must be one of two persons: firstly, the Ambassador's cousin-by-marriage, Madame de Bochetel…"

And of course Sidney must laugh at this… "A woman!"

"A most intelligent, secretive woman — and one Feron obeys. Or secondly — and most likely to my mind — there is Doctor Bruno. I know Sir Philip doesn't —"

Sidney held up both hands in surrender. "No — and most of all, I won't believe that Bruno is a murderer. Most absolutely. As for being Fagot, though … I don't believe that either — but what if I'm wrong?"

For once, he looked uncertain. He looked as though he truly sought Tom's mind.

Tom had little to offer that would be likely or reassuring, though.

"He may well be Fagot, and still innocent of the murders…"

Philip Sidney sighed — a heavy, discontented sigh, before turning to Sir Francis. "What are we going to do about Fagot?"

"Nothing." The dark grey eyes gleamed like glass in the light of the dancing flames. "If Lord Howard and young Throckmorton are behind the murders, then nothing must be done that may frighten them into running or renouncing…"

And trust Sidney to interrupt Sir Francis! "Well, but if they are, then Fagot is not —"

"The trouble is that we can't be sure. Either the conspirators or Fagot himself resorted to murder, but whatever is being plotted at Salisbury Court, it must be suffered to run its course. To run it there, where we have the means of knowing. Thomas…" Sir Francis tapped a forefinger on the carved arm.

"You must make secure of this Feron. See what money he asks — and have Wat arrange the means of acquiring the copied papers. What he offers, we buy — without Fagot."

In the sudden silence, the heaped embers crumbled on the hearth in a hissing shower of sparks. Tom knelt to poke at the fire, before it left them in darkness.

"And what if Fagot killed no one?" Sidney rose to his feet, more agitated than Tom had ever seen him. It made him look younger. "Sir Francis, for all his fiddle-faddle, Bruno has been thrown out of his order, and persecuted, and exiled, and he found a place here at last… Must he also be murdered?"

"You do not believe he is Fagot."

"No — but I may be wrong. Walsingham has been there, has seen how things are, and I have not. What if he is right? And even if he is wrong, what of that woman? Suppose they're not your murderers. They offered you their services — and you will let them be killed?"

"Fagot's services were *sold* to me — whoever he or she is — but that's hardly the matter." Sir Francis rose — a thin, dark shadow limned by the fire's coppery glow. From where Tom knelt, he looked immensely tall. "We have news from Scotland. The Earl of Gowrie teeters, and King James makes ready to escape his rule. It may be a matter of days." The stern gaze fastened on Tom. "Before it happens, Thomas, this Feron must be firmly in our pay."

"He will be, Sir." Tom rose, and Sidney threw him a look of disgust.

"And let Fagot be damned?"

"I will have no swearing, Sir Philip." Sir Francis waited until Sidney looked away, before softening his gaze and his voice. "Unless the guilt is certain, we will try to keep Fagot safe as well. We would have done so already, if he — or she — had trusted us enough. But…"

If an answer was expected, there was none — only the deep quiet of the country night, and the whisper of the rain outside.

When Sir Francis began again, low and firm, and with the terrible finality of stone, Tom knew already what the words would be, words that he had heard before.

"When we consider that the trouble of a few may avoid a general trouble, we must prefer the general to the particular. And this means, Sir Philip…" He paused long enough for Sidney to look up. "This means that you will not warn Doctor Bruno. You will not have him escape Salisbury Court. You are not one of my men, that I can give you orders — but it would be a great disappointment if you were to talk or write or send word to Bruno at all, before this matter is resolved."

Sidney's jaw worked as he held Sir Francis's gaze, gripping the chair's back with white-knuckled fingers, half the offended gentleman, half the child not used to being chastised.

Tom had a notion that they seldom disagreed, these two. He himself did not know how to disagree with Mr. Secretary — and yet found himself disliking very much the thought of the lively, erudite, sharp-witted Bruno lying dead.

The rain petered out at some point during the night, leaving behind a soft, deep quiet. Tom was still wide awake by then, turning and turning his pieces in his mind.

Whenever he stopped, images of Giordano Bruno's dead face floated into his mind — eyes lightless and bulging, mouth agape, a bluish tint to the skin… Sidney's dismay must be catching — for more and more it seemed too harsh a punishment for a man who preached of amity and moderation … foolish, unlikely notions — and yet, to be abandoned to a wretched death for them? No — not for them, in truth, but still, to think of him poisoned!

And if it wasn't Bruno, it must be Diane.

The beautiful Diane — to think of the perfect face livid and contorted in the choking agony of hemlock, the black eyes bulging, all the alabastrine composure lost to indignity and pain and fear…

It bore no thinking.

And yes, Douglas was safely held at Seething Lane, well away from the mysterious Henry Fagot — so there was that. But then, even if Tom was right about him, Douglas had never been the one to cudgel Sauldane to death, and must have hired men to stage the assault against himself. What if he had an accomplice at Salisbury Court? And what if Douglas was innocent after all? What if Lord Howard was behind it all? What if Fagot was instead the murderer…?

What if…?

Votre très humble et loyal serviteur, Henry Fagot…

I heard him in the gallery…

A braw place to see who comes and goes…

Our butler told me so…

Monsieur l'Ambassadeur had letters from his wife…

He said all this in Italian…

A Scot called Fowler — also in the pay of the King of France…

I know very well that he dissimulates in his religion…

I have made the the Ambassador's secrétaire so much my friend…

Fowler is very traitorous…

We were just discussing, were we not, Signor Jauffray…?

He kept a Scot in his house who was being threatened with imprisonment for his religion…

He said this in Italian…

The chief agents for the Queen of Scots…

I know very well…
The secretary will let me know everything he does…
…Says Monsieur Fowler does much better in his own language…
I heard him say this himself…
The Spanish Ambassador…
Much better in his own language…
Votre affectionné Fagot…
I know very well…
A Scot in his house, threatened for his religion…
I know very well…

Tom wrenched awake, sweat-soaked and breathless.

I know very well — of course! The best way of knowing very well a great many things. And a subtle mind, too…

Of course.

In that greying of darkness that heralds dawn from afar, Tom dressed in great haste, went downstairs, boots in hand, and entered the kitchen, where servants were already a-stir for the day. Good Gawton was about, too — it had long been a jest between the cousins that the old man slept fully clothed, standing in a cupboard — and made quick work of providing what Mr. Thomas asked: ink and paper, some breakfast, and a horse to be saddled.

The bread was hot, straight from the oven, and by the time Tom had washed it down with a cup of ale, a note was ready for Sir Francis — a note that, after all, provided some reassurance in more than one way.

The horse was ready too: a sprightly mare, for Mr. Secretary's stable-boys were quick to recognise a weighty errand.

Between the last of the moon, and the first fingers of daylight, Tom mounted and made his way to the carriage path under the elms, and then the road to London.

Now let him just be right…

But, perhaps for the first time since the beginning of this affair, Tom felt confident that he was.

CHAPTER 12

The newness and the exhilaration of hitting the offices in Seething Lane like a whirlwind were mitigated by the fact that, in spite of his half-drunken words, Wat Williams had not mellowed in the least, and was still as crusty as he'd ever been — or else he was suffering through the consequences of more fortifying indulgences.

He was efficient, though — and in a trice notes were written, and Bonetti summoned to deliver whispered words at Salisbury Court … and not a doubt voiced, until the errand-boy had run off and the scrivener was dismissed.

Only then Williams assumed his unpersuaded manner, leaning against the doorjamb and muttering: "Giving ourselves away, are we?"

Perched on the windowsill, Tom explained about Lord Gowrie, and the mayhem waiting to happen in Scotland. "So before then, Feron must be made our man — not Fagot's — and he must be warned… What did you find about him, by the way?"

"Oh ay — Toby was right, you know. Not a scrivener trained. Used to be a merchant, house in Mincing Lane…"

"Well, well, well!" For Mincing Lane was a place of fine houses and gardens, where foreign merchants liked to dwell, if they could afford it. "Grander than I thought…"

Williams shook his head. "Not very — and he lost it years ago anyway. The neighbours don't think too well of him. The English because he was born French, the French because he's become English, all because he wrecked his business and put his wife in the Bedlam…"

The stooping shoulders, the greying head, the clothes well-kept but old… Laurent Feron didn't look prosperous — nor especially cheerful. "A mad wife's charges would weigh hard on a clerk's salary… And a recusant's fine, too. Is he a Catholic?"

"Depends on which neighbour you ask."

Of course — and yet … a lamb in Jauffray's flock, possibly? "Let's hope he is. It would be a sad affair to have him thrown out for a heretic the moment Madame de Castelnau arrives." Tom rose, rolling both shoulders against the tiredness of a restless night, wishing he'd thought to ask Fowler who had been attending that one Mass months ago. "Would Douglas know?"

And small surprise it was that Williams huffed. "Never took much notice of the clerk, he says…"

Another lie, perhaps — or perhaps not. The soirée at Salisbury Court, Feron and Sauldane, standing together in the gallery — and the Scot, only a few steps away, but quite remote from the two he regarded as servants… "He never noticed Girault and his cronies, either, did he?"

"Too far beneath him," groused Williams, with the dour look of one who had been made to feel beneath Archibald Douglas's notice. "And speaking of Douglas, what do I do with him now?"

"Keep him here. Like our Fagot, he's still *sub judice* — but, murderer or not, better have him out of the way for now. With any luck, I'll know by the time I'm back from the Black Friars."

"Ay, speaking of that…" There was more doubtful humming from Williams, though of another colour this time. "Must it be the Blackfriars?"

Hand on the door already, Tom turned to frown over his shoulder. "I rather doubt Feron will like to discuss the matter in a public tavern..."

"Don't take it ill, Mr. Thomas — but I'd like it better if you took Skeres."

"Also, Feron will need persuasion and promises, not browbeating," Tom said — and had to be satisfied with the Welshman's nod of lukewarm agreement. Or not much satisfied, if truth be told: did Williams think he could not look after himself?

And besides, Laurent Feron was a middle-aged scribe with a bad back and a fearful nature, and as for Fagot ... how could they ever be dangerous?

There was little to do, once at the Blackfriars, but pace this way and that in the half-dark hall, the same one where Tom had met Bonetti, with its tall, boarded windows. From outside came a jumble of boys' voices raised in song. Some children's choir or other, according to Sir Francis's clerks — part of More's suit over the whole Blackfriars... Right now, the stone-flagged hall, with all its grime and gloom, seemed hardly worth the bother of going to law. The air, though cooler than it had been, still smelt of dust and dampness, and Tom's steps made a dull echo on the paved floor — until it occurred to him that silence would let him hear Feron approaching.

It was not long before sounds came from the next room. A wooden, wary tread, that paused a few steps away from the open door, so that the newcomer was hidden in the gloom.

"Here," Tom called. "Will you come in, Maître?"

But no maître at all stepped across the threshold with a swish of black cloak, and halted.

It was Diane de Bochetel.

Well, then… "Madame," Tom greeted with a bow, hoping he did not sound as confused as he felt… Diane in Feron's place. Was he mistaken once again, then? He'd come to entirely discard his suspicion that she may be Fagot — but now…

Diane stopped where she was, gripping the doorjamb, peering this way and that in the half darkness. Even across the distance of greyness and bright bars of sunlight, her dark eyes burnt enormous in the pale, lovely face. She made no word, no sound at all.

When Tom made to step closer, she flinched, ready for flight.

He stopped where he was. "Please, come close, Madame. I'm not quite sure what you and I have to discuss, but we can hardly shout at each other across the room…" And, when she kept still, "You do not fear that I'll do you harm, surely?"

The question loosened Diane's chilled immobility. She tilted her head, and was too far away, too deep in the grey shadow, but the hint of a smile was clear in her voice when she spoke. "No, I have no fear of that."

She let go of the door, and straightened, and looked as though she may have fear of nothing.

"Then…" Tom motioned for her to advance, and she did. Now it became clear what had made the curious sound: she wore tall wooden pattens against the mire last night's rain had left in the streets. A sunbeam caught her as she clacked her way to the centre of the hall, rousing copper sparks off the auburn hair that showed under her hood — and then she passed into shadow again.

She stopped a half dozen steps away from Tom. "Well, Monsieur Walsingham?"

"I'm sure you know, Madame, that I was not expecting you."

"No, perhaps you were not — but as for not knowing what is to be discussed… I believe that you lie."

This said with such assured calmness — a statement of fact, not an insult. But this was a game two could play. "I think I should resent this, Madame. Besides, what I said, in truth, is that I am not sure what is to be discussed *with you*. You are here on Maître Feron's behalf, I take it? You've made him so much your friend, after all…"

The lovely face went rigid, the eyes hard. Not in recognition of Fagot's words — no. "My friend!" she exclaimed. "That it is true makes it no less petty. I'd judged you differently, Monsieur."

Burning with contempt, she was — and wrongly, had Tom been right. Only he wasn't, was he? Diane de Bochetel was not Henry Fagot after all. She *was* Feron's friend, though. Oh, the serene, icy Diane, with her bottomless dark eyes and her alabaster beauty, was very much Laurent Feron's friend…

"So had I, it seems." What a naive fool! "Apologies, believe me, would be very awkward at this point…"

And so he *was* petty, after all — something that Sir Francis would most certainly disapprove of. As he would of gaining advantage on a foe, and then failing to pursue it — for a foe she must be. Why, she may even be pretending to be the scribe's lover…

"But then, Madame, I fear you came for nothing. What business I have with Maître Feron, I will only discuss with him."

And this was where the fair Diane's perfection broke into a breathless incandescence.

"Business!" she cried, recoiling. "You call this —" She clamped her mouth shut, just as Tom spoke.

"I'm sure you know…"

Tom went still, and held his breath, as his head filled with the tinkling of glass pieces falling, falling, sliding into place… Not a fearful nature — no: a guilty conscience, rather…?

A heartbeat, then Diane gathered her skirts, and ran in a clatter of pattens.

"Stop!" It took Tom three strides to catch up and grasp her by the wrist, and she tugged, leaning away from him.

"Let me go!" she hissed.

Very grimly, Tom held fast. Oh, what a fool! "Clement Barbier, Madame. What did he ask to hold his tongue?"

The arm that had trembled tense in Tom's grip, went slack at once, the slender figure folding on itself.

Tom didn't let go — not until he had handed her to the bench, and sat her down, looming over her with arms crossed, and his sternest manner and voice.

"Did Maître Feron ever pay him, or was the fellow's fate sealed the moment he asked?"

Not that it mattered much at this point.

Diane seemed to recover a little under the questioning.

"It was me that he asked!" Her smooth voice was gone, broken into a rasp of bitter edges. "Laurent never…" She swallowed, took a deep breath, and raised her eyes to meet Tom's. "In France or in England, a woman's reputation is soon torn to shreds. And I have no money…"

"Save for the price of a vial of hemlock…"

A lowering of the head. "He always wheezed and coughed. I thought…" She looked up again, eyes black as the night. "He was a wicked man, Monsieur."

"What he did was despicable, but —"

"The black rent, the Scots call it. Monsieur Jauffray told me."

Yes — of course he did. "However you name it, Madame, 'tis no more wicked than murder. It must take a tiger's heart to pour the poison in a man's wine, then go to bed, knowing that he..." And a scene flashed in Tom's mind, of the candlelit gallery at Salisbury Court. Crispin Sauldane's fox-like, intent face. Diane's eyes, hard in the golden light. *The wine is being neglected*... "And Sauldane — why, I saw it done! You sent Feron to take care of the wine, and afterwards... Once the poison seized him, Sauldane could never defend himself — not even against a man with a bad back..."

"No!" For the first time there was fear in Diane's manner. "I poisoned him, yes — for he too had found out about me and Laurent... But once he was gone, anyone could have..."

And, fool that he was, Tom found himself sorry for her, and admiring of her courage. "Madame, I believe that you lie. Not entirely — but enough. Does your lover know what you are risking for his sake?"

She leapt to her feet with enough unsteady vehemence that Tom had to take a step backwards.

"My lover, yes!" she hissed. "I am a widow, Monsieur Walsingham. My husband was a cousin of Madame de Castelnau. He was not kind to me. When I lost two babies, he called it my fault, and treated me accordingly. I did not kill him, if this is what you think — but had no tears when the Huguenots did. Madame his cousin took me in, then. In charity, she said, for a barren woman could never marry again. I raised her children, loved them as my own, and she took them from me to send me here to England — a servant in her husband's house. Oh, *Monsieur mon cousin* is kindly, is he not, to all? But think: alone, in a foreign city, among heretics, neither mistress nor servant in a house where no one can be trusted... Laurent was good to me, Monsieur. Good, and gentle, and he loved me as no one had, not since I was a child. I know that he has a wife, and you will think that he is beneath me. I say that love is beneath no one and nothing. Not even…"

She faltered, and her eyes went to something behind Tom. Cursing himself for not making sure the door was closed, he turned around, hand on the hilt of his sword, to find Laurent Feron on the threshold, dishevelled and stooped and breathless. He wore a sword in an old-fashioned scabbard, the way he would a borrowed pair of shoes.

"Madame!" he called.

Tom took a step back and aside, where he could keep an eye on both — lest Diane should choose that moment to flee — and, if truth be told, it was a great relief. Better a dozen murderous scriveners, rather than one woman so brimming with pain…

"Come close, Feron — but not too close."

The clerk obeyed, in that strange crab-wise gait that let him edge towards Diane, his eyes never leaving her. "Madame, what did you say?"

And look at the new sweetness in her manner… "He knows," she murmured. "He knows, Laurent. He did not before — but I was foolish…"

Only then did Feron look at Tom, wary and fierce at once. "Yes," he said. "Yes, she was foolish. I don't know what she said, Monsieur — but here's the way of it…"

"Laurent!"

He ignored the cry, and came to place himself squarely between Tom and the woman. "I killed Clement Barbier, and Crispin Sauldane. Also, I sent those men after that knave, Douglas. They told me later that you were there too, Monsieur. I never meant for you to be harmed…"

Oh this, now! How it would irk the old Scottish devil to have been set upon by a clerk rather than a disgraced earl… "No —

nor, I reckon, did you mean for Mr. Douglas to be killed … but then he didn't know, did he?"

Feron shook his head. "Had he known, then you would too — for a price. Or else Monsieur de Castelnau. But he's a devil, that one, sharp as a viper. It was only a matter of time before he did."

"Sauldane, on the other hand…"

With a groan, Feron took his head in his hands. "That was at the soirée… I don't know what he saw or heard. When I tried to talk to you, perhaps, to keep you away from Monsieur Claude. He watched, and watched…"

"So you followed him when he left, waited for the poison to make him faint, and killed him. Why, you even took his purse so it would look like a robbery."

"I threw it in the Fleet. The purse — I never…" The clerk looked up, eyes full of anguish. "I could not let him go to his Spanish masters! Mendoza would warn His Excellency, I would be a traitor to France, I could no longer…" His gaze travelled to Diane. He could no longer protect her.

How small she looked, hunched on the bench, twisting her hands… Small even as she drew straight. "He would be no more use to your Mr. Secretary!" she said. "You certainly see this, Monsieur. You know that no one else can provide what Maître Feron can…"

Curse her! Curse her for being right — for, murderer or not, they needed Laurent Feron. Needed the papers of Mary Stuart and the King of France. Needed them badly, while the Earl of Gowrie lost his grip on Scotland, while Lord Howard schemed with Madame de Castelnau and the Duke of Guise… It was the safety of England, even the Queen's own life — against justice for two dead men. The general, and the particular. Yes — curse Diane de Bochetel and her keen wits.

Nothing but contrariness made Tom snap: "Do I, Madame?"

And trust her to recover her composure, to see that she had scored a hit. The woman would be calm and beautiful under Spanish fire. "You do," she said, with that hint of a smile. "Not even that Fagot can give you what you need — even if you could trust him, and you do not know, do you? You don't even know who —"

Here a subtler man would not have gloated, would not have matched the woman's smile with one of his own… "Ah, but I do know, Madame. I know who Henry Fagot is. I knew even before you gave him away. The black rent, the Scots call it, don't they? And I was foolish enough to think him a murderer, but —"

"Oh!" With a small cry of rage, she surged to her feet in a whirl of skirts and cape. "Oh, why do you torment us, Monsieur? Taking advantage of a woman's rash words…" She sobbed, and made to push past Tom, and stumbled with her clumsy pattens.

And, knowing well what she was, Tom rushed to catch her before she fell. "Madame — forgive —"

First was a flash of steel, then the bite of pain.

Tom gaped at his left shoulder, at the blood on his sleeve — then at Diane. "Devil seize you!"

Cursing at women is the coward's way, Guildford used to repeat — but, God's pity, this one had stabbed him!

Diane, still grasping his arm, gaped back, round-eyed. "Laurent!" she stammered, and there was the rasp of an unsheathed blade.

Tom thrust the woman away from him. She stumbled back, and fell against the bench, the poniard clattering from her grasp.

Men in fencing books grabbed stray poniards to use as parrying daggers — but men in fencing books had not just been stabbed in their other arm. Even as he drew and turned to face Feron, Tom kicked the wicked thing, and sent it skidding as far away as he could.

A good thing that Feron was distracted with Diane, where she huddled on the floor…

Taking a broad ward, Tom circled well away from her, lest she thought to offer her lover some more help. And wasn't it a wonder how a little stabbing soured a man's admiration?

Feron circled in turn, with that skew-whiff nimbleness of his. His sword was a broad-bladed old thing, slower than Tom's rapier — but heavier.

If you have the patience to wait out your opponent, Thomas, most times he will grow rash and reckless.

Not that Sir Francis would be amused at having his words applied to fencing … or would he? For certainly they worked. Feron stamped forward twice in an angry lunge.

Le grete-steppe, à la façon Anglaise.

They'd all fenced in a small *salle*, in Paris — Tom, Watson, and the Throckmorton brothers, among others — where the master, a Gascon, had been very disdainful of the English style. Which was as may be, and Tom had no difficulty in parrying, and batting Feron's blade away, but the thrust had been, if inelegant, quite forceful. The clerk may not know how to fight — but still he fought dangerously.

Tom pivoted away from another lunge, and riposted, and made a stop-thrust on the next assault, and then once again — for Feron seemed to know no other manner of fencing.

The molinillo was a bit of a hazard, and a skilled opponent would have freed his heavier blade quite easily. Feron was not skilled — and lost his guard so that, had he wanted to hurt or maim, Tom could have skewered him at that point. Dead clerks passed no copied letters, though, and Feron was suffered to break measure, and to charge in again with all his force, unfettered by any necessity but fear and anger.

A feint, a full pass — and there went Feron, grasping his sword two-handed to bat Tom's blade away, to bat it hard. A *botte-de-paysan*, the Gascon would have sneered — but it was enough. Tom nearly stumbled in a flare of pain. His shoulder hurt, blood dripped distractingly down his arm and fingers, and the arm was growing heavy… How long before it undid his balance?

Feron's eyes ran to the floor — Tom's blood staining the flagstones, likely, for the poniard was well away, was it not? The clerk adjusted a white-knuckled grip on the hilt, and advanced again, grim-eyed.

And Tom's arm bled and hurt…

He retreated in a curve, until he found a patch of sunlight — and stood there, his back to the half-boarded window. He moved his tip in an elaborate arc, making the blade glitter. "You haven't considered well, Feron," he called, trying for high-handed unconcern — had he not been somewhat breathless. "They know where I am, at Seething Lane. They know that I am meeting you." Half a step sideways. "And I'm no kitchen servant."

Feron stepped contrary-wise, face contorting. "I wish no harm to you, Monsieur. I wish you didn't know me for a murderer — but you do. I must protect myself…"

Himself, and Diane. Diane was a shadow, bunching itself right at the edge of Tom's vision… He moved a little, trying to keep her in his sight. Feron followed.

"Others will know if I turn up dead. And there's Mendoza's man to consider… We need your work enough that we could overlook your crimes, and even protect you if the Spaniards will not. We could turn a blind eye on Madame Diane, too. But if you kill me…"

Would Sir Francis renounce his mole over the murder of a kinsman? *The general over the particular… He puts the Service before most things…*

But Feron was not to know this. He hesitated, the tip of his sword wavering… A mere moment was all it took.

Tom stepped sideways and backwards again, drawing Feron fully into the sun. The clerk squinted, raising a hand in instinct, opening his guard enough for Tom to step inside it, lock Feron's blade in a grip, and force it from the man's hand. For good measure he hooked a foot behind Feron's, sending him sprawling onto his back.

It was a feat not to go down too, catching himself awkwardly…

Breathless, Tom loomed over the downed man, his rapier's tip an inch from the unguarded chest.

"And now we talk…" he panted.

The roving of the eye, over Tom's shoulder, at something — someone behind his back…

To think his heart had ever stirred for Diane de Bochetel!

"Don't, Madame!" Tom called. "Don't — or…"

Or what, in truth? He tried to turn, and keep the threatening tip at Feron's throat, and an eye on Diane, and there she was, raising, two handed, her lover's dropped sword, and the sun glared in Tom's own eyes now, and his left arm was past lifting…

And then the door slammed open, and a hatless figure sprang in to seize the confounded woman around the waist, spinning her about, until the sword clanged to the flagstones.

"*Eh no, Signora Diana!*" scolded Rocco Bonetti, and he grinned at Tom over her drooping head. "All is well, Signor Walsingham, eh?"

And if not all was well, Lord bless all fencing masters, it was more than enough.

They made Feron and Diane sit on the bench, which they did meekly enough. Feron hunched over, hands clasped between his knees, and jaw working. At his side, Diane sat straight and white-faced, her auburn hair a-tumble down her back, eyes blazing.

Would Castelnau know this proud and contemptuous woman for his quiet cousin? As for himself, Tom must not be thinking straight… Let Sir Francis never know that his cousin found this murderess more beautiful, more alluring than ever…

He sheathed his sword — though not as smoothly as he would have liked, with his bloodied left hand not helping. Bonetti kept his own pointedly drawn, lowered tip swirling in lazy circles. The matter of why he'd come at all would have to wait — although it seemed that he could be counted as a friend.

Meanwhile, Tom pressed a hand on his bleeding wound, and straightened in his most inscrutable, most imperious manner.

"You have killed — and tried to kill — enough to be sent to the gallows, Feron — both in the house of the French Ambassador, and outside, where English justice works. And you are the Queen's subject. You both are murderers — and you, *mon Maître*, have betrayed your French master. If the right word were to be whispered in the right ear … well." He paused — both for effect and to catch his breath. Fates send that these two saw reason soon, for the wound hurt fiercely…

Feron looked up, his leonine head a study in anguish — but it was Diane who spoke, her hand creeping to grasp that of her lover.

"You will not! Your uncle needs him —"

"Cousin." And wasn't he an empty-headed dunce, sticking to petty points, when… "Sir Francis is my father's cousin — and yes, he needs Maître Feron, but only as long as Maître Feron delivers what he has promised. Otherwise, you understand…" He shrugged — one-shouldered, and still it hurt — before turning to lock eyes with the clerk. "But serve Mr. Secretary zealously, Feron, and no words will be whispered — about you … or about Madame's familiarity with hemlock."

Diane exclaimed in disdain. "And are you not just like that man Barbier? Threatening ills if you don't obtain what you want…"

She fell silent when Feron squeezed her hand and rose awkwardly to face Tom.

"I will, Monsieur," he said. "Tell His Honour that I will. All that I promised, all that he will ask — as long as Madame is not endangered, of herself or through me."

Tom hesitated for a heartbeat, before promising what he knew he must promise — impunity for the taking of two lives. A mere heartbeat, and then he nodded. "She will not be — nor will you. Not beyond reason, seeing the nature of your task. And you will find Mr. Secretary generous, besides." And what was it with Diane de Bochetel, that he still felt he had to excuse himself to her — or was it to himself? "And I'm as far as can be from Barbier, Madame. I want nothing for myself. What I do, I do for the sake of my Queen, and of England. Not that this kept you from trying to kill me."

She did not answer, nor did she look away — not until she'd drawn her light cape's hood around her dishevelled hair. Then she slid her hand under Feron's arm, and let herself be led away. Murderers, the pair of them — and never to be punished … unless uncertainty and fear were punishment enough.

They were at the door when Tom called to them. They stopped, and only Feron turned — but what Tom had to say was not for him.

"And remember, Madame: have Maître Feron run, and Mr. Secretary will find him. Or the King of France will, or Philip of Spain. This is what comes of making enemies in all quarters…"

Feron nodded one last time, and then they disappeared.

And not a moment too soon. Tom let his shoulders droop, and hissed in pain.

"Well, *signor mio*, that was well done." Bonetti sheathed his rapier, at last, and came to observe. "You are bleeding like a pig."

"So I am." Sparks were dancing at the edge of Tom's vision, and he blinked. "A good thing that you came by when you did…"

The Italian shrugged. "It took me a while to deliver your other message. Some are easier than others to come by, at Salisbury Court. And while I wait, I see Madame rush out, and then the clerk… And I ask myself: will the boy have someone to watch his back?" Another shrug. "Because, you see, a woman like la Signora Diana… There is little in this world that I put past her — and so, I ran here."

Little in this world, indeed. But besotted fools failed to see this manner of things, and very nearly paid for it with their lives…

"Mastro Bonetti, you have all my thanks."

There went that dazzling smile again. "It seems that you were doing well enough for yourself. But for that devil of a woman, you'd have had no need of … *dannazione*!"

Tom didn't know he had swayed until he found himself grabbed by the arm, dizzy and breathless. "Nothing," he gasped. "It's nothing…"

"Nothing, he says!" the Italian grumbled, slipping an arm around Tom's waist to support him. "Come, let me see what havoc she's done — and thank God it's not your sword arm…"

"Bonetti, I think…" It was hard to walk. It was hard to speak. It was hard to breathe — and, once more, curse Diane and her black eyes… To breathe! Good Lord, had she… "Poisoned!" he gasped. Hemlock on the blade — and now he'd choke to death, and never see Scadbury again, and Sir Francis would never know what… Bonetti knew — but was he to be trusted? Sparks swarmed and crackled around the Italian's swarthy, worried face, the beams of sunlight, so vivid in the dark… Service men died of the blade or the poison… "Tell Wat Williams … Fagot … the Scot…" *We do the Lord's work here, Thomas — and the Queen's. And if our souls must be the price, so be it…*

And then all was blackness.

CHAPTER 13

Lavender and woods wax were the first thing, together with a soft coppery light. And a keening of swallows — unless it was a children's game…

Tom moved a hand, finding crisp sheets. He moved the other, and pain flared in his shoulder.

"Lay still, lay still," said a man's voice — a strange voice in some manner — and Tom blinked to find that, very surprisingly, he was alive.

"Awake, at last," said another voice. "I'll fetch the posset."

A woman's voice. Diane. Feron. Bonetti. Fagot… Tom tried to sit up, only to be grasped firmly and lowered back onto the pillows.

"Don't, *enfant*," the strange voice said — not very strange, after all — just speaking French. And the hovering face that went with it was sad, and noble, and known.

"Oh," Tom said. Not a very intelligent observation. What he meant was, *Why am I not dead?* and *Where am I?* and also, *What of Seething Lane?* and most of all, *What are* you *doing here — you of all men?* If only it weren't all so very muddled, and heavy, and sluggish…

The man at the bedside did not seem to mind. "How are you feeling, Monsieur Walsingham?" he asked. "You lost a good deal of blood. You must restore the humours."

Had the cup been in the priest's hand all the time? Tom let himself be raised, and drank a greedy gulp before it came back to him and made him turn away. Too late… But no — no taste of cat piss. Just a thick, sweet wine, and then the poison had been on the blade — or had it?

"Was there no hemlock, then?" he blurted.

The man frowned at the cup. "But Monsieur…?"

"Not the wine. The blade. I thought…"

And perhaps it was not wise to tell this man, not wise at all, and much, much better to hold one's tongue…

Too late. The harm was done now… But no — no harm, was there? The events in the fencing hall were knitting themselves into some sort of clarity: no harm at all.

Doubt, understanding, dismay, regret chased each other across the chaplain's brow, to settle into the accustomed sombreness. "Yes, you must have," he murmured. "And I should have seen it much sooner, poor Barbier — and then…" He shook his head. "But can it be put on a blade, hemlock?"

Could it, indeed? Had it been? Tom shivered — cold after all the heat of the past days. The Greek Plato … a man touching the legs of the poisoned philosopher, the numbness… He drew up a knee under the sheet, reached to pinch the calf … and felt it quite sharply.

The many uses of reading the Ancients, Watson's voice laughed in his head — for all that a less learned, less fearful dolt could have told by the fact that he was still breathing.

"I don't know that it can," he said — half laughing in tongue-loosened relief. "I've heard one tall tale too many."

There was no answering smile — rather a mild scolding. "But you must lie still. You'll bleed again if you move too much. The barber said that you must not."

The barber… When Tom reached to find his arm and shoulder bound, the chaplain caught his wrist. "Monsieur!"

Tom frowned at the man, with the strangest impression that his thoughts had been tightly rolled up, and were now unfurling into shape again — a shape made, mostly, of myriad questions. "This is not Salisbury Court, is it?"

A shake of the grey head. "Oh, no. It's the house of Sir William More, at the Blackfriars. I had suggested carrying you to the Embassy, I'll say — but your Italian was very scornful of it… Quite rightly so, I fear."

Good man, Bonetti — though there was little chance now that Feron or Diane would try to kill again. "Hardly *my* Italian, but… Is he…?"

"He's gone to advise your people, he said."

Bless Bonetti again. "Thoughtless of him to leave you here, though."

And how the barest hint of a rueful smile changed the sad face! "He threatened me with many ills, should anything befall you."

It's not easy to shake one's head while lying in bed. "I know I summoned you here — but that was when I thought you a murderer. I know better now, and you are risking a good deal, *Father Joffray*." Voice lowered to a murmur, Tom stressed the Scottish pronunciation. "Or should I call you Henry Fagot?"

In the sudden silence, steps creaked on a wooden floor outside, and soon the door opened to admit a stern, grey-haired woman. "The posset," she announced, in the manner of one who did not like to have her home invaded by wounded strangers. Had Bonetti threatened her with many ills, too?

Tom smiled at her, and thanked her profusely, and promised to drink the posset to the last drop.

There was a small table by the door, well out of reach of both men. This severe personage, More's housekeeper, perhaps, set the cup on it, nodded once, and walked away without another word.

Ah well. Tom listened as her steps faded away, and turned to find Adam Joffray watching him through narrowed eyes.

"How did I betray myself?" the chaplain asked.

"You did not. Why, you were most careful — but..." With a sigh, Tom lowered himself among the pillows. "Fagot had to be someone who lived at Salisbury Court, who enjoyed the complete trust of Monsieur l'Ambassadeur, who could make friends with the secretary, who spoke French and at least understood Italian. This left Doctor Bruno or you." Or Madame de Bochetel — but there was no need to tell now, was there?

"Why, poor Bruno! But yes, I think he must loathe the Howards of this world very much."

"Indeed. And it took me a shamefully long time to reflect on two things." He would have held up the first of two fingers, had he not been too tired for that. "First, that Fagot must be able to come and go as he pleased through the whole house — from the Ambassador's study, to the back-passage; second, that he must be the sort of man all will trust with their talk. Not only Monsieur de Castelnau, but his visitors, the butler Girault... All talked freely to Fagot. I should have seen much sooner that they would not do so to the foreign guest. Their chaplain, though..."

"I never betrayed the secret of confession, Monsieur."

"Did I say that you did? But the man who hears their confession, who already knows — this man all will trust, won't they?"

Joffray shook his head. "All but Laurent Feron and Madame Diane, it seems."

"Not with having done murder, no — and all the more because Feron knew that you were Fagot. But Madame told you what Barbier wanted, and you explained the black-rent to her. Didn't you wonder, later, when Barbier died?"

"She only said the man threatened her reputation. Because of Laurent, you see. And when Barbier died, His Excellency's physician called it the asthma, and I believed it…"

"Truly? You stopped sending letters — like one who was afraid."

"I…" Joffray clicked his tongue and turned away. "There was nothing to write, at first — and then you came. Mr. Secretary's man was there, so why write? Then that poor man was killed at the inn, and then…" He turned back, eyes darkened with guilt. "God forgive me — do you think…? The man at the inn, and the Fleming… Had I spoken sooner, would they still be alive?"

And all of a sudden Tom was tired, tired past belief — limbs heavy and mind sluggish, and there was the shrilling outside, and the scent of milk and ginger from the posset, and the torment in Joffray's face… He closed his eyes and sighed. "Hurston's death had nothing to do with you or with Feron. The Fleming… Even if you'd told me your suspicions, there was no way to know what Sauldane knew. I'm still not sure that he truly did, though those two must have believed it."

"But if I hadn't put Feron to it? If I hadn't made him betray his master, made him afraid for his life…?"

"Then those two men would not have been poisoned!" Tom snapped — and regretted it in the next heartbeat. Of all that he had imagined of Henry Fagot — and there had been many things — a conscience was the very last… "But then there would be no door open on the schemes that go on at night in Castelnau's study. Then Howard and Throckmorton and the Queen of Scots would wreak who knows what havoc — and we could not be prepared."

"Havoc…" Joffray murmured bitterly.

"Havoc, yes. An assassination. Even a war — and that would not just touch England…" Tom propped himself on an elbow. "When the trouble of a few may avoid a general trouble, Father, the general must come before the particular."

For the longest time, the man studied Tom, studied him hard. "I cannot decide, Thomas Walsingham, if this makes you a good man, or a dangerous one. And, either way, a liar — for you must know I had no general good in mind when I made up Henry Fagot."

"Nor had you in mind two murders, I'll lay wager."

Adam Joffray shook his head, and when he spoke again, it was in English. "Lay doon, lad. Lay doon, before ye set yerself bleeding again."

Obeying was all Tom could do, thankful that his quivering arm had not betrayed him sooner. Nor did he resist the offer of another sip of wine — to restore the humours — only balking at the posset. And then he lay there, watching Joffray, and waiting.

It was not long before the chaplain sighed, long and slow. "What I had in mind," he began, "what I had in mind was disgust, for the most part. I ran frae the University of St. Andrews at sixteen, ran to France, to Douai to be a priest, turned my back on my family, and they disowned me… I didnae do it for the intrigues of the Queen of Scots, or the Duke of Guise, or Philip of Spain… But the truth is, I wouldnae hae written the first letter, if Lord Howard hadnae come with a certain tale. The story of a Scot, sheltered at Salisbury Court, one who risked prison for his religion…"

"'Twas more than just prison that you risked, though. It can well be the gallows for a priest out of Douai."

"His Excellency said I neednae fear, for all knew me for a Frenchman… That, if Lord Howard had heard of me, so others might, that Mr. Secretary Walsingham has ears everywhere, he wouldnae heed. I thought to flee — but where? I hae nae money, nae family, nae protection save for what Monsieur de Castelnau offers to me."

"And that you questioned."

"Would ye not, in my place?" Joffray turned away, his profile etched in shadow against the square of light from the glazed window. Outside, the shrilling boys had quietened down. "He is a good man — and because he is, he trusts that the world will do well by him. He can afford it, for he has birth, wealth, and reputation. I cannae."

"Hence Henry Fagot. A bold thing to do."

"At first I thought that if yer Mr. Secretary heard of Castelnau's Scot among many other matters, matters of greater weight, then he may take it as a wee thing, and set it aside. And then it struck me that, if I had enough to offer, then perhaps I could buy myself free…"

"…And so you kept writing. Writing in bad French to avert suspicion. It worked, for a while: I believed it must be Doctor Bruno. Not French, and…" Tom found his voice slurring again, and his head heavy. He blinked, and was surprised to find the light had cooled from ruddy to azure. Was he dreaming the distant song of children's voices? There were still many things to know — of Bonetti's hat, of Laurent Feron, of Mendoza's visits, of Joffray's years in Douai… But he was so tired again.

So he asked only one question — one that sounded foolish to his own ears. "Can we trust you, Father Joffray?"

Was that the shadow of a smile, creasing the priest's sad face — or rather a frown? Hard to tell in the twilight. "That Adam Joffray, the lad who ran to Douai… That one withered away a long time ago. There's little more than Henry Fagot left — and he's too afraid, too tired to betray ye, I reckon."

A door slammed somewhere, and there were raised voices. A woman's protestations, and over those a man clamouring for Mr. Thomas… Mr. Thomas Walsingham.

"I think they've come for ye." Joffray's voice — Fagot's — sounded farther away than it had, and outside was the Minotaur, thumping and grumbling, come to the rescue — "Sent by Mr. Sec'tary 'imself!"

Mr. Secretary himself. *Look into Barbier's death. Find Henry Fagot. Gauge the standing of both Douglas and Fowler.*

And, having made what he could of his labours, Hercules let himself drift to sleep.

EPILOGUE

3rd of July

It had always seemed to Tom that Lady Ursula's red roses glowed all the brighter on a grey day.

He sat on the bench under the creeping bush, leaning against the warm wall, head thrown back to squint at the roses against the overcast sky, and was so taken with the exercise, that the first he heard of Sir Francis was a clearing of the throat.

Tom clambered to his feet.

"Don't — don't, Thomas. Sit." Sir Francis sat himself, and motioned that Tom should join him. "How does the arm?"

He had been most solicitous, after Williams had sent word to Barn Elms. There had been orders for Tom to be conveyed to a room all his own in Seething Lane, and tended by Mr. Secretary's own physician, and set to rest, read if he liked, and do nothing else.

It had made for three very long days.

Then this morning Sir Francis had returned, and found the time to briefly see his young cousin, pronouncing that what Thomas needed was the company of trees.

And his own, apparently.

Tom sat straight, and awkwardly adjusted his still aching limb in the sling. "Very well, Sir. Thank you," he lied.

Sir Francis — never one to admit to pain himself — hummed and nodded.

For a while he watched his trees, half a dozen quinces and medlars, and the favourite old plum tree in the corner — a little yellowed by the sweltering summer.

"It will please you to know that we have our first letter from Laurent Feron."

And only then Tom knew he had not believed that the scrivener would keep his word — not truly. "I was not sure…" he murmured.

Sir Francis made no sign of having heard. "And not a day too soon. I had another letter today. It seems that, while you were discovering your murderers, King James escaped the custody of the Earl of Gowrie, and put himself into other hands." He sighed. "There is no knowing what will happen now. Her Highness will not be pleased."

Which was a mild way of predicting the Queen's fury, and Sir Francis would most likely be the one to bring the news…

"At least I'll be able to say that we've gained access to important correspondence. And you can be satisfied, Thomas: in the end, 'tis mostly through your work that we have."

And there was no way in this world that Tom could help the smile at such words, and the blush. "Thank you, Sir," he murmured. And of course it was little enough, and yet it was something, now that Scotland was to fall into turmoil again, and Queen Mary and her party would leap to seize what chance they saw or imagined. Yes, it was something — provided that… "Is the letter helpful? Does the Queen of Scots acknowledge her son's actions?"

"'Tis not from the Queen. Castelnau writes to her — and certainly before anything of King James was known. He writes of Mendoza's visit, and of marrying Anjou to an Infanta."

Tom's stomach dropped. "But we knew of all that!" Two men dead, all the work, the lies, the ugliness of unpunished murder — and all for nothing! "We knew from Fagot and from Fowler…"

"Well, it may mean that they are both trustworthy enough, if nothing else." Never taking his eyes from the garden, Sir Francis tilted his head. "And there will be more and better, Thomas. Joffray fears for his life. Fowler fears for his reputation and for his soul. Feron fears for the woman he loves. Trust would be preferable, or zeal — but if we have to be content with fear, so be it."

Suddenly it all seemed very small and petty — and dubious. "Those two … they murdered two men out of fear, and were prepared to kill again. What if they feel threatened again?"

"I believe that, were anyone else to die around Salisbury Court, even Monsieur de Castelnau would begin to suspect."

And smell treason, surely, if nothing else. So Diane and Feron would live under a double-edged hanging sword of fear, with only treason against France to shield them from a murderer's grisly fate. Not wholly unpunished, after all. And the Ambassador, who had been good to both of them — his scrivener and his wife's cousin…

"I wonder that he hasn't yet. He may not know of Hurston — but still… That it never occurred to him to wonder…"

"Oh, but it did." Sir Francis smiled a little. "I met the good man at Court, and found him full of qualms. He knows of the Fleming."

"Won't it be dangerous if he begins to question how Sauldane died?"

"He will not. 'Twas far from hard to convince him that it wouldn't be wise to pry too closely. Your Sauldane was, after all, Mendoza's man: Spain would resent it if France involved herself in the death of such a character. And Her Highness would like it even less to have Frenchmen and Spaniards brawling in the streets of London. Poor Castelnau is on unsteady ground enough that he will take no risks. He will do nothing to draw attention to Salisbury Court, and those who meet there to plot and intrigue."

And that was something — but still not much. Not enough… "We still don't know where the King of France stands, though…"

"Not truly, no — nor Castelnau himself, except for that matter of Anjou and the Infanta. But I trust that, between Feron and Douglas, we'll soon learn better tidings."

Douglas? The question must have been written plain in Tom's frown, for Sir Francis very nearly smiled. "Did I not say? Another morsel from Feron's copy: Monsieur de Castelnau swallows Douglas whole, and commends him to the Queen of Scots."

Hercules, his third labour won. Or half of it, and in a roundabout manner, but still. So all was well. Or far from well, in truth — for Scotland was ready to burst into flames, and the French and the Scots conspired, and France and Spain courted each other. But at least England — in the person of Mr. Secretary — was warned, and armed, and alert…

Sir Francis rose, and so did Tom, to find himself under Mr. Secretary's scrutiny.

"You are still pale, Thomas… I would have you rest. Your father would never forgive me if you were to come to harm through neglect."

"Oh, I think that he would," Tom said — a silly, petty, childish thing to say.

"Well then, neither my wife nor Frances would — of this I'm sure. You'd rather not go to Scadbury, I take it?"

He'd yearned for Scadbury when he'd thought he was dying — but now he was alive and well…

Sir Francis needed no explanation. "What of Barn Elms, then?"

A great temptation, this, for Lady Ursula and Frances would make much of Tom, and surely Edmund and Father would stop carping when they heard he'd been brought to Barn Elms to recuperate…

"My wife and your cousin were much worried when they heard of your misadventure. They would be glad to have you under their eye. They send their loving greetings, by the way — and Sir Philip sends his thanks."

Of course. Sidney would be at Barn Elms, soon to be Sir Francis's son-in-law, and…

"His thanks?"

"For Bruno. A most vexing fellow — but Sir Philip was relieved that you cleared him of both danger and suspicion."

And in truth Tom was relieved, too. *If men like Castelnau ruled it, this world would be a place of less strife*, Douglas had said. Like Castelnau, and like Bruno, perhaps…

Oh, what baggage! Tom shook his head, half to clear it, half in dismissal.

"I only thought better of a wrong assumption," he said. "And I'm very grateful, Sir — but I would rather stay here, if it is convenient. And go back to work, if I may?"

The scrutiny loosened in the grey eyes, giving way to something akin to a smile.

Sir Francis took Tom by the elbow and walked with him towards the house, just as the first drops of rain fell, filling the garden with a scent of earth, and green, and water.

"As long as you'll let yourself recover fully, Thomas," he said. "There is much that I intend for you, once you are well. In Paris — but mostly here."

And it sounded as though Tom had not failed Mr. Secretary, after all.

HISTORICAL NOTES

Monseigneur, now that I have found something worthwhile, I should like to let you know…
Your very humble and loyal servant, Henry Fagot.

In April 1583 someone began to write to Sir Francis Walsingham from Salisbury Court, the London residence of the French King's Ambassador. They were odd letters. Whoever wrote them was keen to provide, under an obviously false name and in questionable French, bits of unsolicited intelligence about the Ambassador's less public doings — and did so in a manner that showed both inexperience at the game, and a position of considerable trust inside the Embassy.

Sir Francis, who had his own carefully cultivated plants inside Salisbury Court, knew that no "Henry Fagot" existed there, and took the news with an understandable pinch of salt. It was a moment of uncertainty, with Scotland in even greater turmoil than usual. Lord Ruthven's Protestant, pro-English regime stood on dreadfully unsound ground, and Mary Stewart's adherents looked ready to pounce the moment it fell. To this end, Mary's agents were courting French support with the ultra-Catholic faction led by the Duke of Guise. And then, of course, there was Spain, wooing France in turn, in the person of the Duke of Anjou. Anjou, brother and heir to the King of France, and for years a suitor for Queen Elizabeth's hand, had been playing the sovereign in the Netherlands, proving both unpopular and ineffectual. In January he crowned his efforts with a huge military fiasco, when he tried to cheat his way into the Flemish town of Antwerp with a ruse that fooled nobody, and ended in a massacre of French troops. No matter the entity of the disaster, though, Anjou still stood to inherit the French throne, and as late as the end of May there were still Spanish overtures towards a Franco-Spanish match. What the King of France really thought about it all was anyone's guess — and so was what the French Ambassador in London was actually doing. And suddenly, in the middle of all that, "Fagot" up and claimed to have not only the Ambassador's ear, but also the means of leaking out to Sir Francis the Ambassador's private correspondence! It must have seemed too good to be true. Who was this well-placed fellow who wrote (or perhaps affected to write) French like a foreigner? How did he come to know so much? Wasn't he stepping up a little too conveniently?

In the end Sir Francis did act on Fagot's offer — to reasonable success, in view of the Throckmorton Plot — but really, would you blame him if he had sent a trusted man to have a good look at the people of Salisbury Court before he committed himself? And who better than his young cousin, fresh from Paris, and trained in the art of observing people, and unknotting tangles? That said, there is not a single line of ink on paper to prove that Thomas Walsingham was ever involved in all the ado at Salisbury Court — nor, as far as I know, did anybody die in its course.

Still, most of the characters you've met in this story are real. Tom and Sir Francis, obviously — and, as you may or may not remember from book one, Nick Skeres and young Frances — but also Walter Williams and Tom's family back at Scadbury. William Fowler, the wily Archibald Douglas, Rocco Bonetti, and Sylvanus Scory are also real, as are Michel de Castelnau and a good part of his household: Claude de Courcelles, Laurent Feron, my fellow-countryman Giordano Bruno, the butler Girault, the truculent Foxe/Renard with his English wife, and even "Master Herson" over at the (equally real) Half Moon. And while Crispin Sauldane is fictional, his master Philippe Courtois is not. Then, obviously, there is someone else who is very real … and isn't it a nice paradox that the one person who gave us so much detail about the people in this story should remain without a name? Because the fact is that, almost four centuries and a half later, we don't quite know who was hiding under the name of Henry Fagot.

Historian John Bossy has offered an answer in two books: *Giordano Bruno and the Embassy Affair* (1991) and *Under the Molehill* (2001). They contain a good deal of fascinating detective work, and I have made ample use of them in plotting my story. I haven't followed Bossy's lead to the end, though — and not because I think his answer wrong, but because I wanted one of my own — and besides, I had muddied up things with three murders, anyway… So I felt that I could go ahead and make up my own solution to the riddle.

What I can say for myself is that, all in all, I didn't cheat much more than was strictly needed.

A NOTE TO THE READER

Dear Reader,

Thank you for reading Tom Walsingham's second adventure. I truly hope you enjoyed it.

One of the joys of writing a series, as I am discovering, is the chance of developing your characters and their relationships over several volumes. Book one, *The Road to Murder*, with Tom all of nineteen, and entirely new at the game, had a certain coming-of-age feel to it. Now that he is 21, my sleuth is growing into his unofficial job as a solver of riddles for his very powerful kinsman, Sir Francis Walsingham. Part of the challenge was to portray Tom's growth, both as a young man, and as an investigator and intelligencer. I hope I have succeeded. I certainly enjoyed trying, and can't wait to do it again.

In many ways, Thomas Walsingham is an ideal character for the imagination of a historical novelist. We know enough of him that his position with Sir Francis and his subsequent life are documented, offering a historically plausible scaffold for my tales. On the other hand, though, there are huge gaps in his documented career, allowing me all the leeway I could wish in telling them.

So, while there is nothing to prove that Tom was ever involved with the doings at the French Embassy in the summer of 1583, there is also nothing to contradict the possibility that he was.

It is a pet theory of mine that, when it comes to history, the novelist's job is to imagine what we no longer know, on the grounds — and within the bounds — of what we do know.

And of course, the best of it is that historical knowledge is an endless work-in-progress: findings and discoveries happen often enough that, when you think of it, "what we no longer know" perhaps is rather "what we don't know yet". Who can tell what more will resurface, even about a lesser character like Sir Francis Walsingham's young kinsman?

Until then, a novelist's imagination will have to do — and if you liked my efforts, I would truly appreciate it if you'd drop by **Amazon** and **Goodreads**, to post a review, and let other readers know that you enjoyed the novel. I'd also love to hear from you on **Twitter** (where I go by @laClarina) or through **my website**.

Thank you, and meet you again in the next Tom Walsingham book!

C. P. Giuliani

claragiuliani.com

SAPERE
BOOKS

Printed in Great Britain
by Amazon